DOCTOR WHO

THE BURNING
JUSTIN RICHARDS

BBC

Published by BBC Worldwide Ltd,
Woodlands, 80 Wood Lane
London W12 0TT

First published 2000
Copyright © Justin Richards
The moral right of the author has been asserted

Original series broadcast on the BBC
Format © BBC 1963
Doctor Who and TARDIS are trademarks of the BBC

ISBN 0 563 53812 0
Imaging by Black Sheep, copyright © BBC 2000

Printed and bound in Great Britain by Mackays of Chatham
Cover printed by Belmont Press Ltd, Northampton

For Alison, Julian and Christian. With love.

Chapter One
Fighting Fire

The fire was a living thing. Burning. Roaring its way through the roof timbers and running liquid down the front of the building. It licked its way out of the eye-windows of the house, crackling and cackling in the doorway.

The glow was hot on the boy's face as he watched. His eyes were wide, his mouth an open 'o' of rapture. He sat immobile, letting the firelight dance and flicker in his eyes and across his reddened cheeks. The blur of movement, of people running, buckets passed, hoses unwound, hands at the pump, was lost to him. Only the flames mattered, the heat. The burning.

'There you are.' There was relief mixed in with the annoyance in her voice. 'Mum was worried. We all were.'

He did not reply. He leaned slightly to the side, to watch the flames past her. They seemed to erupt from the black silhouette of her body in the autumn dusk.

'Supper's been on the table for an hour,' she said. 'Don't you know what time it is?' More anger now. 'What do you think you're doing?'

'Watching.' His voice was barely more than a whisper. 'I'm watching the fire, aren't I?'

She raised her hand, ready to cuff him for his insolence. 'I can see that,' she hissed. 'But it's time to come home. Long past time. Mum'll learn you to be late when we get back.'

There was a crack from across the street as a wooden beam gave way under the onslaught of the fire. It crashed through the weakened first floor joists sending cascades of sparks flying out of the ruptured roof and through the sightless windows. The girl turned to watch.

For a moment, the briefest of instants, her expression mirrored her brother's – awe, excitement, rapture. For an instant she too seemed to see the beauty and life in the dance of the flames. Her hand rested on her young brother's shoulder, holding it affectionately, protectively.

Then a fireman ran across in front of her, oilskin jacket glistening as the water from the steam pump dried in the heat. Behind him a horse whinnied and trod the air in fright and surprise at the sparks and the flames. The steam pump lurched as the horses moved. Firelight gleamed off the brass of the boiler mounted on its carriage. Black smoke rose from the funnel, mingling with that from the house fire. The people encircling the burning house stepped back, as if part of the dance, as the fire jumped and raced to the adjacent house and started to rip into its roof with a dry throaty cackle.

'Mum says you're to come now,' the girl said. Her voice was husky and dry, barely audible above the cracking and popping of the fire and the cry of the horses and the people. Somewhere down the street a baby cried. At the front of the house the flames balled and gathered, as if preparing for an attack on the house opposite. The fire was gathering itself.

The boy licked his lips.

Chapter Two
Manson's Progress

The tankard had a glass bottom. Harry had told him more times than he cared to recall how he was forced to watch the beer slosh about as Pete Manson drank. Harry had also told him just as often that he didn't care for the view of the inside of Pete's mouth as he drained the pint. But Pete didn't care. In fact, it made him smile almost every time he saw the picture etched on to the base of the tankard emerge from the froth and body of the ale.

Almost every time. But not today. He kept the tankard raised as the last drips of warm liquid ran into his mouth. Even the beer didn't stay cold in winter these days. What was happening to the weather? The picture revealed on the glass disc beneath the ale was a gallows. Not an especially good sketch, it showed a stick-like figure hanging from the noose. There was nobody else depicted. The man was dying in a world of his own. Beneath his perpetual death was inscribed: 'The Last Drop'.

The last drop indeed, Pete reflected as he set down the tankard and wiped his mouth. His last drink in *The Pig and Trumpet*. His last drink with Harry Devlin. His last ale in Middletown.

'Another?' Harry asked, as if offering a reprise.

Pete shook his head.

'This is it then.'

'This is it,' Pete agreed.

'Well.' Harry considered. He pulled himself slightly unsteadily to his feet. 'You'd best be off then.'

'Best be off,' Pete repeated. 'It's a fair walk to Ambleton.' He stood up beside Harry Devlin. He reached almost to Harry's shoulder. He felt his hand smothered by Harry's huge paw as the big man sadly said his farewells. Then abruptly, Pete felt himself dragged into a crushing embrace. When he stepped back, there were tears in Harry's eyes.

3

'We'll miss you, lad,' Harry said. 'You have to go, I suppose.'

Pete looked round the public house. It was almost deserted. By eleven in the morning on a Saturday it should be heaving with life. They should have to shout to be heard. As it was, the loudest sound was the click of the dominoes from the other side of the room. 'I have to go,' he said. 'Nothing to keep me here. Not now the mine's closing. You know that.'

Harry nodded. 'I'd go myself,' he said, staring past Pete as if afraid to look at him. 'If I had anywhere to go.'

Pete slapped him on the shoulder. 'And you've got Rosie and the kids to think about.' He tried to sound bright, optimistic. 'Hey, you're the foreman. You'll get another job easy.'

'Sure I will,' Harry said quietly. 'Mind how you go, eh?'

Pete laughed, but there was little humour in him. 'I'm only going to Ambleton, no harm in that.' He hefted his holdall over his shoulder.

The sound of breaking glass made them both flinch with surprise. A moment later there was another crash as the floor trembled beneath them. A bottle behind the bar edged and jiggled its way to the front of its shelf before toppling forwards and shattering on the flagged floor.

'Not again!' Arthur Melstead said loudly. He dropped the cloth he had been using to polish a glass and started to push bottles back deeper on to the shelves. He grabbed other bottles from the more crowded shelves and dumped them on the bar. 'Give us a hand, will you?' he shouted. He had to shout to be heard above the crash and splinter of glass. A framed map fell from a wall and cracked on to the table beneath. The lamps swung, spreading smoky trails of light in their wake.

'Another tremor,' Harry sighed. 'Best be on your way,' he said to Pete. 'Otherwise Arthur'll have you sweeping up and you'll be here all day.'

Arthur's noisy swearing cut across Pete's reply. Harry turned away. 'All right, all right, I'm here.'

The tremor was subsiding now, the shuddering of the floor, the

4

shaking of the walls abated, faded. Stopped.

Middletown was dead. How many of the houses were empty shells now, Pete Manson wondered? There were a couple of hawkers in the street. A costermonger with a barrow of fruit and vegetables stood alone and forlorn on a corner. He exchanged a sullen nod with Manson.

The community had been and gone. Only the tin mine helped Middletown to cling on at all after the railway ignored the town and came to Ambleton instead. And now even the mine was closing. Empty factories, empty houses, empty ground. Soon there would be nothing left and the place would become in reality as well as name just the midway point between Ambleton and Branscombe-sub-Edge. A place defined by where it was rather than *what* it was, with no identity of its own.

The built-up centre of the town was very small, just a few streets. The housing was mainly stretched out towards where the factories had been. The mine was in the opposite direction, on the Ambleton side, and close to that was the remains of the original medieval village clustered round the small church. The church tower was the highest point on the skyline as Pete Manson left the main part of the town. A point of reference, somewhere to head for.

He passed the Reverend Stobbold outside the Grange. Visiting Lord Urton probably, Pete reflected as they exchanged greetings. Stobbold was the one person who was likely to get more work when the mine closed. Until everyone had realised that there was nothing left for them here and moved on. He reckoned Lord Urton himself would be on his way before long. Without the mine, he had no income. His last desperate gamble to keep it open, to find a new seam of tin, had failed. Local gossip had it that he had spent all his remaining money on building the dam.

They had drained the river, tunnelled underneath it along the dying vestiges of the most promising seam of metal. And found nothing. Just earth. That was when Pete had decided it was time to leave. That was when Lord Urton had announced that he

5

would shortly have to close the mine. There was no resentment, no bitterness amongst the workforce. They all knew the mine hadn't made a profit in years. They all knew that Urton had kept it going, had kept their jobs going, for far longer than made any sense. Now he was ruined, just as his workers were. If anything, Pete and Harry and the others felt more keenly for Lord and Lady Urton than they did for themselves. In a way, they were themselves to blame.

Pete's plan once he got to Ambleton was simple. Find work if there was any. If not, then get on a train and go where there *was* work. London, maybe? Birmingham? He had never travelled further than Ambleton before. Never been on a train even.

In the distance he could see the dam, its pale stonework standing out against the darker rock that surrounded it at the head of the valley. It was a massive – and massively expensive – construction. Building the dam had provided employment for almost a year. More than that, it had imbued them with optimism, with a feeling that the future was assured and bright. For a while. Now it was simply a constant reminder of their folly, of the stark reality of life in Middletown.

It was the movement that attracted his gaze. He stood and watched for a while, shielding his eyes with his hand from the wintry sun. Despite the time of year it was hot, humid. He wondered whether it would be easier if he carried his coat. There was movement on the top of the dam. Tiny specks of red clustered at one end. Without making a conscious decision, Pete found he was heading that way. He could always join up, he thought. Army life couldn't be that bad.

He paused again, watching the tiny figures spreading out along the top of the dam. Several were hanging off the side on ropes, inspecting the workmanship. He had heard they were sending engineers from the barracks at Ambleton to check the structure after the tremors. Maybe they would want help from someone who had worked on the construction. Maybe there was a few shillings' work to be had there.

The dam and the church were equidistant from Manson. If he could see over the hill to his left, he thought, he would see that the entrance to the mine was also about the same distance away. He was in the centre of the triangle formed by the three constructions. More interestingly, he was standing on dry land where only a year ago there had been a river. The moorland was already reclaiming the land. Tufts of grass poked through the damp ground; the rocky outcrops echoed the rest of the moor between here and Ambleton. There was nothing now to show what had been here. Nothing save the dam.

As he stood considering this Pete Manson saw that the tiny figures on the top of the dam had become a blur. They were running to and fro, pausing perhaps to peer over the edge at the dry land one side, the new reservoir the other. They were hauling up the ropes with the tiny red figures clinging to the ends. But the blur was not caused by the motion of the figures. He felt it in his feet first. Then the sensation ran up his legs and he felt his whole body start to quiver as the ground bucked beneath his feet.

The grass was moving. Not just waving in the breeze. Not even trembling with the ground. It was parting, ripped aside, as a dark gash ran across the earth towards him, rupturing the moorland, creating a new river along the bed of the old. It was heading straight for him, but Pete Manson could not move.

It was as much as he could do to maintain his balance. And there was the heat. He could feel it through the soles of his boots. His feet were getting warmer. Burning. There was a hot smell in the air, more than just the sun on the rocks. Like a fire just as it catches in the grate. And the sound seemed to split the air just as the ground was splitting.

He realised that the sound was his own voice, shouting. Screaming. The heat was unbearable now, yet still he could not move. The world shook and blurred around him. A heat-haze of pain and fear. There was steam rising from the jagged black slash that was almost at his feet, running between them. Then, mercifully, just as the heat became truly unbearable, just as the leather of his shoes started to smoulder, the ground disappeared from beneath him and Pete Manson tumbled headlong into the smoking abyss.

Few people waited outside the church. It was as if the uncommon heat of the last month had been vented by the tremors the previous day, sucked down into the chasm that had opened on the moorland. There was a thick frost on the late January turf of the churchyard, the gravestones dripping icicles and glittering in the crystal sun. The congregation stamped and blew their way out of Holy Communion, dutifully shook the hand of the Reverend Matthew Stobbold, and hurried home to the warm.

Lord and Lady Urton waited outside the church, exchanging words of greeting with everyone, no matter from what walk of life or social background. It was their way. Aristocracy with a human face. Lord Urton looked up in surprise at the several uniformed figures that had emerged finally from the church. Their red jackets were a contrast to the greys and blacks of the rest of the people.

Urton had put a brave face on things with the mine workers, knowing as they did that whatever Stobbold might preach about the delights of Heaven, there was bound to be some immediate suffering here on Earth before transcending to glory above. He held out his hand to the tall, straight-backed man in front of him. 'Colonel Wilson, I didn't notice you in church.'

Colonel Wilson shook Urton's hand, then pressed Lady Urton's delicately gloved hand to his immaculate moustache. He was well-built with dark hair and lively eyes. 'We were a little late, I'm afraid. Sneaked in at the back.'

'But why here at all, Colonel?' Lady Urton inquired. 'Why not attend the parish church in Ambleton?'

'We started at the dam as soon as it was light,' Wilson explained.

'Not still checking it?' Urton sighed. 'Thought you were due to finish last week.'

'We were, sir,' one of the other soldiers replied. 'Just about done yesterday in fact.'

'Captain Brookes,' Wilson explained. 'My chief engineer.'

'So why are you still here?' Lady Urton asked. 'The fissure?'

Wilson nodded. 'If it's wise to check the stonework and integrity after a few minor earth tremors in the area, you can imagine the necessity for caution after a thing like that opens up across the moors.'

Behind the soldiers, Lord Urton could see Matthew Stobbold approaching. He had removed his white surplice and carried it over his arm. In the hand that emerged from the folded material was held a prayer book. He was within earshot and caught the end of the Colonel's comments.

'Subsidence, do you think?' he asked, beaming round as the group moved slightly to allow him to join them. Stobbold was a slight man in his fifties. His hair retained its brown colour, but was receding from the centre of his forehead. His features were not prominent but his deep set eyes twinkled with an intimation of good humour and optimism. 'I mean from the mine workings.'

Captain Brookes was shaking his head. 'Don't think so, sir. For one thing, the fissure only catches the end of the workings. And it runs across them rather than following their path.'

'And it's too deep, so far as we can tell,' Wilson added. 'Still too hot to get a good look, but it seems to reach beyond the depth of your mine, sir.' He nodded to Urton.

'Yes,' Urton agreed. 'The workings themselves are quite shallow. Used all to be open cast, you know. But as the seams run away from us we dig deeper, following their path.'

As they spoke, Betty Stobbold joined them. She stood quietly beside her father, relieving him of the surplice and prayer book. He smiled at her a moment as he let her take them, before returning his attention to the conversation.

Lord Urton watched her as she stood meekly and waited. She looked after Matthew, had kept house for him since her mother died. It couldn't be much of a life for a young woman, but he had never heard her complain. When she had been born, almost seventeen years ago now – how time simply flew past – Urton and his wife had discussed whether she would be a good match for their son. Marrying into the clergy was hardly a step up the social ladder, but Urton was keen to maintain his links with the local community, to continue the tradition and succession that he was himself a part of.

Except of course that it would never happen now. Urton had no son, no children at all. His lineage would end with himself and his wife. And perhaps, since the fortune was gone and the mine was worked out, that was after all a good thing. He became aware that Betty was watching him, having noticed his attention. She smiled, guileless and pretty with the sun on her freckled face. He smiled back, a flicker of joy in his increasingly unhappy life, and turned his attention back to the conversation around him.

'Some of the lads,' Captain Brookes was venturing hesitantly, 'they say that, well… ' he broke off as if embarrassed.

'What do they say?' Urton prompted.

'They say,' Wilson finished for him, 'that this fissure goes down into hell itself. That Middletown is about to be swallowed into oblivion.'

Stobbold gave a snort that mixed amusement and disdain. 'As if heaven and hell were physical places within our own world. Reality is far more mundane, though I fear Middletown may well be sinking into oblivion. But for economic and social reasons rather than superstition and devilry.'

Captain Brookes blew on his hands and stamped his feet uneasily. 'Whatever the cause of it, though,' he said, 'we still have to check the dam. Every foot of it.'

Lord Urton looked down at frozen ground. 'Wish I'd never built the blasted thing,' he said. 'For all the good it's done. Now you tell me it may be falling down anyway.'

'I hope not,' Wilson said quickly.

'It might as well,' Urton said.

'I beg to differ, sir.' Wilson glanced at Captain Brookes, as if for support. 'Now that it's there, with that head of water built up behind it, any structural problems could be disastrous.'

'The water wouldn't just flow back into the old course of the river,' Brookes explained. 'Not if the dam burst. Well, it's difficult to know what it would do. But Branscombe-sub-Edge is below the old river level...'

'That's why we're giving it our full attention,' Wilson finished.

'And if it is about to give way?' Lady Urton asked.

'Oh no immediate worry, your ladyship,' Wilson reassured her. 'If there's any problem we can either repair it, or dismantle the structure carefully, in a controlled manner.'

'Like closing the mine in stages,' Urton muttered. 'Get out slowly and carefully and hope it isn't too painful an experience.' He shook his head and toed at the frosted gravel of the path. When he looked up, he fixed Stobbold with a stare. 'We'll let you worry about the theological implications of it all,' he told him. 'Just warn us if Old Nick's coming to dinner, won't you?'

The group broke up, their laughter echoing off the frozen stone work of the church and the gravestones. Lord Urton and the clergyman walked together, following the soldiers. A few steps behind them, Lady Urton walked with Betty Stobbold.

'And speaking of dinner,' Lord Urton said to Stobbold as they approached the lynch gate, 'don't forget it's the first Thursday of February coming up.'

'I'm looking forward to it,' Stobbold confirmed.

'Good. Good,' Urton hesitated. Then he confessed: 'I've, ah, I've asked some people to join us. From London.'

Stobbold made no comment, waiting for Lord Urton to continue.

'Recommended to me by a friend in the Royal Society. They're from some sort of offshoot that examines... these sorts of things.'

'What sorts of things?' Stobbold asked. 'You mean the tremors, the fissure?'

'Ye-es. That sort of thing. Apparently it's called the Society for Psychical Research.'

Stobbold said nothing for several moments. Then he smiled. 'Sounds interesting,' he said. 'I'm sure we shall have a lively and informative discussion.'

They shook hands at the gate and parted company. Matthew and Betty Stobbold headed off towards the Rectory, while Lord and Lady Urton turned the other way, towards the town and the Grange. They walked in silence for most of the way. They had been married for so long that the quiet was neither embarrassing nor ominous.

It was Lady Urton who spoke first. 'Who is that?' she asked.

As they approached the driveway that led up to the Grange, the road curved upwards. There were frost-hung hedges on either side, but on the westward side there was a break where a section had died away. The gap afforded a view across the moors, towards the mine. They both stopped and looked out over the workings that had been the Urtons' fortune for generations, and was now their nemesis. There was not much to see, some small wooden huts clustered round a tunnel leading into the hillside was the only evidence that there was a mine there at all.

But beyond the mine, to the side of the hill, a crooked black line broke the frosty surface of the moor; the ragged fissure that had opened the previous day. It was towards the fissure that Lady Urton was pointing. Her husband screwed up his eyes and peered into the distance. Sure enough, he could just make out a tiny dark figure beside the abyss, standing at its very edge. Behind him stood a horse-drawn cart. Urton fancied the figure was staring deep down into the very depths of the earth itself, but it was impossible to tell from this distance.

'I have no idea,' Urton replied. He shivered. There was something, he wasn't sure what, some feeling of 'presence'. He looked again at the distant figure. Still it did not move, though he could see the horse tossing its head. 'You carry on home,' he said to his wife.

She regarded him for a short while. It was as close as she came to questioning any decision he made. 'Don't be long,' she said softly.

'Hmm?' He was still watching the black speck. 'Oh no,' he agreed. 'I just want to… ' He frowned as he turned back down the road. 'I'm sure it's nothing,' he said. But when he set off towards the tiny figure, it was with an urgency in his step and a feeling of foreboding in his stomach.

12

Chapter Three
Under Mine

The man did not seem to have moved at all by the time that Lord Urton reached him. The horse stamped its hooves impatiently and blew hot steamy air from its nostrils. It calmed slightly as Urton approached, hoping perhaps that his presence signified an end to its stationary ordeal.

'Can I help you?' Urton called as soon as he was within earshot.

The man did not look up. He was staring into the dark reaches of the crevice that had opened up across the moorland. He gave no indication that he might have heard.

Urton ventured closer, impatient now. The cold was seeping through the soles of his boots. He sympathised with the horse. 'I said, "Can I help you?"' he repeated as he closed on the man.

'Lord Urton? How good of you to come.' He answered without looking up.

Urton stopped dead in his tracks. 'You have the advantage of me, sir.'

Now the man did look up. His eyes were alive with inner intelligence and flicked back and forth as he surveyed Urton. 'Yes,' he said quietly, a half-smile on his face. 'Yes, I think perhaps I do.'

'And may I ask what your business is?' Urton asked.

'Am I on your land?' The man's tone implied that he already knew the answer.

'No, sir. This is common moorland.'

The man nodded, then indicated the fissure. 'But a most uncommon feature, you will agree.'

Urton, despite himself, joined the man at the edge of the gaping hole. He peered into the depths, half expecting to see the fires of hell burning distantly at the bottom. But there was nothing, just empty velvet blackness. 'It appeared yesterday,' Urton explained. 'There was an earth tremor.'

'Mmm. I felt it. I was on my way here.'

'From where?'

'Does it matter?' the man asked.

Urton shrugged. 'That depends on the answer. And on what your business is here at Middletown.'

The man drew in a deep breath of cold air. The horse was stamping and whinnying now, and he moved to calm it, taking hold of the reins that were tied back to the cart. 'I understand,' the man said, 'that you are the proprietor of the mine that runs under this moorland. That runs almost to this...' He paused and nodded towards the slash across the landscape. 'This uncommon feature.'

'I am.' Urton was studying the cart. It was loaded with crates and packing cases. Heavy, by the look of them. 'For all the good it is.'

'Then my business is with you.'

Urton blinked and almost took a step backwards. 'What business?' he demanded. His immediate suspicion was that here was yet another creditor come to collect his dues.

'There is a possibility, I wouldn't phrase it any stronger than that at the present, but a possibility nonetheless that I might wish to purchase the mine from you.' His mouth twitched into a smile. 'For all the good it is,' he added.

'Purchase?' Urton's voice caught in his throat as he repeated the word.

'As I say, a possibility.' He patted the horse's head with sudden tenderness. 'Or if you decide when you hear what I propose that a partnership would be more appropriate, then so be it.'

The man started walking, leading the horse across the moor. Urton watched him for a moment, then followed, hurrying to catch up. They were heading, he noticed, towards the mine.

'And what is this proposal?' Urton asked as he regained his breath. 'I must confess myself to be intrigued by any suggestion that can find profit in a worked-out mine.'

'Worked out?' The man was still smiling. 'That rather depends on what you hope to dig up.'

'So you propose... what?' Urton watched the man closely as

they walked, waiting for a reaction. 'I'm afraid I don't know your name,' he added when the man said nothing.

'No,' he agreed. 'No, you don't. I am a traveller.'

'From where?'

'Oh, travellers are not from anywhere. They travel.'

'And may I ask where you have travelled from?'

The man blinked, a sudden contortion of the area round his eye as if the whole area of muscle had spasmed. 'I have travelled extensively,' he said. He enunciated each word with a precise deliberation, as if each carried a significant meaning. 'I have seen such things,' he went on in the same exact manner, 'such things as would turn your hair white.' He stopped abruptly, and turned to look at Urton. 'More things in Heaven and Earth,' he murmured. 'Enough to engender a whole new philosophy.' Then, as abruptly, he resumed his march across the empty barren land.

They continued in silence for more than a minute before Urton asked: 'And what will you do with the mine? If I agree to sell?'

The man almost laughed at this. He let go of the horse's reins and let it continue on its own beside them. 'If you agree to sell,' he said, 'I shall reopen it, of course. And provide gainful employment to the good people of Middletown again. Eventually.' His tone was lighter now. His eyes almost glittered with enthusiasm as he spoke. 'We shall have to start small, limit our operations until... Well, until we can expand our venture, shall we say?'

'Employment.' Urton licked his lips.

'There are conditions, of course.' Again, the man stopped abruptly, leaving the horse to continue on its way. He turned abruptly to face Urton as the cart rumbled past them over the frozen ground.

'Such as?'

'I shall want to conduct a thorough survey. And while I do so, I shall need somewhere to stay. Somewhere to stay and to store my... belongings.'

They both watched the cart as it continued on its journey. 'I believe you are not using the west wing of your house at present,' the man said quietly, turning to face him. 'Since you had to let the servants go.'

Urton met the man's stare. 'You are very well informed.'

'Indeed I am.'

'But you'd be more comfortable, I'm sure, in town. The Midland Hotel has excellent facilities, I'm told.'

He was shaking his head. 'But hardly so convenient for the mine. Or its proprietor.' The man started after the cart again. His voice floated back on the chill air. 'So that's settled then.'

Urton shivered. He did not care for the gentleman at all, whoever he was. Probably it was a waste of time, but if there was a chance of a future for the mine. For the town...

Only Devlin and a few others were still employed by Urton. Their job – their last job for him – was to close down the workings, making them safe. They were almost done. The passages were shored and the smaller less secure tunnels filled in. When they were finished, the entrance to the mine would be closed off.

But today was Sunday, a day of rest. So the mine was deserted and silent. Its entrance was a hollow archway of darkness set into the side of a shallow hill. Several wooden huts clustered nearby. They were in a state of disrepair that embarrassed Urton. But there had been no reason and no money to refurbish them. Soon they would be demolished anyway. If they were still standing.

The horse stopped outside the entrance, shying away from the dark. The man, the traveller, kept walking until he was framed by the arched blackness. He turned to face Urton.

'I shan't be long,' he said. 'Just a preliminary look round.'

'Of course,' Urton replied. 'I'll get a couple of lamps.' He made for the nearest hut.

'Just one will suffice,' the man said. 'I shall not require your company. You may wait for me here.'

'I beg your pardon?' Urton was not used to being brushed off so casually. 'This is still my property, I will remind you, sir.'

'Then,' the traveller replied easily, 'you already know what it looks like. Please be good enough to allow me to form my own impressions. Alone.'

Urton said nothing. He opened the door to the hut and retrieved an oil lamp. There was a box of lucifers in the same cupboard. He and adjusted the wick, and went outside again.

The traveller was still in the arched entrance to the mine. The edge of it was bricked like a railway tunnel. He was standing staring into the blackness. He nodded slowly, as if appreciative of what he saw so far. He took the lamp from Urton without comment, and lifted it so it was level with his head. The pale yellow glow illuminated the sloping floor of the passageway as it led down into the workings. Into the earth.

Urton watched the glow of the lamp fade and diminish as the traveller walked into the darkness.

When he could no longer see the dying glimmer of the light, Urton turned his attention to the horse and cart. The horse was stamping its feet again impatiently, and he spent a few moments calming the creature. He patted its head, looked into its eyes and spoke calmly and gently to reassure it. When it was stilled, Urton moved to the cart, patted the flanks of the horse as he went, still talking quietly to the horse, to himself.

'Now, let's see who your master is, shall we?' he murmured as he inspected the crates loaded on to the cart. They were large packing cases and tea chests, lids nailed firmly down. From the stains and dents, and from the destination and shipping labels pasted across their sides, it looked as if their owner was indeed well travelled.

Urton worked his way along the cart. He examined labels and stencilled destination names. His fingers brushed over Cairo and Bombay. They lingered on Antikytera and Hissarlik, tapped with interest on Karnak and hovered over Santorini. But while the place names seemed preserved, there was nothing to indicate a precise address or a contact name.

But then, towards the back of the cart, Urton found a label that was half torn off, a customs label from Dover. It was less faded than most of the other labels and Urton assumed it was recent –

the traveller's most recent disembarkation, perhaps. A flap of gummed paper was folded back across the label, and Urton slowly and carefully unpeeled it, folding it back into place. 'Name:' it said, printed in bold block letters. And after that, written neatly in blue ink was: 'Roger Nepath.'

Urton read the remains of the label several times. Then he folded the label back over itself, as he had found it. He was thoughtful as he walked round the other side of the cart. He did not bother to check the labels on this side, but made his way back towards the entrance of the mine. He patted the horse on its chestnut flank as he passed, saying nothing.

When the traveller returned, an hour later, Urton was sitting on a large rock just outside the entrance to the mine. He was tossing a stone from one hand to the other, so deep in thought that he failed to notice the approaching light until it was almost at the mouth of the tunnel.

As the man emerged from the mine, Urton looked up. He let the stone drop to the ground and roll away. 'Mr Nepath,' he said, watching the man's grimy face carefully. 'I trust you had an informative time?'

Nepath's clothes and face were blotched and stained with dirt and grime from the mine. His eyes were alive and pale, widening as Urton spoke. 'Indeed,' he agreed. 'An extremely informative time. As I see you have had.' His gaze switched to the cart. The horse met his stare impassively. 'You should not always believe everything that you read,' he said.

'Is that so, Mr Nepath?' Urton found he was rather enjoying the man's discomfort. 'I like to have things defined,' he went on. 'I like to know where I stand.'

Nepath regarded him. If he found it ironic that Urton was still seated on the rock, he did not say so. 'Not always easy. In this day and age.'

'You mean the tremors?' Urton asked. 'The peculiarities of the weather this winter?'

'Amongst other things,' Nepath agreed. He set the lamp down on the ground and inspected his grubby hands, peering with apparent interest at his nails. 'There are more things –'

'In heaven and earth,' Urton finished. 'So you said.'

Nepath smiled at him, white teeth emerging from the shadowed face. 'Do not believe you can find an explanation for everything, Lord Urton,' he warned. And his tone suggested that it *was* a warning.

'I am a rational man,' Urton replied. 'Which is why I have invited some gentlemen from the Society for Psychical Research to offer us what explanations as the new sciences can offer.'

'Really?' Nepath gave his strange, convulsive blink. 'That may be... interesting. Under the circumstances.'

Urton stood up and brushed his palms together. He noticed that they were sweating slightly. In fact it seemed suddenly to be uncommonly warm. As if hot air were blowing out of the entrance to the mine. 'And what circumstances are those?' he asked.

'Come with me,' Nepath said. 'And I will show you.' He lifted the lamp and turned back towards the mine.

Urton hesitated. Partly he wanted Nepath to realise that he was not following and have to wait for him. But the man seemed oblivious. After a few moments, Urton followed, hurrying to catch up with the smoky gleam of the oil lamp.

The pool of light cast by the lamp made Nepath glow. It seemed to suffuse him, exude from him as they walked deeper into the mine. Nepath kept to the main passageway. It was high enough to allow them to stand. The floor was worn flat from years of footsteps and cartwheels. The walls were rough earth shored up with cracked timber. Every so often a heavy wooden frame was braced into the tunnel.

As they penetrated deeper into the workings, the passage narrowed and the roof dipped. The walls were less well shored and dripped with moisture. They were, Urton knew, under the old river bed now. The ground had still not dried up, though the tin

19

seam had. They passed openings and side tunnels, Nepath leading the way in silence.

They were almost at the end of the tunnel by the time Urton asked: 'Where are you taking me?'

Nepath did not pause. The end of the tunnel was in sight now, a dripping mass of mud bulging towards them. 'There is something I think you should see. Before we discuss terms.'

The air was heavy and humid. Urton licked his lips. the whole area smelled damp, yet there was another smell mingled in with it, a musty, almost smoky, smell that he had not noticed before. 'There's nothing here,' he said.

'Oh, but you're wrong.'

Nepath had gone. His voice floated out of the ether, and Urton looked round in surprise, the light already fading. Then he saw the shadows lengthening on the wall beside him, and turned quickly to the narrow opening that Nepath had pushed through. Urton followed, forcing his way through the crack. It was not a tunnel as such, not one that his men had opened. It reminded him of the fissure across the moors, only upright. A jagged slash down the wall of the tunnel.

It opened out almost at once, and Urton found himself standing in a huge cavern. 'Well, I'm blowed,' he said quietly. 'I never knew this was here.'

'Perhaps it wasn't.' Nepath was already striding across the cavern.

The walls were sloping mud and earth, the ceiling a vaulted mass of rock packed tightly above them. Urton guessed that the weight of the water above had bedded it down over the years. Stalactites hung low, and he had to duck between them. He brushed against one as he passed, surprised to feel it warm and dry as it grazed by his cheek. Usually, he knew, they were damp and clammy.

Nepath was waiting for him by a flat piece of wall on the far side of the cavern. His eyes were gleaming in the hazy light from the flickering lamp. He set it down on a narrow shelf of cracked rock as he surveyed the wall.

'Is this it?' Urton asked. His voice was hushed, but it still echoed round the chamber. 'A rock wall?'

'This is it,' Nepath confirmed. He pressed his hand against the bare rock, and it seemed to Urton that it sank slightly into the surface, as if there was a skim of mud across it. But when Nepath pulled his hand away a few moments later, it had left no imprint.

'I wish Patience could see this,' Nepath breathed. 'After all these years. Searching.'

'Patience?'

Nepath turned. His face was aglow, his lips curled back into a huge smile. 'My sister,' he explained. 'You will meet her soon.'

'Oh?' Urton stepped forward to examine the wall. 'It's just rock,' he said perplexed. 'Or packed earth.'

'She will be staying with us.'

Urton swung round. 'Staying? Now see here, Nepath –' he began, his voice booming round the cavern, echoing back to them.

'Lord Urton,' Nepath cut in loudly, 'I am now, I feel, in a position to offer you a partnership. Join us, Patience and I, in our venture.'

Urton gaped. He looked from Nepath to the bare rock wall and back again. 'Because of this?' he asked. 'Is this what you wanted to show me? What you came here to find?'

Nepath nodded. His face dipped in and out of flickering shadow.

'But – why, for God's sake? What does it mean?'

'Feel it.' Nepath's voice was stern, emphatic.

Despite himself, Urton found he was reaching out towards the blank rock. His fingers touched the smooth surface, and he snatched them away at once. 'It's… It's warm.' He frowned, placing his hand gingerly against the rock. It was indeed warm. Not unpleasantly, but more than he could explain. Urton knew about rock and earth, about his mine. The wall should be damp, cold and clammy. Not warm and… spongy. He pushed, feeling his hand sinking slightly into the surface. He snatched it away and stared at his palm. It had come away clean.

Then he leaned forwards, and peered closely at the surface. It appeared unblemished.

'Feel it,' Nepath repeated, his mouth uncomfortably close to Urton's ear, his breath hot on Urton's cheek.

'No,' Urton said. 'No, I don't think –'

But Nepath cut him off. 'Feel it!' he shouted. And his hand slammed into the back of Urton's head.

'*Feel it!*' The words re-echoed round the chamber, hammering again and again into Urton's senses as his face slammed into to rock wall. He tried to cry out, but his face was smothered, covered, sinking fast and deep into the sweaty rock. The wall seemed to be pulling him into its glutinous surface. Smothering him. It was hot, getting hotter, searing its way through his skin, his flesh. Urton was screaming, but the sound was absorbed into the rock. And he felt it push back, flowing into his mouth as he cried out. Hot in his blistering throat. Scalding.

'Feel it! Feel it flow into you, through you!' Nepath's voice was all there was now.

And the burning.

Chapter Four
Warm Reception

It was their custom on a Sunday evening to sit round the fire. Rosie was in the back room getting the tea. James was reading aloud from the Book of Psalms.

Harry Devlin was proud of his family. But at the moment his pride at hearing his eldest son reading was tempered by the knowledge that in another week he would no longer have a means of providing for them. He remained calm and impassive, trying not to let his anxiety show. Rosie was terrified at the prospect, he knew. They had talked quietly and emotionally during the evenings and into the nights while the children slept in the next room.

He stilled little Annie's fidgeting with a glance, catching her eye and nodding towards James as he continued to read in a monotone of concentration. He read well. Better than Rosie. As well as Harry did himself. And Lawrence was catching him up. Of his three children, Lawrence would be the brightest. That was why Harry continued to let James read out loud on a Sunday. Wouldn't do for Lawrence to be seen to overtake him, not yet.

It took him a while to realise that James had finished. He sat with the Psalter open on his bare knees, waiting for a cue from his father. The fire crackled and popped in the grate.

'Well done, lad,' Harry told him. 'That was good. Very good.'

'Shall I read another?' There was an edge of worry in the boy's question. He was nearing the end of his concentration.

Annie shuffled uncomfortably on her seat. She was past her limit. Harry got to his feet and tousled James's hair. 'No, lad. That's enough for today.' He winked at Lawrence, and smiled to Annie as she looked at him expectantly. 'You can get down now. Get yourselves cleaned up for tea.'

There was sudden noise as the children raced off, each wanting to get to the pump first. A moment later came the shouts and remonstrations of their mother as they hared round the tiny kitchen and got in the way.

The knock at the door was loud, even above the sound of the children. Insistent.

Harry sighed and crossed the room. The front door opened directly into the living room. Off the living room was the kitchen. That was it. Upstairs were two small bedrooms, one shared by Rosie and Harry and the other where all three children kept themselves warm in a single small bed.

He lifted the catch and swung the door open. He was half expecting to find Pete Manson on the doorstep, grinning in his inane way and offering to buy Harry a pint. It wouldn't surprise Harry if Pete was back from Ambleton within the week. Strange he hadn't heard from him – a note had been sent to the pub. Some message. They had worked together for a long time. They were friends.

But the figure on the doorstep was not Pete Manson. The man was too tall, wearing a hooded cloak that was altogether too lavish for Pete to afford in a month of Sundays. His face was shrouded in shadow, and he shuffled past Harry and into the room unbidden.

Only when he was inside did the figure push back the hood. Harry had been on the point of demanding an explanation, of throwing the man back out into the street. But now he just stared. The firelight flickered behind the man's shape, silhouetting him, glowing round him.

'Your Lordship!' Harry said aghast. 'I'm sorry, I wasn't –'

Lord Urton gestured for him to be silent. 'No matter, Devlin.' His voice was crisp and precise. It lacked the friendly expansive tones that Harry was used to from the mine.

'What can I do for you, your lordship?' Harry ran a finger round his collar, feeling the sheen of sweat. Suddenly he was feeling hot.

'I want you to work for me,' Urton said. 'At the mine.'

Harry frowned. 'I *do* work for you at the mine,' he said. 'For the

24

next few days, any road.'

Urton shook his head, the hint of a smile touching his mouth. His eyes glittered in the firelight.

'Who is it, Harry?' came Rosie's voice from the kitchen, followed immediately by her call to the children to be quiet.

'It's for me,' Harry called back, not taking his eyes off Lord Urton. There was something about him, about his manner…

'We're going to re-open the mine,' Urton said softly. 'You and I. And my partner, Mr Nepath.'

'To dig for… what?' Harry asked, amazed at his own impertinence. Why not just accept it? This was the best news he could have imagined, yet he felt nervous. Apprehensive.

Urton ignored him, or perhaps did not hear. 'We shall need a few men. Just a few to start with. Until the machinery arrives.'

'Machinery?' Harry shook his head.

'The latest mining equipment from London and Birmingham.' Urton turned towards the door. 'We have some serious excavating to do,' he said as he crossed the room. 'Be at the mine tomorrow morning at eight o'clock sharp.' He opened the door, turning back towards Harry as he crossed the threshold. 'There is something you have to see,' he said.

Then he stepped out into the darkness, closing the door behind him.

Harry stared at the door for a while. He was still there when Rosie put her hand gently on his shoulder. 'Tea's ready,' she said.

He flinched, in surprise, then followed her through to the small kitchen. Suddenly he felt cold.

The glass roof was black from the smoke. The air was full of it, a dense cloud that did little to muffle the noise of the people and the engines. Professor Isaac Dobbs pushed open the door of the carriage and stepped down on to the platform, waving for a porter. Dobbs was in his later years, his hair a shock of tousled white that seemed out of place in the grimy station.

'You know,' he said to his companion as a porter hurried up to their first class carriage, 'it is difficult to see that science has much further to progress. We can travel even to these remote places at the speed of steam and we have within our grasp the secrets of the universe.'

The younger man smiled in reply. 'Oh I think there is a good deal of room for advancement still, Professor. Whole areas that are as yet unexplored. That is why we are here, after all.'

Dobbs waved the porter in the direction of their baggage and watched as the man easily loaded the suitcases on to a trolley. 'I think we shall find a rational explanation well within the boundaries of our existing understanding, don't you?' he told the younger man. 'There is surely no mysticism or quirk of supernature to be discovered here.' He levelled a stare at his companion. 'Despite your rather fanciful and I might add unproven whims and ideas.'

The younger man did not answer. He followed Dobbs along the platform, the porter pulling his trolley after them. The porter's whistling seemed to cut through the smoke and steam and rise above the noise around them.

There were several taxi-cabs waiting outside the station. The cabbies were wrapped up in dark cloaks against the cold, the reins emerging from layers of dense fabric to connect the drivers to the horses which blew more hot steam into the heavy atmosphere. Dobbs waited for the porter to lead them to the frontmost cab. As the bags were loaded, he gave instructions to the cabbie.

'Middletown, if you please. We are expected at Lord Urton's house within the hour. Do you know it?'

The cabbie nodded, his face emerging into the glow of the gaslight for a moment as it tilted forwards. 'I know it,' he said.

'How long will it take?' the younger man asked as he clambered after Dobbs into the cab. 'Time is of the essence.'

'This time of day, shouldn't be more than an hour. Could be a bit less.'

The young man paused, mid-way between the ground and the

compartment. 'Thank you,' he said. 'That's very helpful.'

As they left the cobbled streets of Ambleton and headed through the countryside all light disappeared. There was heavy cloud, and nothing was visible through the windows. Dobbs shifted nervously in his seat, checking his pocket watch every few minutes.

'I hope we shan't be late,' he muttered. 'I do so hate to be late.'

'A few minutes at most,' the younger man said with a smile.

'And if we get lost?'

'The driver knows the way. Probably he travels this route many times a week.'

They travelled on in silence, a frown settling on to Dobbs's face. After a while, Dobbs unbuttoned his coat and let it hang open, revealing his jacket and waistcoat beneath.

'Do you feel it too?' the younger man asked.

'Feel what?' Dobbs snapped. 'Not some more hocus pocus of yours, I trust?'

'A feeling of... oppression.' He sucked in his cheeks thoughtfully. 'As if there's about to be a summer storm.'

'It is the middle of winter, in case you hadn't noticed.'

'Mmm,' agreed the other man. 'Although it *is* getting warmer. Don't you think?'

'No. I don't.'

'Yet you have unfastened your coat, professor.'

Dobbs checked his watch again, as if to imply that it was to facilitate this that he had opened his coat. 'May I remind you, yet again... ' he said with exaggerated patience.

'I think you are about to,' his companion murmured.

'...That the Society for Psychical Research,' Dobbs continued with a glare, 'is an offshoot of the Royal Society. Not some crackpot mystic organisation given to experiencing feelings and documenting gossip. We are scientists, we apply precise rigorous rules to the study of these so-called psychic phenomena.'

'Even so, there is a difference, wouldn't you agree Professor, between approaching that application from a position of scepticism and approaching it with a mind open to the possibilities that they imply.'

'Hah. We have the tools of explanation already to hand,' Dobbs retorted. He gave a slight gasp as the cab lurched over a bump in the road. When he had recovered, he went on: 'What is not exposed as trickery or imagination can be deciphered by the application of modern science.'

'I beg to disagree.' The other man seemed to be enjoying the familiar debate whereas Dobbs resented the need for it yet again. 'We have the tools of *analysis*. Explanation should surely follow. It is not… ' He looked round as if for inspiration. 'Not a taxi-cab to be jumped on before we know where our destination might be, where our journey may lead.'

Dobbs leaned forward, his face set in an expression that was dangerously close to a grimace. 'Primitive man must have marvelled at the supernatural magic of a lightning storm. Even our grandparents had no explanation for the phenomenon. Yet we know it to be an electrical discharge caused by a change in atmospherics. This warmth, this oppression you claim to feel is almost certainly a phenomenon of the same ilk.' Satisfied, he leaned back in his seat and turned his attention to the blackness outside.

'Once again, I fear we must agree to differ,' the younger man sighed. 'But one day, one day we shall come across something which your science cannot readily explain.'

'That may be, young man,' Dobbs said, his mouth curling into a faint smile. 'But whatever Lord Urton may suspect, I doubt very much that we shall come across it in this benighted neighbourhood.'

They drew up at last, several checks of Dobbs's pocket watch later, outside a large house. Lights were burning in several of the ground floor windows, but the upper floors appeared to be in darkness. The structure was cold and stark, a solid blotch against the darkened sky.

There were lights outside the porch, and in their yellowed

suffusion Dobbs and his companion dismounted from the cab. The young man made his way to the front of the cab, and took the bags and cases as the cabbie handed them down.

'Your horse,' the young man said.

'What about her?'

'She's been ill.'

The cabbie paused, suitcase hovering above the young man's head. After a moment the suitcase continued its journey to his outstretched hands. 'Yes, she has.' There was a note of caution in the cabbie's tone.

'But she's fine now,' the man assured the cabbie. He reached up for the last case. 'Born under Aries unless I'm much mistaken. Given to moments of headstrong behaviour. Got a weak stomach.'

'I'll say.' The cabbie climbed back down to his seat. 'Found a pound of cheese in the gutter. Must have lain there a week or more. Made her sick for days.'

'How much do we owe you?' Dobbs asked, cutting across the conversation. He did not wait to hear the answer, but motioned for the other man to pay. Dobbs made his way to the porch and rang the bell. His coat flapped loose in the night air. There was indeed an uncommon warmth and humidity to the evening.

The taxi-cab departed in a clatter of hoof beats on the driveway. They waited outside the front door in silence. Eventually, deep within the house, they could hear footsteps approaching. The bolt was drawn back and when the door opened it revealed a middle-aged woman dressed in a neutral charcoal dress that complemented her undistinguished grey hair. Her face was long and her hooked nose threatened to reach down to her upper lip as it curled upwards to meet it. She surveyed the visitors through narrowed eyes.

'Professor Dobbs,' Dobbs informed her, 'and Mr Gaddis. To see Lord Urton.'

The woman did not move or speak.

'We are expected,' Gaddis told her.

'I understood your visit was cancelled.' The woman's voice was

29

cracked and reedy. 'You'd better come into the hall.'

Dobbs and Gaddis exchanged glances before following her inside the house. The hallway was short and led into an open area at the base of a large staircase that swept upwards into the darker reaches of the upper storey. There were portraits in the alcoves and several doors leading off. The woman left them there and her harsh footsteps clattered off into the depths of the house.

'Hardly an auspicious start,' young Gaddis commented.

'A misunderstanding, I am sure,' Dobbs said. 'It will soon be resolved once Lord Urton knows we are here. Since we are responding to his invitation he can hardly express surprise.'

'But I do, gentlemen.' The voice came from behind them, and they both turned to see who had spoken. 'Did you not get my telegram this morning?' He was standing in an open doorway, just outside the pool of light from a wall lamp.

'We have been travelling all day, sir,' Gaddis said.

'I assume that you are Lord Urton?' Dobbs inquired.

'I am indeed,' the man told them, stepping into the light. He was a thin man, his slight frame making him appear taller than he really was. His face was also thin, with angular features and a narrow nose. His high forehead led to swept-back hair, white and grey intermingled with the original brown. His eyes shone with inner brightness as he surveyed the two newcomers. 'And I assume that you are Professor Isaac Dobbs and Mr Alistair Gaddis.'

'We are. And may I ask what your telegram said, sir?' Gaddis replied.

Urton thrust his hands into his jacket pockets as he approached them. 'That much as I appreciate your interest, gentlemen, your services will no longer be required. I fear you have had a wasted trip.'

'Perhaps we shall be the judges of that,' Dobbs told him. 'While you may have extended an invitation to us, I think it would be premature for us simply to leave the matters you mentioned uninvestigated.'

'But there is nothing to investigate. A few earth tremors, that is all.'

Dobbs shot a glance at Gaddis. 'Nevertheless, whatever deductions you may have drawn, sir, we should analyse and investigate the situation before we draw conclusions as to an explanation.'

Urton removed a hand from his pocket and stroked his chin thoughtfully. 'I cannot, of course, order you away,' he said. 'But please be aware that circumstances have changed here. I think you will be wasting your time.' Abruptly he turned away. 'Now, gentlemen, I am rather busy. I shall have Mrs Webber organise a carriage.'

'A carriage?' Dobbs was astonished.

'To return you to the station in Ambleton,' Urton said without turning back.

'At this hour, sir?' The elderly man was almost spluttering with anger and incomprehension. 'But there will be no train back to London tonight. And in any event the journey will take hours.'

'It took us all day to get here,' Gaddis pointed out severely.

Urton turned back with a sigh. 'Then to the Midland Hotel,' he told them.

'Hardly hospitable, sir,' Dobbs said, calming slightly to adopt an air of righteous indignation. 'You promised us rooms here at your house. Even if you have changed your mind as to the necessity of our services, the least you can do is honour the promise you made as to our accommodation.'

'This is a large house, sir,' Gaddis pointed out. 'I suggest there must be some lodging available. If only for one night.'

Urton stared at them. His expression did not soften. But as he opened his mouth to reply, a voice cut in from the other side of the stairs.

'Indeed there must.' It was a woman's voice, clear and sharp. 'And whatever the case, you will at least join us for dinner.'

Lady Urton joined her husband, feeding his unhelpful arm round hers as she smiled at her guests. She was as tall as he was. Like him she was not young but not yet old. Her hair appeared to retain its natural dark colour and was tied up on her head with a precision and care that was echoed in the rest of her appearance.

Her face was not conventionally pretty, but there was an aristocratic presence to it that made it attractive despite being overly angular. 'I'm sorry if my husband has been a little surly, but he seems to have a lot on his mind at present.'

'We have guests,' Urton said stiffly.

'Indeed we do,' Lady Urton replied quietly. 'So let's start treating them as such, shall we, Robert?' She turned back to Dobbs and Gaddis. 'Your luggage is outside?'

Dobbs nodded, unsure what to make of this turn of events.

'Then I shall have it brought in. Mrs Webber will show you where you can rest and recover from your journey, and she will call you for dinner in an hour.'

'Eloise,' Urton said, 'I really don't think –'

'We have yet more guests for dinner,' his wife interrupted. 'It's the first Thursday of February, or had you forgotten. Matthew will be here soon. Another two diners are easily accommodated.' She smiled thinly. 'Will you excuse us, gentlemen? My husband and I have several things to discuss.'

'Of course, Lady Urton,' Dobbs said. 'And thank you.'

'Not at all. Mrs Webber will be with you in a moment. I am afraid we are rather short-staffed at present, so she has much to do.' She led her husband away. His expression as he glanced back at them was unchanged.

She waited until they were in the drawing room before she rounded on him. 'Just what do you think you are doing?' she demanded. As if in response to her sudden anger, the fire in the grate behind her flared and sputtered.

Lord Urton stared back at his wife impassively.

'You invited these men here, remember that. The least we can do is show a little decency and hospitality.' She shook her head and sighed deeply. 'I don't know what's got into you this last week, Robert, I really don't. You seem happy enough to invite that ingrate Nepath to stay despite the fact we can't afford the staff to help look after him.' She turned away so that he could not see the moisture in her eyes. 'Yet the gentlemen you yourself have invited are slung out to the Midland Hotel.'

'There is no room for them here.' There was a lack of emotion in her husband's reply. In angered her that he could be so callous, that he seemed not even to wish to discuss the matter.

'There is plenty of room here,' she told him. 'Even with Nepath taking over the West Wing, even with the crates and trunks of... of goodness only knows what that arrived this morning. And with Matthew Stobbold coming for dinner, there will be plenty to eat as well.' She turned back to face him again. 'Or have you also taken against the local clergy and postponed Matthew's visit?'

'I had forgotten he was coming,' Urton confessed.

'You mean you would have put him off?' She could not believe she was hearing this. She paused, considering. When she spoke again her voice was softer, more measured. 'It's since Nepath arrived,' she said. 'What is it, Robert? What's going on?'

He met her gaze and she saw something flickering in his eyes. A reflection of the fire perhaps. 'Nepath,' he said quietly. 'Yes, we should talk to Nepath.'

'You're right,' she agreed. 'I think we should.'

She let him lead the way to the stairs that led up to the West Wing of the house. The servants' quarters had been above the West Wing, but the only servant they had been able to keep on was Mrs Webber. Now Nepath had the entire area. The rooms were all off the corridor from the top of the stairs, the main reception room was half way along.

She rarely came into this part of the house, and had not visited it since Nepath's arrival the previous weekend. The room was large, occupying the space over the main drawing room on the ground floor of the house. There was another, slightly smaller, reception room off the side of it.

As her husband opened the door, she was astonished at what she saw. There were lighter patches where pictures had been removed. The furniture too had been taken out of the room and the carpet rolled back to expose bare, dusty floorboards.

In place of the furniture there were display cases running the entire length of the room. There were wooden specimen tables with glass tops in the centre of the room. Glass-fronted cases lined the walls, their shelves for the most part bare.

Every spare area of floor between the cabinets and cases it seemed was occupied by tea chests and trunks. Scrunches of newspaper and other packing materials, straw even, were pushed into the spaces below the cabinets. And in the middle of this confusion, Roger Nepath sat massively on the floor, cross-legged. He was examining a small statue that seemed to be carved from dark, smooth stone. It was the image of a woman, her breasts and stomach emphasised and long hair curled round her stone head. The feet were splayed out and exaggerated. The hands were moulded to the sides of the figure.

'What is going on?' Lady Urton asked, her voice husky with surprise and irritation. 'Where is the furniture? The table...'

'Quite safely stored away, I do assure you.' Nepath pulled himself to his feet and picked his way across the room towards Lord and Lady Urton. He was a big man, broad and tall. His face had a quality like etched granite and his steel-grey hair served to emphasise the lack of colour in his face. 'As you can see,' he said waving a hand over the crates and cases, 'the bulk of my collection arrived today, mercifully intact. I was just unpacking a few items.'

'You seem,' Lady Urton said in a low voice, 'to be installing yourself for a lengthy stay.'

'Yes, I do, don't I?'

Lord Urton spoke for the first time since they had left the drawing room. His voice was level, a monotone. 'The work at the mine may take some considerable time.'

'So you have told me,' his wife said with rather more emotion. 'And when, may I ask, am I to be told what this work entails?'

'Oh, but you did not, I think, come here to discuss the mine,' Nepath said easily. He was standing directly in front of her. He still held the carved figure, one hand caressing the smooth surface as he held it up for her to see. 'She is beautiful, don't you think? From

34

South America. Perhaps as much as four thousand years old.' He stared into the small statue's blank eyes. 'Imagine how many hands have touched this surface, how many memories are locked within her structure.' He looked back up suddenly. 'You have come perhaps to advise me that it is almost time for dinner?'

'I have come,' Lady Urton said in a steely voice, 'to insist that whatever you are doing to my husband is to stop this instant.'

Nepath raised an eyebrow. Lord Urton neither moved nor spoke.

'I am doing nothing,' Nepath said after a short pause. 'Tell her, Urton.'

'He is doing nothing,' Lord Urton said at once, his voice maintaining its earlier flat tone.

'And you expect me to believe that?' she demanded. 'He's not been himself since he met you, since you came to this house. Anyone can see that.' She took a step towards Nepath and was pleased to see that he instinctively stepped back. His foot caught on the edge of a packing crate and he stumbled slightly. 'I want you out of my house and out of my life,' she said.

Nepath's expression did not change as he regarded her. 'I can see that you are upset,' he said slowly. 'And we can't have that, can we?'

'We can't have that,' Lord Urton murmured in response.

'We have other guests,' Lady Urton went on. 'Invited before you arrived. So, you see, I'm afraid we shall need the space.'

'Indeed?' Nepath nodded in apparent understanding. 'Yes, I thought I heard the door bell. Who are these guests, may I ask?'

'You may not.'

His eyes narrowed, just slightly, just enough to betray his anger. 'I was addressing Lord Urton,' he said in a low voice.

'Professor Isaac Dobbs and Mr Alistair Gaddis of the Society for Psychical Research,' Lord Urton responded immediately.

'Really?' Nepath seemed if anything to be amused at this information. 'How very impressive.'

'Then I shall take it you will leave tomorrow,' Lady Urton cut in.

'Dinner will be at eight. I will leave you to make your own arrangements for transporting yourself and your… ' She looked round the room again. 'Your belongings.'

'You are too kind, Lady Urton. My sister and I shall join you for dinner at eight, then.'

'Your sister?' She glanced at her husband, but could not tell from his neutral expression whether this was news to him or not.

Nepath froze, a sudden look of puzzlement on his face. 'But you have not yet met Patience, have you Lady Urton? She arrived this morning. With my… belongings.' He stepped away from her, heading towards the door that led to the outer room. 'Please,' now he was the perfect gentleman, beckoning for Lord and Lady Urton to follow him. 'Please, come through and let me introduce you.'

A smile spread across his face as they followed, carefully picking a path through the open crates and packing materials.

'I am sure my sister can explain everything, put your fears well and truly to rest, Lady Urton.'

He opened the door to the other room and stepped back to allow them to enter first. Lady Urton looked closely at Nepath as she stepped over the threshold, but she could read nothing in his expression.

The room was in near darkness. A single gas lamp burned on one wall, casting a pallid glow over the immediate area. Beneath the lamp, the light spilling over it and into it, was a large display case. Like the cases in the larger room, it was largely made of glass. It was difficult to make out anything else in the room.

Nepath stepped past her. She was aware of her husband behind her. 'I thought you said…' she began.

'Lady Urton,' Nepath interrupted. 'Please allow me to introduce my sister.' He stepped towards the light, extending a hand.

She followed his hand, saw where he was pointing. Saw what he was pointing at. For a moment she stood absolutely frozen, her blood running cold. When she started screaming she found she could not stop. There was a part of her that tried to rationalise what was happening, that listened to herself, to her cries echoing round the room. There was a part of her that heard Nepath speaking to her husband.

'I think it is time you explained matters to your wife, my dear Urton.' His voice was calm, cloying, menacing.

There was a part of her that was aware of her husband beside her, of his hands reaching for her, of the hissing and spitting of his fingers as they touched her throat. A part of her felt the blistering heat as his fingers scorched their way through the skin, smelled the charred flesh, saw his thumbs closing on her eyes as her vision blurred in a heat-haze of the most excruciating pain.

Her screams were breathless, stuttering and dying in the torrid atmosphere. But through her pain and her disbelief, through the searing, molten remnants of her eyes she could still see the after-image of what Nepath had shown her. His sister.

There was a part of her that was aware that she had stopped screaming, that her husband's white hot thumbs were pressed deep into the scorched sockets of bone where her eyes had been, and were still pressing.

Until there was only the burning.

Chapter Five
Heated Conversations

The heat of the preceding days had given way to a sudden dry, cold calm. He had noticed the change even as he drove the cart up the drive to the manor house. He could have walked, but he was late already. It was as if, he reflected as he stood on the doorstep, a pressure valve had opened and the heat had been released into the upper ether. As if it had evaporated to allow the winter to reclaim her territory and take her proper course.

The door opened and Mrs Webber's familiar form stood framed in front of him. Her mouth twisted into the closest approximation of a smile that his experience led him to believe she was capable of.

'Doctor,' she said, 'how good to see you again. Come in.' She stood back and allowed him to enter the house. He handed her his hat and his top coat and she carried them through, leading him to the drawing room. 'Dinner will be at eight, Doctor,' she informed him.

There were two men in the drawing room. He did not recognise them. One was an elderly man, though he seemed full of energy. White hair erupted from his head like wire. The younger man was more sombre looking, with dark hair and long sideburns. His face was round and made him look younger than he probably was.

'Good evening,' he said as they stood in response to his entrance. They had been sitting opposite each other, warming themselves by the coal fire that burned in the grate.

'Good evening, sir,' the older man replied. 'Are you Mr Nepath?'

He smiled. 'Alas, no. I assume from your question that you are not associates of Mr Nepath?'

'We are not,' the younger man said. 'I am Alistair Gaddis. This is Professor Dobbs of the Royal Society.'

'I am impressed. A scientist.'

'Indeed,' Dobbs told him. 'Did I hear correctly, sir, that you are a doctor?'

'I am. Of divinity. So I am equally used to being called Reverend.' He tapped his clerical collar and smiled. 'Matthew Stobbold, DD. I am delighted to meet you both.' He sat down in a free chair. 'Robert – Lord Urton – had mentioned that he was expecting some guests from the Society for Psychical Research. Yourselves?'

'Yes,' Gaddis answered, sitting down again.

'Forgive me,' Stobbold said. 'I was afraid that you would be attention-seeking sensationalists rather than men of science and learning. I am, I must say, relieved.'

Gaddis and Dobbs exchanged glances. 'The Professor is more the scientist than I am,' Gaddis admitted. 'But I trust we shall alleviate your fears nonetheless. While we are here, at least.'

Stobbold sensed there was a tension between the men, something unspoken. He had an idea what it might be. 'I am also relieved,' he said slowly, 'that Lord Urton still extends his invitation to you both. He has been of late somewhat capricious.'

'Capricious?' Dobbs's anger was evident in the way the word exploded from him.

It was a similar exorcism, Stobbold reflected, to the way the heat of the atmosphere had been abruptly vented. 'You have found him so as well?' he hazarded.

'He tells us,' Gaddis explained more calmly, 'that there is regrettably no room for us at his house. That our engagement and invitation here is in effect terminated. Forthwith.'

'Fortunately,' Dobbs said, recovering something of his composure, 'Lady Urton seems more aware of her social duties and manners.'

Stobbold sighed. Here was yet more evidence that Lord Urton was not himself. He had yet to meet the mysterious Roger Nepath, but he fancied that here lay the root cause of the problems he had himself observed. 'And how did you find Lord Urton?' he asked. 'Was he civil? Lucid?'

'Decidedly lucid, and extremely uncivil I should say,' Dobbs replied.

'Yet...' Gaddis started. They both waited for him to continue. After a while he said: 'I did not get the impression that he set out to anger or annoy us. There was little emotion in his arguments, merely statement of his position and his intentions.' He glanced at Dobbs again, as if for approval, before saying to Stobbold: 'I can usually gauge the emotions of a person, determine whether their outward demeanour and inward sentiments are in agreement.'

Dobbs snorted, but his reply was good natured. 'Load of mumbo-jumbo rubbish if you ask me. Completely unscientific. But,' he conceded, 'Mr Gaddis is usually proved correct in his diagnoses.'

A gong sounded in the distance, and Stobbold looked to the clock on the mantelpiece. Eight o'clock exactly. Some things at least remained constant.

'And how did you gauge Lord Urton's inner emotions?' he asked Gaddis as he showed them the way to the dining room. 'Did you get the impression that he is under some stress, perhaps?'

Gaddis paused in the doorway to the dining room as he answered. 'I got nothing,' he said simply. 'No impression at all. No emotions, no feelings.' He shook his head, as if still unable to credit it. 'Nothing,' he said again, his voice a hushed whisper.

Unusually, Stobbold noticed, a fire had been set in the dining room. Normally the grate was bare, a screen in front. But today, perhaps due to the reversion to the cold weather, a good fire was burning. Stobbold walked past it, and stood behind his accustomed chair. Dobbs and Gaddis also stood waiting on the opposite side of the table.

'Gentlemen, please do be seated.' To Stobbold, Lord Urton looked his old self. He was smiling, welcoming, as he strode into the room and took his own seat at the head of the table.

Lady Urton followed him in and sat beside her husband. Normally, she sat at the other end of the table, but Stobbold made no comment. He smiled at his friends.

'I have been making the acquaintance of Professor Dobbs and Mr Gaddis here,' he said. 'They were explaining to me how you had invited them to help investigate the somewhat uncommon phenomena of the last months.'

Urton sniffed. 'No doubt they also appraised you of the fact that we have no room for them here, and that I have suggested they remove themselves to the Midland Hotel if they wish to remain in the area,' he said. 'As for these uncommon phenomena as you refer to them, as a man of the Church I would assume you were able to distinguish between such things and the vagaries of the weather.'

'You put this fissure that has opened up across the moorland down to the weather, Robert?' Stobbold chided gently. He smiled to mitigate the comment. He was aware of a bell jangling deep within the house, but neither Lord Urton nor his wife seemed to remark it. Nor did they reply. Urton's eyes were wide as he stared at Stobbold. There was a light in them, something moving within or behind them. It took him a moment to realise that it must be the reflection of the fire. It was in Lady Urton's eyes too, he noticed. Dancing yellow and orange across the iris.

'You mentioned, Lady Urton, that you might possibly be able to find some space for us to lodge here after all,' Gaddis said politely into the awkward silence.

Her eyes snapped from Stobbold to look at Gaddis. 'No,' she said. Her voice was a level monotone, no hint of regret or sympathy. 'That has not been possible.'

Gaddis frowned at the reply. His mouth opened, then closed again without comment. He looked at Stobbold, who had the impression that the man was trying to tell him something. But before their unspoken communication could proceed further, the dining room door opened again.

Mrs Webber ushered two men into the room. One entered without comment, taking the seat beside Stobbold, smiling a mixture of greeting and apology as he took his place amongst them.

But it was the other man who drew their attention. He was a large man, which accounted in part for the sudden sense of presence as he entered. But it was due to more than that. His eyes

41

were bright and alert. His suit was immaculate down to the ruby-red cufflink studs visible at his wrists. His hair was grey but it was impossible to discern his age. His face was craggy, as if hewn from rock. His lips were pale, almost as grey as his hair, and drawn back over perfectly white teeth in a smile which owed more to the skull beneath than to his apparent demeanour.

'Gentlemen,' he acknowledged as he took the place at the end of the table. 'Lady Urton.' He busied himself with his napkin and glanced impatiently at Mrs Webber as she wheeled a trolley beside his chair and served him first with the soup.

'Mr Nepath, I presume,' Stobbold said quietly.

'You presume, do you?' the man demanded without looking up from his bowl. He signalled with a dismissive flick of his hand that he had sufficient soup. 'I am Roger Nepath.' Now he did look up, and despite himself Stobbold felt the force of the man's stare press him back into his seat. 'And you, sir, are the Reverend Matthew Stobbold, doctor of divinity.' Nepath laid down his soup spoon and sat back in his chair, teeth glinting. 'I count it no surprise that you appear to have taken the opposite seat from our friends of the scientific world.' He glanced at the man sitting beside Stobbold. Whether this was intended to include him in the comment or to chide him for his choice of seat, Stobbold was unsure.

'You think there is no place for science in religion?' Stobbold asked.

'I take it that by religion you mean Christianity,' Nepath replied. 'I understand that science offers rationalisations for those matters for which Christianity will brook no explanation.'

'I would not presume to limit my reference to Christianity,' Stobbold said. He smiled to show that he meant no ill will toward the man. 'I have knowledge of many religions, and some understanding of science.'

'Have you really?' Nepath, for the first time in the conversation, seemed interested.

Stobbold leaned back to allow Mrs Webber to serve him. 'I

42

assume that you believe the ideas of Mr Darwin conflict with the Christian view of the world. That your understanding of Christianity assumes that it is a narrow church with no room for the beliefs of others.'

'Enlighten me,' Nepath said. His voice was hardly more than a whisper, his eyes glinting with interest.

'Darwin's theories are not incompatible with the main tenets of my own beliefs,' Stobbold said. 'There are those of us who do not view the entirety of the Bible, complete with its own internal contradictions, as literal truth. If Darwin offers a scientific basis for the world that we interpret through the teachings and ministry of Christ, then so be it.'

'And the garden of Eden?' Dobbs asked.

'A parable or a literal truth.' Stobbold shrugged. 'Just between us here, it matters not either way. You talk of science offering an explanation,' he said to Nepath. 'But it is *meaning* that is important.'

'Well put,' the man beside Stobbold murmured, drawing a glare from Nepath.

'Thank you. This soup is excellent, Mrs Webber,' Stobbold said as he tasted it. The woman half-smiled back as she withdrew from the room. 'And as for other religions,' Stobbold went on, beginning to enjoy himself, 'some are obviously primitive attempts to interpret the world that merit little attention. But those religions that believe in a single altruistic god may all stem from the same divine inspiration. Whatever we choose to call our Father, He remains the same. It is, if you will, the spirit rather than the letter of Christianity that is important.'

'You have studied other religions, you said,' Gaddis said to Stobbold.

'Some,' Stobbold confirmed. 'Though I am sure that my researches scarcely do them justice. There is a limit to what you can learn from books and libraries.'

'Indeed there is,' Nepath said. His lips were curled into a sneer. 'There is no substitute for first hand knowledge. For travel.'

'I take it that you have travelled?' Dobbs asked.

'Extensively.'

'And what is your opinion?' Stobbold's neighbour asked.

'My opinion?'

'You seem ready to disagree with others, I assume it is because you have formulated a contrary opinion from your own experience rather than out of...' he shrugged.

'Caprice?' Nepath suggested. He was staring at Stobbold as he spoke. 'I have travelled further than you can imagine.' His voice was low, husky. His gaze slipped away from Stobbold, and he appeared to be staring into the distance as he spoke. 'I have seen such things in my search for... enlightenment.'

'And have you found it?'

'I have found many things. Many pieces. Enough to know that the notion of a single all-encompassing God is the easiest of belief structures. How much more imaginative, how much more scientific, to associate an explanation, a god, with each phenomenon.'

'You do not, then, see an organising principle behind the universe?' Stobbold asked.

Nepath blinked, a sudden convulsive movement as if he had been jolted back to reality. 'There are more things in this world,' he said slowly, 'than our tiny minds can comprehend. Science may offer paltry explanations to nugatory questions. But the great debates of life and of the world continue despite it.' He leaned forward, elbows on the table. 'I have seen sights that you could never imagine let alone comprehend. I have made discoveries that science cannot and never will explain, sir.' He pointed at Dobbs and Gaddis, a gesture that was almost violent it was so sudden. 'You are the worst of them,' he said, his voice heavy with contempt. 'You seek to explain the inexplicable, to assign meaning to that which is beyond meaning, to trivialise with science that which transcends such human concepts and boundaries.'

'And on what do you base this argument?' Dobbs demanded. He

glanced at Gaddis, then at Lord Urton who sat silent and impassive.

'On my own experiences.'

'On your extensive travel?' Stobbold asked.

'Indeed. My sister and I have been to places you have never dreamed of, seen sights that would leave a so-called rational man gibbering and insensible.'

'And does your sister share your enlightened point of view?'

'She does. As she would tell you, were she able to join us.' Nepath's expression seemed to soften at the mention of his sister. 'But sadly she is rather tired from her journey.' He shrugged and seemed to attempt a smile. 'I must show you my collection, gentlemen. Forgive me if I seem a little intransigent, but if you see something of the pieces I have collected on my travels perhaps you will begin to appreciate my enthusiasm for this dialogue.'

Mrs Webber was back now. She cleared away the soup bowls and began to serve the main course.

Nepath continued to speak. 'I must also apologise for the fact that my extensive collection is partly the reason why there is no room for you to lodge here. It takes up a lot of space, I fear.' He cut into his meat with vigour. 'But I understand that you will not be in the area long.'

'That depends,' Gaddis told him, 'on what we discover.'

Nepath gave a short snort that evidently implied he thought there was nothing *to* discover.

'May I ask what your own opinion is on these strange events and phenomena?' Stobbold asked.

'I have no opinion.'

'I find that hard to believe,' the man beside Stobbold said lightly. Again, Nepath glared at him.

'For your information,' Nepath said, 'there is obviously nothing to investigate. A few earth tremors that have opened a crack in the ground. A late warm spell, some thunder storms. Locals who are more superstitious than objective and still smarting and sensitive from the loss of their livelihood. Nothing that your science cannot explain in a morning's work.'

Dobbs sighed. 'I think, from what I have heard so far from yourself and Lord Urton, that this may indeed be the case.'

Nepath smiled again. But neither Lord Urton nor his wife commented. They continued to eat slowly and mechanically.

It was the man beside Stobbold who responded. His voice was low, but forceful and hard-edged. 'You will forgive me, Mr Nepath,' he said, 'but it seems to me that you are seeking to explain the inexplicable.' He paused to take a mouthful of food. 'To assign meaning to that which is beyond meaning,' he went on, his voice slightly indistinct as he chewed. He seemed oblivious to Nepath's face darkening with anger as he stared back at the man. 'To trivialise with science that which transcends such human concepts and boundaries,' he finished.

There was silence for several moments. Stobbold was surprised, and also a little amused by the man's comments. He had assumed, since they entered together, that this man was a friend or at least a colleague of Nepath's. But there was no friendship in the stare that Nepath had fixed on him.

'And on what do you base this suggestion?' Nepath asked. His face was thunder-dark and his voice grated with anger.

'I too have travelled,' the man replied, meeting Nepath's gaze. 'Extensively, I expect.'

'You don't seem very certain,' Nepath said.

'Only scientists are certain. Those of us who have travelled, explored, discovered, who have been to places undreamed of, seen sights that science cannot and never will explain, we keep an open mind.'

They ate in silence for several minutes. Mrs Webber returned and cleared away again. Stobbold took several opportunities to examine the man beside him. He tried to glance at his neighbour without the man noticing, but was embarrassed to see that every time, the man met his gaze with piercing blue eyes that shone with intelligence. His face was young, yet Stobbold got the impression he was older and more experienced than he looked.

The man's hair was long and dark, curling almost to his shoulders. He wore clothes that almost made him seem overdressed. But beneath the long velvet jacket, the waistcoat was showing threads, and the cravat was torn where the single tarnished pin stuck through it. By contrast, the wing collars of his shirt emerged brilliant white from beneath the dark cravat.

The man caught Stobbold's eye again, and raised an eyebrow. He nodded, almost imperceptibly, towards Lord Urton at the head of the table. His head tilted slightly to one side, questioning. Stobbold followed the man's glance. Lord and Lady Urton's stoic reticence worried him as well, and he struggled to think of a way of reopening the conversation such that they might join in.

'You mentioned the loss of livelihood,' he said at last, addressing his comment to Nepath, but including Lord Urton with a quick glance. 'I understand that you are intending to reopen the mine. Indeed, that you have already begun some preliminary work.'

As Stobbold had hoped, Urton answered. But only after a look from Nepath that might have been a warning. Or permission. 'That is correct,' he said. His voice was flat, devoid of the enthusiasm and excitement that Stobbold remembered had accompanied their conversations about his plans for the mine in the past. Before the dreadful realisation that whatever Urton did, the mine was worked out, that there was no more tin to be found however deep or wide they dug.

'And you have some new stratagem for making a profit?'

'Mechanisation,' Nepath replied.

'I see.' Stobbold continued to speak to Lord Urton despite Nepath's intervention. 'And you believe that will help?'

'What has been the problem?' Gaddis asked politely.

'The problem is one of quantity,' Urton said. 'With the new mining machinery now available, we can remove the ore with less overall expense and thus we need less in order to turn a profit.'

'But surely the equipment, the machinery is itself costly,' Dobbs suggested. 'I saw a demonstration recently of a new powered drill and trepanner for use in mining coal. It was an enormous and enormously expensive piece of machinery.'

'Capital expenditure,' Nepath snapped. 'The variable costs will plummet.'

'You still need to raise the capital,' Gaddis pointed out.

The man beside Stobbold cleared his throat. 'There is another consideration,' he said. 'Since we are speaking of livelihood.'

'And what is that, Mr –' Nepath broke off. 'I did not catch your name, I'm afraid.'

'The only way that your variable costs will be lower than when the mine operated before is if you intend spending less on the running of the mine.'

'Obviously.'

'And, I would suspect, for a labour-intensive operation such as this, that cost would be mainly labour. Am I correct?'

Stobbold could see where the man was going with this argument. 'You intend to employ fewer people.'

The man nodded. 'Many fewer, if you are to more than offset the running costs of the new machinery.'

'You seem very well informed,' Nepath said, his eyes narrowing.

'And those who are employed,' the man went on, 'will be slaves to the machines. They won't be directly productive, hewing the ore from the rock themselves. They won't be taking pride in their achievements, literally weighing their success each day. They will become machines themselves, mechanised. The group becomes more important than the individual.' He sighed, as if deeply saddened by the thought. 'So it begins,' he murmured, so quietly that Stobbold alone heard him.

'And where on your extensive travels did you forge this particular opinion, sir?' Nepath demanded icily.

The man smiled back pleasantly. 'Oh, here and there. It is more of a synthesis of ideas than a single thought. And please,' he continued, 'call me Doctor.'

'Doctor?' Nepath said. 'Just "Doctor"?'

The Doctor seemed not to have heard. 'But tell me, where on

your own travels did you find you formed most of your opinions and thoughts? Which location was the most inspirational? I am fascinated to discover what a fellow traveller has found.'

Nepath leaned back in his chair, folding his hands in front of him as he considered his answer. 'Inspiration is to be found in all manner of places, all manner of experiences,' he said.

'Perhaps just an example then?'

The large man seemed to come to a decision. He reached inside his jacket and pulled something from round his neck. It gleamed in the firelight as he drew it over his head. A metal chain, silver perhaps, Stobbold thought. And attached to it was a small figure, also silver. Nepath leaned forward and held out the necklace. The Doctor reached across and took it. He held it up so that everyone could see it as he examined the small figure.

'A good luck charm?'

'I suppose so. It has certain sentimental values.'

The Doctor hefted it experimentally. 'Heavy. Silver?'

Nepath nodded, watching as the Doctor handed the figure and the chain to Stobbold. It was a male figure, naked with a large belly overhanging thin legs, about an inch and a half tall. The face was round, the features intricately cast in the heavy metal. On its head the figure wore a head-dress, like a crown, but made of fire. The chain was threaded through a hole in the centre of tallest tongue of flame. The figure was certainly not attractive, but there was something intriguing about it, a quality that drew the eye, inspired the curiosity. Almost reluctantly, Stobbold passed it to Lord Urton.

Urton took the figure and passed it straight on to his wife. She too did not even look at it, but handed it directly to Gaddis.

'I obtained it in southern India,' Nepath said, watching Gaddis's interest keenly. It is a representation of the god Agni.'

'God of fire,' the Doctor said.

Nepath's attention snapped towards him. 'You *are* well informed.'

'As I said, I have travelled.' The Doctor leaned forward so as to point out features to Gaddis, who held the figure dangling from the chain so that all could see it. 'His belly is full because fire consumes everything. Note the flames on the head-dress. They assumed there was an essentially human form for the gods of the elements. Anthropomorphism in their deities.'

Nepath too was watching the small figure as it spun slightly on the chain, reflecting the light from its polished surfaces. 'Wherever there is fire, Agni is born,' he said. There was a note of reverence in his voice – unmistakable to Stobbold. 'Because he is present in every home, he can hear all secrets,' Nepath went on.

Dobbs took the necklace from Gaddis and returned it to Nepath. 'Superstitious mumbo-jumbo,' he said. 'Though I dare say the silversmiths make a profit from it.'

Stobbold could see from Nepath's expression that the man was not amused. 'In your *scientific* opinion,' Nepath said shortly.

Dobbs nodded dumbly, apparently taken aback by the strength of Nepath's retort. Stobbold quickly intervened. 'I do apologise,' he said to Lord Urton, 'but I shall shortly have to take my leave.' He folded his napkin and placed it beside his empty plate. He smiled round at the others. 'It is my daughter's seventeenth birthday today. I promised I would return and bid her good night. She does not like to be kept up late.'

In response, the Doctor pulled a watch from his waistcoat pocket and consulted it. 'Indeed,' he agreed, nodding his head emphatically. Stobbold could see the face of the watch clearly – the white background, the Roman numerals. But it had no hands. 'How the time goes,' the Doctor added as he returned it to his pocket and for a moment his eyes met Stobbold's. Then he folded his napkin, set it down exactly as Stobbold had, and stood up. He gently pulled on the back of Stobbold's chair encouraging him to stand. 'We must be on our way,' he said to the assembled diners.

Stobbold turned as he rose, the question obvious on his face.

The Doctor frowned in response. When he spoke, his voice was an impossibly quiet whisper. Stobbold seemed to hear it inside his head rather than through the air. 'I am sorry,' the Doctor murmured. 'I understood that Lord Urton had agreed with you that I should lodge at the Rectory.'

And, because it seemed such a reasonable request, because it seemed merely to confirm how Urton's manners and humour had deserted him, because he did not wish to embarrass the Doctor or Lord Urton or the others, Stobbold said: 'Of course, Doctor. We must be on our way. Betty will be wondering where we have got to.'

Everyone else rose to their feet to bid their farewells. Lord and Lady Urton were reserved and clinical in their demeanour as throughout the meal. Both Dobbs and Gaddis seemed genuinely friendly. Nepath was polite, but beneath his smile was a hard edge, a suppressed anger. It was only as they finished shaking hands and made their way to the door that it occurred to Stobbold that they had all assumed that the Doctor was his guest, that they were together. Yet Nepath had asked the Doctor his name. And neither Lord nor Lady Urton had made any allusion to seeing the Doctor again soon, or given an indication that they had met before.

The realisation caused Stobbold to pause just inside the dining room door. Mrs Webber was standing in the doorway, ready to see them out. He turned back to face the Doctor. The Doctor had also paused, his head cocked slightly to one side as his eyes again met Stobbold's. As if Stobbold had given him the idea he turned back towards the table.

'I understand that Professor Dobbs and Mr Gaddis must also find accommodation.' As they nodded their agreement, the Doctor turned back to Stobbold. 'Perhaps they would be glad of a lift?' But there was more in his meaning than in his words.

Stobbold cleared his throat. 'Of course,' he said. 'They are welcome to join us at the Rectory, if they do not mind being a little cramped. It is not,' he said pointedly, 'a large house. But what room we have is of course at the disposal of our friends.'

Dobbs and Gaddis exchanged glances. Dobbs murmured a few words which Stobbold did not catch, and then both men rose to their feet.

'You are too kind, sir,' Dobbs said. He looked from Lord Urton to Nepath, his feelings apparent. 'Extremely hospitable.'

Nepath seemed to grow larger at the implication. He drew himself upright and turned to face Stobbold. For a moment, for a split second, something in his attitude made Stobbold shudder. But then Nepath's face split into a smile. 'I feel awkward, I confess, at having been the instigator, however unwittingly and unwillingly, of these gentlemen's situation.' He was holding the tiny figure of Agni in his hand, extending that hand towards Stobbold as he approached. 'Your daughter's birthday, you say?'

Stobbold nodded. He made to speak, but his throat felt hot, constricted and no sounds came out. He found himself taking the necklace from Nepath.

'Give her this,' Nepath said. 'With my… blessing. A gift. Recompense in some small manner for your enforced hospitality.'

'Thank you,' he stammered. 'But surely… Great sentimental value, you said…'

Nepath dismissed the objection with a wave of his hand. 'My collection of such trinkets is enormous,' he purred. 'I can spare you a little good luck, I think.' He reached out and put his hand under Stobbold's, folding Stobbold's fingers round the pendant.

Stobbold was aware of Gaddis and Dobbs now standing beside him at the door. The Doctor was waiting in the corridor outside with Mrs Webber. Stobbold looked down at his closed fist, and drew a deep breath. Then he pushed the necklace into his pocket, nodded to Nepath, and hastened from the room. Behind him he could hear a log shifting in the grate – the sudden flurry of disintegrating wood and the hiss of rising sparks.

Chapter Six
By the Light of the Fire

A light sprinkling of snow misted the late evening sky. Dobbs and Stobbold watched as the Doctor and Gaddis hefted the luggage on to Stobbold's cart. Once loaded, there was little room for anyone but Stobbold himself.

'Don't worry,' the Doctor assured him. 'The walk will do us good.' He seemed to know the way to the Rectory.

'I'll ask Betty to make up rooms for you. They should be ready by the time you and your colleagues arrive,' Stobbold said as he took the reins.

'Colleagues?' The Doctor frowned. Then his face cleared. 'Of course, yes,' he said.

A thought occurred to Stobbold, as he encouraged the horse to start moving. 'Don't you have a coat?' he asked. The man was standing there in only his jacket, snow scratching at its surface and evaporating.

'I did have one, once,' the Doctor said. 'And a hat. But they weren't really my style. So I picked this up instead.' He gestured down at the bottle-green velvet. 'It seems much more me, somehow.' He turned back to Dobbs and Gaddis.

It took Stobbold only a few minutes to get back home. The snow was beginning to settle on the driveway as he stabled the horse and called for Betty to help him with the bags. He could have left them until the others arrived, but that was less than hospitable.

Betty stood in the doorway and watched as he reached down the last of the luggage. 'I take it,' she said, 'that these are not birthday gifts from Lord and Lady Urton.'

'You take it correctly, my dear.' He caught his breath in the cold air and went to kiss her. He could feel her stiffen as she awaited an explanation. 'We have guests,' he said. 'I'm sorry.'

'How many?'

'Three. Betty, darling, there was nothing I could do. They need somewhere to stay.'

She regarded him for a moment in the moonlight. A flake of snow landed on his shoulder and she brushed it off. She sighed. 'Of course not,' she said. 'It's a cold night.' She smiled weakly. 'I'll make up beds. I think we have enough sheets.'

'Thank you.' He collected the first of the luggage and struggled with it into the house. 'I don't know what I'd do without you.'

She was already disappearing upstairs. 'Nor do I,' he heard her say. 'But maybe one day we shall find out.'

He smiled as he returned for the rest of the cases. It did not occur to him that she might not be joking.

The snow was deep enough now for them to leave footprints. She could see the faint trail of dark blotches behind the three men as they approached the Rectory. She stood at the window of a small bedroom, shaking a pillow into its case. The pale light within the room reflected her image back at her – white face framed by dark hair. She could only make out the vague shape of herself as she focused through the glass on the approaching men.

As she watched, one of them, the one with long dark hair, suddenly threw back his head and laughed silently. She could imagine the sound, the humour and mirth and life in it. She could tell he was not from anywhere nearby. She could tell he had a life, interesting things to do, interesting people to meet and places to go.

The men passed beneath the window, out of sight as they reached the door. Just their footprints were left, fading beneath the virgin snow that fell into them. She refocused on the glass in the window, on her reflection, and tried to smile. Her image did not smile back.

Drawing a deep breath, she turned and threw the pillow on to the bed, pummelling it into shape.

Despite himself, Professor Dobbs was enjoying the conversation. The Doctor showed a remarkable grasp of the latest discoveries and a keen interest in Dobbs's opinion of them. He also seemed exceptionally curious about Gaddis's fields of expertise.

'You pick up some resonance, some vibration or feeling from other people?' the Doctor asked as Gaddis explained about how he had felt no emotional feedback from Lord Urton.

They were approaching the Rectory and their feet were melting holes in the thin crisp of snow adhering to the gravel driveway.

'Nothing. And again, when Lady Urton joined us for dinner – nothing.'

'Yet you discerned her emotions, her tension with her husband earlier, you said.' The Doctor nodded as he walked, head down, staring at the snow. 'How curious.'

'It's a rare gift,' Gaddis agreed. But Dobbs thought the Doctor had been referring to the emotional state of the Urtons.

'A question of tuning, I suspect,' the Doctor said. He looked up and smiled, his face caught in the moonlight as it reflected off the gathering snow. 'I think we are all aware of the emotions of others, tipped off by a million signals and receivers. Clues we have either forgotten or never knew how to interpret.'

'Oh?' Gaddis seemed unsure.

'And you are lucky enough to be tuned into this non-verbal communication.'

'There you are Gaddis,' Dobbs said with a snort of laughter. 'A scientific, rational explanation for this gift of yours.'

'An interesting theory, no more,' Gaddis replied with a sniff of disdain. 'I think there is more to it than that.'

At this the Doctor threw back his head and laughed. 'You're right of course,' he said through his sudden mirth. 'There is always more to it than that.' As abruptly, he was serious again. They were almost at the door now, and the Doctor turned to Gaddis. 'What do you get from me?' he asked, his voice a hush of mist in the cold night.

'From Lord Urton, I got nothing,' Gaddis said slowly. 'And later from lady Urton too.'

The Doctor nodded with an eagerness that contrasted with his slight frown.

'From you...' Gaddis paused, his eyes narrowing in concentration. 'From you, Doctor, I get too much.'

The door was opening, and the Reverend Matthew Stobbold welcomed them into his house.

Both weary from a day's travel, Dobbs and Gaddis took their leave of Stobbold and the Doctor almost immediately. Stobbold helped them with their luggage and Betty showed them to the rooms she had prepared.

It was only as he returned downstairs that Stobbold realised that they had taken all the luggage to Dobbs's and Gaddis's rooms. He found the Doctor in an armchair in the drawing room. He was leaning forward, chin resting on his cupped hand as he stared into the dying embers of the fire. Stobbold raked through the cinders, sending up a shower of sparks, then added more coal.

'I could not help remarking,' he said as he took the armchair opposite the Doctor, 'that you seem to have no luggage.'

The Doctor did not move. His attention was still firmly fixed on the fire. 'Mmm,' he murmured. 'Just one small box. I prefer to travel light.'

They sat in silence for several moments, Stobbold unsure quite what to say. It was the Doctor who broke the silence. 'Won't you introduce me to your charming daughter?' he asked.

Startled, Stobbold turned, and found Betty standing in the doorway. He was not sure how long she had been there, but she was leaning against the door frame, watching him.

'I'm sorry, Betty. I was just...' His voice tailed off. He was not altogether sure what he had been doing. He stood, and went to his daughter. Behind him the Doctor was also getting to his feet. 'This is the Doctor.'

Betty nodded. She was smiling, a genuine smile, not just a formality born of politeness. 'Doctor,' she acknowledged.

He gave a short bow. His mouth twitched into what might have been a smile. 'I'm afraid,' he said gravely, 'that I haven't brought you a present.'

She laughed. Stobbold loved his daughter's laugh. He had

forgotten how much until he heard it again above the crackle of the fire. And he found that he was laughing too.

'That's quite all right, Doctor,' Betty said. 'It's the thought that counts.'

'I know, I know,' the Doctor assured her. 'And thoughts are so much more difficult than gifts.'

'Gifts, of course.' Stobbold exclaimed. 'I'm so sorry, my dear. I have something for you.' He went out to the hall in search of his coat. 'I had forgotten.'

'But, father, you've already –'

'Oh, not from me.' He rummaged through his pockets, coming at last upon the pendant. 'It's from Mr Nepath.' He examined the figure on its chain as he came back into the drawing room. 'Though whether you will appreciate it…' he began dubiously.

Betty was already lifting the ornament from his hand, holding it up to twirl in the firelight. 'It's beautiful,' she said. The light reflected off the surfaces of the silver, glittering in her eyes. 'Such detail…' Carefully, she lifted the thin chain and hung it around her neck, continuing to look down at the small figure resting on her blouse.

'It's some Indian god,' Stobbold explained. 'Their god of fire, apparently.'

'Agni,' the Doctor said from across the room. The name sounded harsh and ugly when he said it. Betty let go of the figure.

'Thank you,' she said.

'Well, as I say, it's from Nepath,' Stobbold reminded her. 'But happy birthday.'

'It's lovely.' She leaned forward and kissed him on the cheek. 'Thank you for everything, father.' Then she turned and walked quickly from the room. 'See you in the morning,' her voice floated back to them, followed by the sound of her footsteps on the stairs.

When he turned back, Stobbold saw that the Doctor was once again in the armchair. He held a small box, a plain black cube about two inches along each side. He was turning it over in his hands, as if looking for a way to open it. After a few seconds he tossed it into the air, caught it, and stuffed it into his jacket pocket.

'Are you not tired, Doctor? After your travel?'

'Oh, I'm used to travel,' the Doctor said. 'It's sitting still doing nothing that tires me.' He turned to face Stobbold, and their eyes met. 'Are *you* tired?'

And suddenly Stobbold found that he was not. He was wide awake and alert. Curious, even. 'Can I offer you a small glass of sherry, perhaps?' he asked.

The smile spread slowly across the Doctor's entire face, as if thawing it out after a hard winter. 'I'd like that,' he said. 'Yes, I'd like that very much.'

They sat in silence for many minutes. Stobbold watched the Doctor. The Doctor watched the fire. Occasionally, the Doctor raised his sherry glass and took a sip. The firelight, captured in the facets of the crystal, threw patterns dancing across his face.

'That was an eloquent speech you made to Nepath about reopening the mine, using machinery,' Stobbold said after a while. 'It was good of you to think of us, of the wider picture.'

At first the Doctor did not answer. He did not even indicate that he had heard. But eventually, he drained what remained in his glass with a single swallow. He held up the glass and twisted the stem slowly between his thumb and forefinger, letting the light spin off it. 'Not that it will make any difference,' he said. 'Does it worry you,' he went on slowly, 'that we live in a deterministic universe?'

'You think that whatever is going to happen *will* happen, despite what we may do and say?' Stobbold asked. 'Like the mine?'

'What do you think?'

'I think that's a very simplistic view,' Stobbold said. 'I think that God moves in a mysterious way.'

'Like evolution, you mean?' There was the glimmer of a smile on the Doctor's face.

Stobbold smiled too. 'You are surprised to find a man of the church accepting so easily what Darwin propounds?'

'I'm sure it wasn't easy.'

Stobbold's smile froze. 'No,' he said quietly. 'No it wasn't.'

'Do they remind you of the snow?' the Doctor asked.

Surprised out of his brief reverie, it took Stobbold a second to respond. 'Does what?' he asked.

The Doctor gestured towards the fire. 'The sparks. See how they rise, carried upward on the hot air? They twist and turn, they collide and fall. Completely random.'

'I see. You are comparing the way the sparks rise in this manner to the way that the snow is falling outside? The way the flakes twist and turn, the way they too collide at random.' Stobbold nodded, wondering where this was leading. 'Yes, I agree there are similarities.'

'And differences, of course. One up, the other down. One hot, the other cold.'

'One destroying, the other creating?'

'If you like.' The Doctor set down his glass on the table beside the chair. He leaned forward, his eyes glittering as he fixed Stobbold with an unsettling stare. 'But Newton told us over a hundred years ago that this is not random at all. Given an understanding of the forces that are acting – of gravity, of convection, of friction with the air, of opposing forces when the particles collide – we can predict the path of any particle.'

'Yes,' agreed Stobbold slowly. 'I suppose so.'

'And if we can predict the path of any particle, we can predict the path of every particle. And we know then how and when they will collide, what changes in their velocity and direction will ensue until the next collision.'

'Well…'

'Expand this notion further and we can predict the motion and life of any particle of any kind anywhere. Forever.' He leaned back in the chair, his face creased into a frown. 'Doesn't that scare you? The notion that we live in a clockwork universe?'

Stobbold considered this. 'You are saying, I think, that God set things in motion according to His plan. But that if Newton is correct, then we could predict that plan.'

'Yes.' The Doctor's response was a harsh whisper.

'Which in turn means that there is no place for free will in the universe. Everything is pre-ordained. Predestined.'

'As you said, like the sparks, like the snow,' the Doctor said quietly. 'God moves in a mysterious way.'

Stobbold pulled himself to his feet and fetched the decanter. He refilled first the Doctor's glass then his own. He set the decanter down in the hearth. He had a feeling they would need it again before the night was out. 'It seems to me,' he said as he settled back into his chair, 'that you are considering the human spirit to be composed of, what shall we say, Newtonian particles? Atoms?'

'You think the soul is exempt from the laws of physical science?'

'I hope so, indeed. If that is not the case, tell me Doctor, how can you live with the universe?' Stobbold took a sip of the warm sherry. It was viscous and sticky, sweet and cloying. 'It was you yourself who preached the dangers of mechanisation to Mr Nepath this evening. Are you now saying that we have already lost our individuality, our free will?'

It was the Doctor's turn to consider now. He blew out a long breath before he answered. 'No. No, I hope that is not the case. My feeling is that we have a lot to learn yet, that there is more to life than Newton.'

'Indeed.'

'After all,' the Doctor added, again smiling, 'if our wills were not free would we ever be permitted to doubt that they were?' With that he lapsed into silence again.

'An interesting discussion,' Stobbold said when it became plain that the Doctor was going to add nothing further. 'For myself, I have always found the difficulty not to be whether I may take decisions at all, but in taking the right ones.'

The Doctor nodded. 'With free will comes responsibility,' he said. 'And that is what I believe Nepath and Lord Urton have failed to appreciate.'

'Conscience comes with consciousness?'

'Well put,' the Doctor said. 'Well put indeed. There is a Newtonian order to the decisions we make. Each decision breeds another which twists and turns on its way, colliding with other decisions and affecting them, affected by them.' There was an edge to his voice now, an encroaching, rising passion. 'Thus conscience doth make heroes of us all. So Luther interprets his stomach cramps and his misgivings, and he nails his own conscience, itemised, to the door of Wittenburg church. A decision taken. He makes his stand.' The Doctor's expression was one of intensity again, one side of his face shadowed from the firelight by the wings of the chair. 'He can do nothing else.'

The sudden intensity of the Doctor's short speech surprised Stobbold. He was not sure whether he was supposed to take it seriously or not, whether to react. How to react. 'Are you a theologian, Doctor?' he asked, suddenly aware that he had invited into his house a man about whom he knew practically nothing.

'Perhaps,' the Doctor conceded.

'Meaning you don't wish to say?'

The darkness had spread across the entirety of the Doctor's face now. A mask of shadows. 'Meaning I don't know,' he breathed.

Stobbold frowned. 'So, why are you here?' he asked. 'I understand that Professor Dobbs is a scientist. Mr Gaddis seems to be more of a humanitarian, if I can put it like that. But what is your interest in the fissure?'

'The fissure?' The Doctor's tone was once again light and easy. 'What fissure is that?'

Stobbold caught his breath in a half-laugh of surprise. 'What fissure? Why the one that has opened across the moorland, across the old river bed. You must have seen it.' He paused, another thought occurring to him. 'I thought that was why you came here. You are with Dobbs and Gaddis, are you not?' He was leaning forward in his chair for the response, holding his glass so tight that the edges of the cut glass bit into his palm.

'I never met the gentlemen before today,' the Doctor confessed.

'Though they seem pleasant enough. This really is excellent sherry, you know,' he added as if the whole conversation had been cautiously edging towards soliciting his opinion on the matter. 'Thank you.'

'You're welcome,' Stobbold responded mechanically. 'So why are you here?'

In answer the Doctor leaned awkwardly to one side. Stobbold wondered for a second if he was about to topple forwards out of the chair. But in fact he was reaching into his jacket pocket with one hand, his other unwilling to relinquish the sherry. 'Because of this,' he said quietly as he pulled something our.

It was a cube, completely black, apparently solid. It was about two inches across each side. The surface seemed to be smooth, glossy, reflective. So black that it almost seemed not to have a colour at all. Stobbold could see his hand reflected in the cube, split across its surfaces as he reached for it. The firelight danced on its sides. But before his fingers closed on the thing, the Doctor tossed it suddenly in the air, caught it within his palm, and returned it to his pocket.

'What is it?' Stobbold asked.

'Someone on the stairs outside,' the Doctor replied. And Stobbold realised that he too had heard the sound. They both turned towards the door.

The hallway outside was in near darkness. The flickering light from the drawing room cut across the floor, deepening the shadows to either side. As they watched, another shadow – a silhouette – crept forward into the light, making its way across the opening towards the front door.

'Betty?' Stobbold crossed the room quickly. She was at the door when he reached her, already undoing the catch.

'What is it, my dear?' She seemed not to respond to his voice. He was aware of the Doctor emerging behind him from the drawing room, watching them. He turned his daughter towards him, feeling her slight resistance. Her eyes were open, but unfocussed, unseeing as he looked into them. Her dark hair was down over her shoulders, contrasting with the white linen of her night dress. As he turned her back towards the light from the drawing room, he caught sight of the chain around her neck. Her hand was at her throat, holding the figure of Agni. Like a talisman.

'Is she given to sleepwalking?' the Doctor asked. His voice was low, so as not to startle her.

'Not so far as I have been aware.' Stobbold led her gently back towards the stairs. 'I'll take her back to her room. Best not to wake her.'

'Yes.' The Doctor's voice seemed distant. 'I suppose so.'

She allowed herself to be helped up the stairs, Stobbold's arm around her shoulders. He guided her to her room, and she climbed into bed, pulling the covers back over herself. Her eyes closed, and in a moment she seemed fast asleep. An oil lamp was burning low in the corner of the room. She liked to have light as she slept. The glow permeated the room, ageing the white of the sheets, of her night dress to a pale yellow.

He sat beside the bed for a while, listening to her regular breathing, watching the covers move gently in response. She was so like her mother. So very like her. As he sat there, time was suspended, the world stopped. There was nothing but the two of them. Until the grandfather clock in the hallway jolted him back to the present, and Stobbold quietly, softly left the room.

Downstairs, in the drawing room, he found the decanter returned to its proper place in the Tantalus. The sherry glasses had been washed, dried and replaced in the cabinet. The fire was dying in the grate, embers glowing faintly amidst the dusty residue of the coal. Stobbold lifted the curtain and peered out into the night. Snowflakes were falling gently past the windows, twisting, turning, colliding apparently at random. Of the Doctor, there was no sign.

Chapter Seven
The Fires of Hell

By morning, the world was completely white. Professor Dobbs was aware of the covering of snow even before he opened the curtains. There was a brilliance, a brightness to the light that shone through the material. He had lived through enough winters to know instinctively what that meant.

It was eerie, seeing the morning mist hanging low over the white-shrouded moorland beyond the Rectory. Eerie, yet beautiful. Somewhere out there in that white wilderness was the fissure. A mystery. Since he was a child he had felt compelled to investigate the mysterious, to explain the odd. He had read Wilkie Collins when he was barely in his teens, moved on to Poe before he was twenty. A study of science had seemed an obvious progression, an outlet for his inquiring mind.

He saw something of the same enthusiasm for the unexplained in Alistair Gaddis. Had his own enthusiasm, Dobbs wondered, been as uncontrolled, as unfocused? And if it had, was he now a victim of the constrained and straitjacketed thinking which he had so resented in his elders when he first started on his career, which he had so disparaged in his peers when he first joined the Royal Society?

Staring out now across the strange, pale horizon-less landscape where land and sky met in a misty blur, he found it hard to believe he had ever lost his wonder at the intrinsic beauty with which the world fitted together, the way that everything had its appointed place and could be explained by its context. He could feel the enthusiasm welling up within him, the excitement at being so close to taking another enigma, another oddity and slotting it into its proper place in the order of things. Of explaining the inexplicable.

Betty Stobbold had prepared breakfast, and Dobbs was

surprised to find he was the last to rise. He ate quickly, kept company by Stobbold. The Doctor and Gaddis had already breakfasted and had retired to the drawing room.

'I shall be interested to hear your views on the fissure this evening,' Stobbold said over the toast. 'Today is my day for visiting, otherwise I might be tempted to join you on your little expedition.'

'You would of course be most welcome,' Dobbs told him. 'As would your friend the Doctor, of course. Your hospitality is much appreciated.'

'My friend...' Stobbold replied. 'Yes.' He finished his toast. 'You are welcome to stay as long as you wish.'

Normally Dobbs preferred to work alone, or in the company only of Gaddis who was by now used to his ways and methods. But he found himself genuinely delighted that the Doctor was able to join them on their first visit to the fissure.

The mist had lifted by the time they were ready to set off. Gaddis was carrying a satchel of equipment, and Dobbs wielded his favourite walking stick. The Doctor appeared unchanged from the previous night.

'So which way is this fissure?' Gaddis asked the Doctor as they reached the end of the Rectory drive.

'Which way?' He seemed surprised at the question. 'I have no idea. I thought you were the interested parties.'

'You mean you haven't seen it? Haven't been to look?' Dobbs was astounded.

The Doctor shook his head. 'I only arrived yesterday evening, like yourselves.'

'Oh.' Dobbs and Gaddis exchanged glances. 'I apologise, Doctor,' Dobbs said. 'I assumed, we both did, that you had been staying with your friend the Reverend Stobbold for a while.'

The Doctor's eyes glinted in the sunlight reflected off the snow. 'As a scientist, you should always question your assumptions,' he said. 'Don't you think?'

Dobbs frowned. 'Are you a scientist? Is that what you're saying?'

But before the Doctor could answer, Gaddis cut in. 'Shall we go back?' He suggested. 'Ask Miss Stobbold?'

'About our assumptions?' the Doctor asked in apparent surprise.

'About the location of this fissure.'

'Oh, I'm sure there's no need,' the Doctor said. He set off down the lane, heading away from the town. 'Stobbold said it was on the moorland, running across the old river bed.'

'And that is this way?' Dobbs asked as he caught up.

'Yes.' The Doctor hesitated. His breath hung in the air a moment as he seemed to consider, then his face cracked into a grin. 'That is my assumption.'

The Rectory was on the edge of the community. Only the church seemed to be further out of the town. They speculated at the way Middletown had grown, pulled towards the mine workings and the factories. A movement away from the church and towards modern industry, towards mechanisation. Before long they were crunching through the unbroken snow across the empty moorland.

'What's that?' Gaddis asked, shielding his eyes against the low sun.

Dobbs struggled to see what he was pointing towards. His eyes were old, and he was losing the sharpness of his distant vision. There was something, though. A smudge on the horizon.

'Stobbold mentioned that the fissure cuts across the old river bed,' the Doctor said thoughtfully. 'I would say that was a dam.' He turned a full circle as he looked about him, snow churning at his feet. 'This whole area is slightly lower than the surrounding land,' he observed. 'Another reason they could not expand this way, I would think.'

'The river?' Dobbs asked.

The Doctor nodded. 'I wonder why they built the dam.'

'Something to do?' Gaddis suggested with a smile.

'Not completely without merit,' the Doctor observed seriously. 'Providing employment would be a concern, I imagine. Good for morale to have such a large project ongoing.'

'But surely there would have to be some practical application,' Dobbs pointed out.

'One would assume so.' The Doctor clapped his hands together, though whether this was to ward off the cold or to signal an end to the conversation was unclear. 'This way,' he said brusquely and set off towards the distant dam.

'Well,' Gaddis observed after several minutes of silent progress, 'let's hope that when we do find this fissure we don't fall into it.'

'We won't,' the Doctor told him. He was a few steps ahead.

'Might be hidden in the snow you mean?' Dobbs said to Gaddis. The Doctor did not break his stride. 'It isn't.'

'How do you know?' Gaddis asked.

'Because I can see it,' the Doctor told them.

They need not have worried about the fissure being concealed by the snow. It split the moorland like a jagged cut, a wide, dark, serrated hole. There was no snow either side of the fissure for several feet, and the grass that poked through the rocky ground looked dry and dead.

Dobbs knelt at the edge of the snow and felt the bare ground beside the fissure.

'Warm?' the Doctor asked.

'Warm enough for the snow not to settle.'

'Hmm. Deep then,' the Doctor commented. He took a step closer to the edge, leaning forward and trying to peer into the depths of the hole. Wisps of smoke were curling from the abyss and rising, twisting into the sky.

'We can worry about the depth later,' Dobbs decided. 'First we should plot its size and position on a map. Mr Gaddis, if you would be so kind?' He held out his hand.

'What?' Gaddis had been watching the Doctor. 'Oh, of course.' He pulled the satchel from his shoulder and opened it. From inside he took a folded map of the area.

Dobbs relieved him of the map and opened it out, holding the large paper flapping in the light breeze. The Doctor turned back from the fissure, the wind ruffling his hair as it rippled the map.

'How do you propose to plot it?' he asked. 'Looks about, what, ten feet across? We'll have to find the ends to work out its length. And it may be changing of course.'

'We can check that,' Gaddis assured him. 'We'll take bearings on each end today, then again tomorrow and see if they have changed. Try again in a week and we should know if there's any movement and how rapid it is.'

The Doctor pursed his lips together, sucking in his cheeks. 'Not much by way of precise landmarks for triangulation,' he observed. 'If you want an accurate measurement.'

'There is the dam,' Dobbs pointed out. 'And the church spire.'

'The mine too, if that's what it is over there.' Gaddis nodded as he reached inside the satchel again.

Dobbs and the Doctor both looked where Gaddis had indicated. Sure enough, Dobbs could just make out a few low buildings huddled together, brown wood just visible through the snow that clad them and masked their shape against the hill that might have been material worked out from the mine.

'I think perhaps your idea of precision is a little different from mine,' Dobbs heard the Doctor murmur. He ignored the comment and took the compass from Gaddis.

But any irritation was lost as he watched the needle. 'How very peculiar,' he said. He gave the instrument a little shake and looked again. 'What have you been keeping with this?' he asked Gaddis. 'Nothing magnetic, I hope?'

Gaddis frowned in surprise. 'Of course not, Professor. Is there a problem?'

Dobbs held out the compass. 'Indeed there is –'

Gaddis reached across to take back the compass, but the Doctor beat him to it, lifting it from Dobbs's surprised hand and turning immediately away.

'Excuse me,' Dobbs exclaimed.

'Doctor, may I?' Gaddis reached out again.

The Doctor remained oblivious to them both. His attention was focused on the compass. He stared intently at it for several seconds, then swung suddenly round, never taking his eyes from it. Moments later he was bounding across the landscape, keeping parallel to the fissure, Gaddis and Dobbs trailing in his wake. He stopped at last, licked his finger and held it in the air. Then he shook his head in apparent irritation and drew a heavy sigh.

'Doctor, the compass,' Gaddis said, annoyed. 'If I may have it, please?'

'Oh, of course.' He tossed it towards Gaddis, and turned away again towards the fissure, as if he had completely lost interest. 'It won't tell you anything,' his voice floated back.

The compass had landed in front of Gaddis, upside down on the damp ground. Dobbs watched as the younger man picked it up and brushed the surface with the side of his hand. It took him only a second to see that the Doctor was right. The needle of the compass was spinning, turning back and forth, unable to settle on a single direction.

'What does it mean?' he asked in surprise. 'Professor?'

Dobbs shrugged. 'It is as if there were another magnet nearby,' he said. 'Sufficient to divert the needle from pointing North.'

'But why does it swing back and forth so alarmingly?'

'Of course it's a magnetic influence.' It was the Doctor who replied. He was still staring at the fissure, facing away from the others. 'It swings because the magnet the Professor postulates is so large.'

Dobbs coughed, a way of showing both amusement and disbelief. 'But there is nothing here, Doctor. Nothing so large that it could exert such an influence.'

'Unless...' Gaddis walked slowly over to join the Doctor. 'Do you mean..?'

The Doctor waited until Dobbs had joined them, staring down at the smoky hole, before he answered. 'Exactly,' he said in a low voice. And despite the warm air he could feel rising from the fissure in front of him, Dobbs shivered.

'I have come across,' Gaddis said slowly, hesitantly, 'some sites, usually ancient sites, where there seem to be lines emanating.

Under the surface. Hidden.'

'Lines?' Dobbs asked. 'What do you mean, hidden lines? If they're hidden, how do you know they're there?'

'You can... feel them. That's the only way I can describe it.'

Dobbs snorted in derision. 'Feel them! How scientific an observation is that?'

'Go on,' the Doctor said gently. He shot a glance at Dobbs, remonstrating.

Gaddis shrugged. 'Well, that's it, really. I don't know what they are. I just wondered –' He shrugged again.

'Whether we might not have some similar phenomenon here?' the Doctor finished for him. He was nodding vigorously. 'Good thought, good thought.'

Dobbs had listened to enough of this, and could contain himself no longer. 'It is not a good thought,' he exploded. 'Mysterious invisible lines of goodness-only-knows-what –'

'Magnetic influence?' the Doctor suggested.

Dobbs ignored him '– snaking out across the landscape from a perfectly natural fissure caused by seismic activity. Utter nonsense, Mr Gaddis. And I'm surprised you even give it credence, Doctor,' he added.

'I take it you are not convinced.'

'No, sir. And even if I were, I struggle to understand how we would test this theory or what we should make of it were we able to test it.' Dobbs folded his arms, daring one of them to answer.

It was Gaddis who spoke first. 'I have found that dowsing gives a good indication of the path of –'

'Dowsing?' Dobbs stared. Was he hearing correctly? 'Dowsing?!'

'What's wrong with dowsing?' the Doctor asked, his voice making the question sound reasonable.

'Ancient old wives' balderdash without a shred of scientific foundation or experimental value, not testable or verifiable in any way.' Dobbs paused for breath. 'Is that a serious question? What's wrong with it?'

The Doctor seemed unperturbed by Dobbs's outburst. 'Yet you

were willing to consult a compass,' he said. 'How very eccentric.'

Dobbs drew himself up as tall as he could, hands on his coat lapels as he looked down his nose. 'There is at least one eccentric person here,' he said, his gaze flicking from the Doctor to Gaddis and back, 'quite possibly two. And I am confident that neither of them is me.' He waited for this to sink in, and then added: 'Now, let us have no more talk of such idiosyncratic methods and confine ourselves to observable, verifiable science, shall we?'

'Don't argue with him, Doctor,' Gaddis said, his eyes fixed on Dobbs. 'Once he gets like this, there's no reasoning with him.'

'Reason, sir, has nothing to do with parading across the countryside with a pair of sticks in front of you,' Dobbs snapped back.

'I've observed as much myself,' the Doctor replied. But Dobbs was not sure which of them he was agreeing with.

'So let us instead decide what we should do in the absence of a reliable compass. Hmm?'

'You can do what you like, Professor,' Gaddis said. 'Despite your blinkered comments, I intend –'

'I think,' the Doctor interrupted loudly, 'that we should go for a walk.'

They both stared at him. 'Go for a walk,' echoed Dobbs.

The Doctor nodded. 'That's the spirit. Yes, exactly. To see if we can discover the extent of this natural seismic phenomenon. Don't you think?'

'You two do what you like,' Gaddis said again. 'I intend –'

'To see how far the fissure extends that way? Off towards Ambleton?' the Doctor finished for him. 'Very wise. The Professor and I shall see how far towards the dam it reaches. Won't we?'

This last was addressed squarely at Dobbs. He blinked, frowned. He tried to think of a response. But in all honesty this did seem like the best plan. 'Of course, Doctor,' he said. 'Just what I was about to suggest myself. We shall observe this phenomenon and measure it as best we can. Then meet back here to compare notes at, when shall we say, noon?'

'An excellent plan, Professor,' the Doctor said clapping an arm round his shoulder and leading him along the edge of the thawed snow. 'See you later, Mr Gaddis,' he called back.

Professor Dobbs did not bother to look back. He did not particularly want to see if Gaddis was mirroring their progress, walking back beside the fissure. He was not interested in what Gaddis might be doing. And he regretted that for the rest of his life.

The fissure narrowed to a crack as they progressed. After about half a mile, it petered out, the light covering of snow reasserting its supremacy over the landscape.

'Have you ever encountered anything similar, Doctor?' Dobbs asked as they stood at the end of the fissure and looked back along its length.

'Not that I recall.'

'What do you suggest now?' Dobbs was not used to deferring to others, particularly anyone younger than himself. But the Doctor exuded a sense of experience, of confidence.

'It would be useful to get an overall impression,' the Doctor said. 'If we could see it from above...'

'From above?' Dobbs frowned. 'Really, Doctor, unless you have a hot air balloon readily accessible I doubt whether that would be possible.'

'Oh I don't know.' The Doctor was looking past Dobbs, staring into the distance. 'A vantage point would suffice, I think.'

Dobbs turned to see where the Doctor was looking. 'A good thought,' he conceded. 'From the top of the dam we should be able to examine the extent of this trench.' He peered into the distance. There seemed to be some movement on top of the dam, tiny dots of colour moving back and forth behind the railings that ran along its length. 'I do believe there is someone up there already,' he declared. 'Sightseers, perhaps?'

'Soldiers,' the Doctor said.

'Soldiers? But why? What can they be doing?' Dobbs turned

back to the Doctor. But he was gone. He looked all round in a sudden panic, had the Doctor vanished into thin air? But no, he was striding out across the frozen landscape towards the dam.

'Why don't we ask them?' he called back to Dobbs as he went.

Dobbs hefted his walking stick and followed.

From the top of the dam the figures were two small black dots, ants making their way across the snowy moorland. Colonel Wilson watched the tiny figures as they approached. He was leaning on the iron railings that ran along the top of the dam. The metal was cold even through the leather of his gloves.

'Do you know them?' he asked Captain Brookes. The figures grew closer and there could no longer be any doubt that their destination was the dam.

Brookes produced a set of field glasses and examined the two men through them. Then he handed the glasses to Wilson. 'Can't say that I do, sir.'

'Nor I,' Wilson agreed as he watched them reach the base of the dam. The younger man started up the service ladder set into the side of the structure, close to the rock wall that delineated the cutting through which the river had run. 'Griffiths!' he shouted, waving the sergeant over. He pointed at the figures making their way up the ladder. The older man was being left behind by his more agile partner. 'Find out who they are and what they want, would you?'

'Of course, sir.'

Leaving Sergeant Griffiths to worry about the newcomers, Wilson turned his attention back to the work. 'Another hour, would you say?'

'The lads are just double-checking the last section, sir. Then we have to pack up the equipment. Two hours at the most.'

On the other side of Brookes, Wilson could see the first of the two men climbing off the ladder to stand on the walkway at the top of the dam. He was talking with Sergeant Griffiths, pointing out across the moors, back in the direction he can come from. As they conversed, the older man heaved himself up beside them, almost exhausted, the air misting as he breathed out heavily.

Wilson sighed, and made his way along the dam.

'Bracing isn't it, Colonel,' the younger of the men called out as he came within earshot. The man's long hair was blown back from his face by the wind and his jacket was billowing out behind him.

'It is indeed, sir,' Wilson agreed, surprised that the man recognised his rank. 'A couple of the men have lost their caps in the reservoir. It's actually quite calm now, but it can kick up a fair storm when it sets its mind to it. Quite bracing if you happen to be hanging over the side on a rope, I can tell you.'

'I'm sure.'

'May I ask your business here, sir?' Wilson said. Though he was prepared to be civil and polite, he was not really in the mood for a chat about the weather. He nodded a dismissal to Griffiths, and the sergeant seemed relieved to be on his way.

'Do we need any?' the man asked. 'And do you need to know if we do? I assumed this was public property.'

Wilson regarded the man closely. His tone was not unpleasant, and his eyes were alive with intelligence. Maybe it was just his manner that made him seem insolent. 'Your business is your own, of course, sir,' Wilson conceded. He had to be careful, he had no idea who this man was or what position he might hold. He did not recognise either of the men as locals, and that in itself marked them out. 'But we are currently checking this structure to ascertain whether its integrity has been damaged by recent events. Under the circumstances...' he let the implications hang.

The man cocked his head to one side as he listened. Then he nodded towards the dark gash of the fissure than ran across the landscape below them. 'By recent events, I take it you mean that.'

'And the tremors, sir, yes.' He decided on a different approach. 'May I at least ask you your names?'

It was the older man who replied. He seemed to have got his breath back now after the climb. His voice was authoritative, but tinged with respect. 'Of course. I am Professor Isaac Dobbs of the

74

Royal Society, and this is...' He waved a hand in the air as if hoping the name would come to him. 'The Doctor,' he said at last, his tone suggesting that this much was self-evident.

'We're very interested in recent events, as you call them,' the Doctor said quickly as Dobbs finished. 'In particular we wanted to take a look at that fissure from up here. Get an idea of the size and shape of it.' He leaned closer to Wilson. 'Make deductions and test assumptions,' he added knowingly.

Scientists, Wilson could cope with. He was an engineer himself by profession – an engineer and a soldier – so he had an appreciation of the sciences. 'I see, Doctor. Well, please help yourself to the view. My men are just finishing, but if we can offer any help or insight which might be of assistance, please do ask.'

'You're very kind,' Dobbs assured him.

'Is it safe?' the Doctor asked.

'Sorry, sir?'

'The dam. Apart from the danger of losing our hats, I mean.' His hand flew to his head suddenly, and he seemed surprised when it met his wind-blown hair.

'It appears to be safe, yes sir. The tremors and the fissure don't seem to have affected the structure at all. But we'll check again in a week in case there's any movement.'

'Very wise.' The Doctor had turned. He was staring out across the reservoir on the other side of the dam. The surface was partly frozen, islands of ice floating just under the surface of the artificial lake. In places the ice emerged from the water and was dusted with snow.

'Did you know,' the Doctor said quietly, 'that snow screams when it hits water?'

'No, sir. I didn't know that.'

'Nor did I,' Dobbs said in surprise. 'What do you mean?'

'Oh it's too high-pitched a cry for us to hear,' he mused in the same quiet voice. 'But just because we can't perceive it doesn't mean it doesn't happen.' He swung round to face Wilson. 'Thank you, Colonel,' he barked loudly. 'You may carry on.'

Instinctively Wilson saluted. 'Sir.' Then he frowned. 'Are you a military man, sir? I hope you don't mind me asking.'

'Of course not.'

'You mean you're not in the military?'

'I mean I don't mind,' the Doctor confirmed. 'A military man,' he murmured as Wilson turned to go. 'Perhaps. We all have our wars to fight, you know.'

'Indeed, sir.' Wilson shuffled, embarrassed, not sure if he had been intended to hear the remark. 'Excuse me, sir.' He made his way back to his men, thoughts of the two scientists already demoted. Just an hour or so, and he could be on his way.

The strongest dowsers did not need a rod or a plumb bob, Gaddis had been told. They could just feel the influence – the flowing power – within themselves. In their bones.

His grandmother had taught Gaddis the art. She had Romany blood in her, or so she claimed. She had taken him out in the meadow behind her cottage and led him towards the stream, sticks outstretched, searching for the water running below the surface. She knew where it was, of course. She had the gift herself, and had been delighted at her grandson's instant aptitude.

But Alistair Gaddis needed a medium, something for the power to be channelled through. Finding no suitable sticks, he was using his house key. He had threaded a length of twine through it and held it out before him, allowing it to swing gently back and forth to describe an oval in the air as he walked.

He knew that Dobbs believed that dowsing was nonsense. The one semi-civilised conversation they had shared on the subject, many years ago now, had been enough for Gaddis to realise that Dobbs missed the point and always would. The professor had been forced to admit that dowsing might on occasion work. But his explanation was a subconscious realisation on the part of the dowser, an assimilation of clues and evidence from the surroundings that gave an indication of where water might be found. The movement of the sticks or the pendulum was merely, Dobbs maintained, a subconscious outlet for that realisation.

When they had moved on to discussing other lines of power, of magnetism and more esoteric forces, Dobbs had ended the conversation. He could never admit what Gaddis knew. What he knew from his own experience. He had felt the movement of the sticks unbidden in his hands, seen the pendulum swing awry without his assistance.

Now, as he worked his way along the side of the abyss, Gaddis was not examining the landscape for tell-tale topographical evidence. He had already found two lines of power, both of which pointed in the same direction. When he found the third and started to follow it he decided that he had found the focal point for whatever force emanated from the fissure. His concentration was focussed on the key as it swung in its arc.

So focussed that he did not see the figure approaching him until it was within twenty yards.

'I thought so.'

Dobbs had examined the fissure from the windswept top of the dam for as long as his old skin could bear the bite of the wind. He had made estimations of the size, sketched outlines of the shape, wondered at the depth. The Doctor had pointed out where there were jagged patches along the edge of the snowline where the snow had receded still further. As if the heat from the fissure were concentrating its efforts on particular points where it struggled to push back the snow.

Now they were walking round the frozen edge of the reservoir. The Doctor had said he wished to examine a slight inlet along the side, pointing it out to Dobbs's bleary eyes. They had a while yet until they were due to meet Gaddis, and Dobbs had no objection to a walk in the Doctor's company.

He leaned heavily on his stick and watched the Doctor slip and slide his way down towards the water's edge. Sure enough, as the Doctor had described, he could now see that the water here was steaming. Probably it did not need to be very hot in this weather for the effect. But it was unsettling nonetheless. He tried to recall if he had ever witnessed such a phenomenon before. He could remember walking across the frozen Thames when he was younger. But had the water steamed like warm breath in the cold air as it thawed?

'The ice is simply melting, surely,' he called after the Doctor who was now crouched by the misty edge of the reservoir.

'I don't think so.' The Doctor's voice carried back easily through the cold air. 'It's actually bubbling in places.'

'Bubbling?' Dobbs pulled himself upright and took a few steps forwards. But his feet slipped slightly and he felt decidedly unsteady. So from only slightly closer he called: 'Are you sure?'

'It's not something that allows for doubt.' The Doctor sounded put out by the question. He was leaning forward, into the mist. When he turned and started up the slope towards Dobbs, his hands were cupped together in front of him. They were steaming.

'Here,' the Doctor said as he stood in front of the Professor. He nodded towards the shallow water cupped in his hands. 'Stick your finger in.'

Even as he said it, even as Dobbs reached forwards, it was obvious that the water was hot. It was not bubbling, but a hazy mist shimmered from its surface. A drop squeezed out between the Doctor's hands, running down to his lowest knuckles and dripping to the ground. The snow where it landed shrank away from the warmth. Dobbs wondered for a moment if it was screaming as he dipped his finger cautiously into the liquid.

He nodded. 'Warm.' His eyes met the Doctor's. 'What do you think that means?'

'I don't know.' Suddenly the Doctor opened his hands and the water splashed to the ground, making a series of spattered depressions in the snow – a central hole with jagged patches along the edge where the snow sank away. 'Now,' the Doctor said as they both stared after the water, 'lick your finger.'

'I beg your pardon?'

'The wet one. Lick it.'

Reluctantly, Dobbs licked at the tip of the finger with which he had tested the water. He frowned. 'Acidic?'

The Doctor nodded. 'That's what I thought. Interesting, wouldn't you say?'

He saw the man's shadow cast across the snow before he saw the man himself. Gaddis looked up in surprise.

'What are you doing? I've been watching you.'

'I'm sorry, I didn't see you.' Gaddis gulped. 'If I have strayed on to your land, sir, I do apologise.'

But Lord Urton's tone was one of interest rather than accusation. 'What are you doing?' he repeated. 'Are you looking for something?'

'Yes, in a way, sir.' As his apprehension faded, Gaddis became eager to explain. 'You see, I'm using the key as a pendulum. I'm dowsing, looking for hidden paths and lines.'

'What sorts of paths and lines?' Urton was standing with his hands behind his back, regarding Gaddis intently.

'Well, I'm not sure really, sir.'

'And have you enjoyed any success?' His hands were in black leather gloves as Urton stepped forwards, towards Gaddis. 'You did seem to be following a path of sorts.'

Gaddis nodded. 'I'm not sure what it is, some line of power, of influence. There are several.'

Urton was still approaching him. He was slowly teasing off one of the gloves.

'The strange thing is,' Gaddis went on, his attention on the hand as it emerged from within the glove. What was that hissing sound he could hear? His imagination? 'The strange things is,' he repeated through dry lips, feeling the skin stick as they pulled apart, 'that all the lines seem to lead towards the same place. Towards –'

But Urton cut him off. 'Yes.' His voice was still quiet, still reasonable and calm. 'Yes, I do know.'

The hissing was louder now. There was no mistaking it. Like boiling water hitting ice. Urton raised his other hand, and slowly pulled off the remaining glove. Gaddis watched, fascinated, transfixed, as Urton let both gloves fall to the ground. A cloud of steam exploded from the light snow as the gloves landed, scorched their way through.

Now Gaddis *did* take a step back. But too late. Urton's bare hands hissed towards his face, spitting and steaming in the cold air. Gaddis felt the heat of them as they closed on his neck. He opened his mouth to speak, to cry out. But already the air was squeezing out through the hole in his windpipe and all he could manage was a dry rasp of pain. His nostrils were full of the stench as his flesh seared away. Steam choked out of his ruptured throat, rising in front of him and obscuring his vision, smearing out Urton's smiling face.

The cold was eating through his boots. Dobbs stamped his feet hard on the frozen ground as he walked, trying to work some life and feeling back into them. They were beside the fissure again now, walking along its widening length.

'But to raise the temperature of the water in that inlet,' Dobbs said, 'the whole reservoir must be affected to some extent.'

'Heat cannot of itself pass from one body to a hotter body,' the Doctor agreed. He was walking briskly, but otherwise showed no indication that he was feeling the cold. 'Which does rather suggest a source of extreme heat somewhere below the surface.'

'Or on the shore, perhaps?' Dobbs suggested.

The Doctor shook his head. 'We would see it. Melted snow, smoke. At that sort of heat there would be combustion.' He paused, peering into the distance ahead of them. 'No, no, no,' he decided. 'It's in the water. Or below the bed of the reservoir.'

Dobbs blew out a long misty breath. 'But to generate that sort of temperature, Doctor?'

The Doctor was walking forwards again, slowly, cautiously. 'I know. Extreme heat like that might come from the very heart of the planet itself.'

'This fissure?' Dobbs nodded towards the smoking hole beside them. 'It is hot, I grant you. But not so hot as you are suggesting.'

'But who knows how deep it goes? Maybe it runs under the surface, under the reservoir, heat bottled up and looking for an outlet of some sort.'

'Leaking into the reservoir? Is that possible?'

'Anything is possible.' The Doctor pointed across the snow, away from the fissure to their left. 'What's that?'

Dobbs turned to look. 'Wouldn't the water leak back into the fissure?' he asked. But the end of his question dried as he saw what the Doctor was pointing at. 'Good grief.' Dobbs broke into a stumbling, unsteady run.

Dobbs arrived at the body first, glancing back to see the Doctor apparently in no hurry to catch him up. The corpse was lying in an island of grass. The snow seemed to have retreated from it, as if trying to distance itself from the death. The ground was hard and parched, the grass dry and dead. The body was lying on its back. It was charred almost beyond recognition, the clothing fused to the blackened remains, the dark brittle bones visible where the flesh had peeled back. The head was a dark wreck of bone and cartilage, teeth grinning up at the sky.

Retching suddenly and dryly, Dobbs sank to his knees beside the body. His hands were knotted about his walking stick, as if he were planting a memorial to his friend. The Doctor's shadow fell across the dry ground.

'The leaking water would be vaporised by the heat,' he said. His tone seemed unchanged from their earlier conversation.

'What?' Dobbs barely heard the words.

'We have more evidence here of the extremes of temperature.' The Doctor knelt down beside Dobbs, poking a finger into the side of the corpse. The black flesh crumbled like charred paper, flaking to the ground. The Doctor held up his finger, and blew. A mist of fine black soot was carried away by the air and sprinkled itself across the brilliant white of the nearby snow.

'He's dead, Doctor.' Dobbs's voice was a hoarse whisper of disbelief. 'Dead.' He shook his head and stifled a sob.

'Very dead,' the Doctor agreed, standing up. 'Nothing we can do for him now, but it suggests that there is a degree of urgency to our investigations.'

Dobbs pulled himself upright beside the Doctor. 'Don't you understand?' he pleaded. 'Gaddis – Alistair. He's dead. I can't…' He was trembling. 'I don't…' He stared back at the blackened wreck. 'Dear God, what will I say to his mother?' His hand was at his mouth. He swallowed, his throat dry and dusty.

The Doctor was staring off into the distance, back towards the dam. He seemed unaffected by the grotesque discovery. Suddenly, Dobbs was angry at that. 'Have you no feelings, sir?' he demanded. 'Damn it, answer me!' He grabbed hold of the Doctor's sleeve.

When the Doctor turned, he seemed surprised, eyebrows raised. Almost in embarrassment, Dobbs let go of the Doctor's coat. He felt drained, empty. Cold and numb inside.

The Doctor glanced back at the body. He leaned down and carefully brushed a fleck of dust from the charred remains of a lapel. 'Intriguing, isn't it,' he murmured.

Chapter Eight
Curio

The sun was low in the sky. The snow on the streets had turned to dark slush beneath the carriage wheels and horses' hooves. Outside the barracks, soldiers wheeled and turned on the parade ground as the drill officer barked orders through an exhalation of mist.

The Doctor paused to watch the patterns the identical troops made as they marched back and forth, followed instructions, kept in step, responded immediately and mechanically.

Further down the same street he passed the entrance to the station. The cabs and carriages drawn up outside were a counterpoint to the parading soldiers – a medley of shuffling, stamping, haphazard vehicles and animals. The patterns they made were non-patterns, chaotic and indiscriminate, yet there was an underlying order to it.

The figure ahead of the Doctor was dressed in a long grey coat that reached almost to the ground. His gait was purposeful as he continued down the street and he carried a leather holdall. The Doctor waited until he was almost lost amongst the people on the pavement, then followed.

They walked for ten minutes. The figure did not once look back, gave no indication that he thought he was being followed. Or if he did, he did not care. Eventually, he stopped outside a shop. He looked in at the window, then pushed open the door.

The Doctor watched, expressionless. The shop was one of the larger antique dealers in Ambleton. It also dealt in second hand books and other curios. Through the window, the Doctor could see the grey man as he walked round the shop examining the items on display.

Crossing the street, the Doctor went instead into the shop next door. Give the grey man time to make his pitch. He did not look to see what sort of a shop it was, and once inside he paused to look around. It was dim and dusty and smelled of machine oil. At the back of the shop a small man wearing a smeared apron looked up from his work table. He had a jeweller's glass in his eye, as if filtering his view of the Doctor. The only light came through the stained windows and from the lamp that burned on the table, illuminating the man's work.

At once the man returned to his task. 'Feel free to look around.' His voice was husky and grating, as if the mechanism were worn. He waved a hand dismissively in the air. 'If there's anything in particular…'

'I shall ask,' the Doctor assured him. He approached the table, looking to see what the man was working on. Beside him, arranged along the aisle that led to the table, shadowy figures and shapes held their peace. Across the table small pieces of machinery were arranged. Cogwheels and springs, half-assembled mechanisms, drilled metal plates and a collection of brass screws.

There was a sudden metallic click from beside the Doctor, and he froze. Slowly, he turned towards the sound. In the shadows he could make out a figure as it leaned towards him. Its movements were jerky and uneven. A scraping, mechanical sound accompanied the movement and the Doctor saw now that the small figure was a monkey. Its eyes shone out of the darkness as it lifted a paw towards him. There was something clutched in the paw, the Doctor noticed. He saw also that the creature was dressed in a dinner suit. There was the stump of a cigar clamped in its mouth.

'The spring slips.' The man's voice carried apologetically above the sound of the monkey's mechanism. 'There is a loose floorboard there somewhere. It is enough sometimes to set him off.'

'That's fine.' The Doctor watched in fascination as the monkey's hand reached its mouth and he saw that it was raising a lighter. The flame flared for a second, then died. The monkey's paw dropped slowly away, clicking back to its original position. 'What would you evolve into?' he wondered out loud. As if in reply, a stream of smoke ·blew out from the automaton's mouth, enveloping the Doctor in a purple haze. He cleared his throat and continued towards the table.

'This will be a music box,' the man explained. He swept his hand over the table to indicate the parts. 'A dancer inside. She stands up when the box is opened.'

'So she will appear to emerge from the box to dance.' The Doctor nodded enthusiastically. 'Very clever.'

The man shrugged. 'Straightforward enough. It is amazing how small we can make the mechanisms now.'

'Is that so much of an advantage?'

'It means we can better conceal the workings. And we can make the automata smaller also. People prefer smaller ones these days.'

'And they say bigger is better,' the Doctor mused.

'Do they?' He did not seem interested.

The Doctor watched the man work for a minute. 'I was in Turkey once,' he said. 'Well, I think it was Turkey, I have trouble remembering.'

'Mmmm.' The man held up his work to catch the light, nodding with satisfaction.

'They had an automaton there that played chess.'

'Really?' The man continued to nod. 'That would not be too difficult. Some pre-set moves. Two players, a board. Plenty of room for the mechanism.'

'Except,' the Doctor went on, 'that it really *did* play chess. A man, made of hollow metal with flexible arms. He sat beside a board and people paid to play chess against it. It usually won.'

The man let the eyeglass fall from his eye into his palm as he regarded the Doctor. 'Surely that is not possible.'

'That was why people paid. In fact it was very simple.'

The man leaned forward eagerly. 'Tell me.'

The Doctor shrugged. 'It was a midget.'

'I beg your pardon?'

'It was a midget,' the Doctor repeated. 'Hidden inside the metal man. He was quite good,' he added.

'That's cheating,' the man said, his tone betraying his contempt for the very idea.

'That was what the people said when they found out,' the Doctor admitted. 'Though given that the automaton is an imitation of real life, using a live person to imitate an automaton has a certain symmetry. Don't you think?'

The man grunted in a way that suggested strongly that he did not.

The Doctor shrugged. 'I thought you might be interested, that was all. Another example of the utility of smaller mechanisms. I can see that you're busy.'

'Feel free to look around,' the man said.

'Thank you. I will.' The Doctor turned and looked back down the aisle of automata. The monkey had finished puffing smoke and was silent and still once more. Further along the line, a diminutive butler held a tray of glasses in one hand and a bottle in the other. A lion crouched over a terrified woman whose hand was up to ward off its jaws. A soldier stood, rifle shouldered. A steam train waited patiently on a circle of track on a table close to the door.

'Perhaps another day,' the Doctor said as he walked past the mechanical figures. 'When I have the time.' He turned at the door. 'Thank you,' he said.

The man glanced up again briefly, but the Doctor was already stepping out of the shop. He turned abruptly, and went into the antique shop next door.

It was an impressive collection, but not worth anything like what the man was asking. Garfield Gelt shook his head sadly and made an offer.

'Is that really the best you can do?' the man asked. He was a big man, broad and powerful, and the way he leaned forward was intimidating.

Gelt simply shrugged. 'I might manage slightly more.' He picked up a figurine made of silver and examined it for the third time. He sighed. 'Very impressive, I agree. But what can I say? The market just is not there for these… items. Not for something so…'

'Eclectic?'

'Yes, a good term.' Gelt looked up to see who had spoken. He had not heard the door of the shop open, but the voice was not the big man's. Sure enough, standing beside them was a newcomer. His eyes were wide with interest and intelligence, his face framed by a cascade of brown hair. Was there a hint of grey in it, or was it a trick of the light? Something about the man spoke of more years than his appearance would indicate.

'Why, it's Mr Nepath, isn't it?' The newcomer seemed surprised to find the big man there. He extended his hand, and the other man shook it warily.

'Doctor. What brings you here?'

'Oh this and that. One thing and another.' He pushed past Nepath and examined the items spread across the counter. 'Quite a collection.' He turned to Nepath. 'Are you selling? I thought you valued your bric-a-brac more highly than mere money.'

'Some duplicate items. Close matches, that's all,' Nepath said, his eyes narrowing. 'Hardly bric-a-brac.'

'My apologies.' The Doctor picked up a smooth sphere of metal cloisonné finished. 'Chinese?' he asked.

Nepath took the sphere from him and replaced it on the counter. 'Tibetan.'

'Of Course. So how much do you want for it?'

'Now wait a moment, sir,' Gelt said quickly. He did not want to see the items disappear from under his nose. They were worth rather more than he was offering, he knew. They might take a while to sell, but eventually he would more than make his money back.

'Are you interested in them, Doctor?' Nepath asked, cutting across Gelt.

The Doctor seemed to consider a moment. Then he shook his head. 'Not in these,' he said. His fingers brushed against a figure of the goddess Kali fashioned from bronze. 'Beautiful though they are.' He paused, and looked closer. 'Interesting,' he murmured.'

'What?' both Nepath and Gelt asked at once.

'I hope you're not trying to pass this off as genuine fifteenth century work,' the Doctor said to Nepath. He winked at him. 'A seventeenth century copy, surely. The increased emphasis on the shape of the bowls she holds is unmistakable. See how shallow they are, how the flames spring up from them.' He continued before Nepath could respond: 'So why are you selling? Short of storage space in Lord Urton's house?'

'If you must know,' Nepath said, 'It is a question of cash flow. You know the problem, I feel sure.'

'No, actually.' The Doctor smiled at Nepath.

Gelt cleared his throat. He upped his offer, enough he hoped to regain Nepath's interest. 'Three hundred and fifty,' he said. 'No more.'

'A good price,' the Doctor agreed. 'If that's guineas.'

Gelt felt a sudden butterfly of panic. Were the two of them working together? Had this Doctor come in so as to get the offer increased?

'Unless you would care to improve on it, Doctor,' Nepath said.

The Doctor smiled and shook his head. 'I think not. But thank you all the same. I do have an interest in such things. But in genuine artefacts.' His eyes widened. 'Not bric-a-brac.'

Nepath flinched.

Gelt felt hurt despite himself. 'Do you mind, sir?'

'What would you be interested in, Doctor?' Nepath asked softly.

The Doctor's reply was equally quiet. 'What have you to offer?'

Nepath's fingers drummed on the top of the counter a moment. 'You are a man of means, I take it.'

The Doctor shrugged, raised an eyebrow. 'Men of means don't advertise the fact,' he said modestly. He brushed a speck of dust from his stained coat.

'I shall be needing further funding shortly,' Nepath said. His voice was slightly hesitant, as if he was unsure whether to confide in the Doctor or not.

'For the mine?' the Doctor asked.

Nepath nodded. 'Modern machinery is expensive.'

'And you are in a hurry.'

'I see we understand each other.'

'I doubt it.' There was an edge to his voice, though the Doctor was smiling thinly as he said it.

'I am having an exhibition of the more, shall we say, *unusual* items in my collection. At the Grange.'

'How nice for you.'

'Only those who can appreciate their true value are invited.'

'Together with their wallets, I assume.'

Nepath blinked, one side of his face convulsing with the movement, as if it was stiff and hinged to the eyelid in some way. 'You are a man of rare insight. Perhaps you will see something that interests you?' He reached inside his coat and drew out a card. He handed it to the Doctor.

'Perhaps I shall.' The Doctor put the card inside his own jacket pocket without looking at it. 'How nice to see you again, Mr Nepath. I trust your business here is successfully concluded?' Without another word, the Doctor turned and walked from the shop.

'I hope that he is correct in his assumption,' Nepath said.

It took a moment for Gelt to realise that Nepath was addressing him. 'Oh, yes sir. Indeed, sir. Let me find the cheque book.' As he handed over the money order, Gelt asked: 'Was he right?' He pointed to the figure of Kali. 'Is it a late copy?'

Nepath took the cheque. 'Oh yes,' he admitted. 'He was right. About that.'

After leaving the antiques shop, Nepath went straight to the bank. The Doctor watched him emerge a while later. He was not actually counting bank notes, but it was apparent to the Doctor what he had been doing. Keeping well back and in the lengthening shadows of the early evening, the Doctor followed.

As the Doctor had suspected, Nepath was making for the

railway station. The Doctor watched from an adjacent platform as Nepath spoke with a porter, followed the directions he was given, and arrived at length beside a goods train. Beside the train were several men - impatient men from the way they shook their heads and stamped their feet. One of them spoke with Nepath, and the Doctor saw the money exchange hands.

He did not wait to see the train unloaded or the machinery put on to the waiting carriages for transport to Middletown. He lingered just long enough to satisfy himself that it was indeed mining equipment that Nepath was buying - or more probably putting a deposit down for. That would explain why he needed an amount of money today and would need a great deal more in the near future.

There was a cab waiting outside the station and the Doctor clambered in without giving the driver a glance. Once on his way back to Middletown he examined the invitation card which Nepath had given him. He had no intention of buying anything at the exhibition. But he did have every intention of attending.

Chapter Nine
Souvenir

The chairs were arranged in a semicircle around the main display table. For the moment there was nothing on it apart from a felt cloth. As they arrived, the guests had been allowed to browse the display cases and cabinets round the walls. Each of the items was labelled, and it was explained that the items for sale were all marked with a reserve price. If they were not priced, they were not for sale. Not for any amount of money.

Most of it meant nothing to Sir William Grant. He pushed his ample form through the gap between the edge of the ring of chairs and a glass-topped cabinet and made his way to the central seat. Whatever Urton had organised for him, whatever this chap Nepath had to show, it had better be good. He was a busy man. A visit to the barracks at Ambleton might be overdue, but there was no point in admitting he would have had to make the journey anyway. Let them believe he was there entirely for this exhibition. Whatever it turned out to be.

As he waited impatiently, Grant looked round at the other guests. Most were obviously men of means. They wore expensive suits and talked in low voices. They nodded at various items on display, and made scratchy notes in small pocket books. Lord Urton stood by a door at the back of the room, strangely reticent. Usually he was a social man, but today he seemed withdrawn, reserved.

As Grant turned his attention to the table in front of the chairs, a man sat down in the seat next to him. The man seemed as disinterested as Grant himself, stretching out his legs towards the table. Grant turned to look at the man. His face was set in a neutral expression, and his dark hair cascaded down over the shoulders of his bottle-green velvet jacket. He looked almost completely out of place amongst the suits and the polished shoes. His eyes were closed.

Before Grant could look away, one of the man's eyes opened and stared at him. Then the other. The man sat up straight, drawing his legs in. 'You're not interested in the displays?' he asked, his tone mild and polite.

'No more, it seems, than you are.'

'So why are you here?'

'I could ask you the same question.' Grant felt slightly put out by the man's interrogation. He turned away in an attempt to close the conversation.

'No, no.' He was not to be put off. 'I asked first.' The man leaned slightly across so that his shoulder nudged against Grant's 'Come on,' he encouraged, his head bobbing in mock-conspiracy. 'You can tell me.'

Grant shrugged him off. 'Do you mind, sir?' he said loudly. Several heads turned as people reacted.

The man sighed and stretched out his legs again. 'Sorry,' he mumbled. 'Just being friendly.' He crossed his ankles and folded his arms as if sulking. Then suddenly he was upright again, extending his hand. 'I do apologise, I haven't introduced myself. I'm the Doctor.'

Grant shook his hand quickly. 'Grant,' he grunted back. 'Sir William Grant.'

'Delighted.'

They sat in silence for several moments. Around them, the guests continued to examine the displays.

'What are you a doctor of?' Grant asked eventually. He was bored. Even talking to this Doctor was better than sitting in silence and drawing attention. Better to seem engaged in conversation. Keeping busy.

'Well, actually,' the Doctor said slowly, 'I don't really know.' He stared off into space for a moment, then shrugged and sighed. 'I hope it's something impressive though,' he added quietly.

'Don't know?' Grant said in surprise.

'But that's enough about me, what about you?' The Doctor turned on his chair, drawing one leg up underneath himself and facing Grant. 'What do you do? What's your disinterest here?' He grinned suddenly.

'I am responsible for equipment procurements for the army, sir,' Grant said in what he hoped and intended was a suitably impressive tone. 'I am here by invitation. I must confess I am not entirely sure why Lord Urton felt this exhibition would be of use, but he was most insistent I come.'

'Good old Urton.' The Doctor swung round again. 'I think we're about to begin the auction,' he said.

As he finished speaking, the door beside Lord Urton opened and a man entered the room. He was a large man, with a craggy face and grey hair that was brushed immaculately. He strode purposefully to the table in front of Grant and the Doctor and waited. It did not take long for others to notice he was there. They began to drift towards seats, and before long there was a silence of anticipation.

'Good afternoon, gentlemen,' the man said. 'I am Roger Nepath, and I thank you for coming, just as I thank Lord Urton for his hospitality. Many of you have come a considerable distance, and I know you will not be disappointed.'

As he spoke, Urton removed a piece from one of the cabinets and carried it to the table. He set it down in front of Nepath. It was a bronze figure, about eight inches tall. A naked woman, her hair tied back. She was dancing, one hand on her hip, the other held aloft. In the upraised hand, she held a bowl of fire.

'A bronze statuette from Mohenjodaro. Over four thousand years old,' Nepath said. 'I trust you have all had ample time to examine her. You will have noticed that she is a ritual dancer, naked apart from the necklace and bangles, wed to the temple god.'

There was a general shuffling as people leaned forwards in their seats. Several already had their pocket books raised, ready to bid.

But Nepath was not yet finished. 'She was discovered in seventeen ninety-three by the Daniells brothers in the cave temple of Kanheri. The temple was hewn from the living rock by –'

'Is the fire significant?'

Nepath blanched at the interruption.

'At all?' the Doctor went on. He was again sprawled in his seat, legs out and arms folded. 'It's just that I notice almost all the items you have here display some affinity with fire. Either explicitly or by association.'

Nepath answered slowly. 'Fire is a theme of my collection, yes. How observant of you, Doctor. There is no especial significance in this particular case.'

'Any of them?'

'I beg your pardon?'

There were impatient shuffles and murmurs now. The bidders were anxious to get started.

'Sorry,' the Doctor went on. 'I was just wondering, before we start, whether there is any significance to the fire motif in any of the items that you have up for sale. It just seems to me that there isn't. That you are withholding any and all pieces where the fire is, what shall we say, integral?' He paused, then nodded as if pleased with his choice of word. 'Yes, integral to the work.'

Nepath's reply was an impatient rasp. 'And if I am, that is surely my prerogative.' He drew a deep breath, and went on: 'Since you are so interested, Doctor, perhaps you would start the bidding. The reserve on this piece is one hundred and ten guineas.'

The Doctor held up his hands as if in deferential surprise. 'Oh I'm not interested in bidding,' he said quickly. 'But you please go on.' He smiled. 'Don't mind me.'

The dancing statuette eventually went for over two hundred guineas. But by that time Grant had already lost interest. Beside him the Doctor's eyes were again closed, and at one point Grant could swear he heard the man snore.

It took almost three hours to conclude the auction. By the end of it Grant was thoroughly bored and the seat had become decidedly uncomfortable. The final piece, a figure of a man with four arms dancing within a circle of fire that ran from his feet over the top of his head, his hair splayed out to touch the edges of the ring, went for a staggering amount of money. To Grant it was merely another bronze statue. He had watched figures and boxes and bowls and ivory sold for what seemed to be quite unsupportable sums.

Nepath drew the proceedings to a close and once again thanked everyone for their presence and for their patience. People slowly began to leave, ushered out by Lord and Lady Urton. A woman with a face like a well-worn hatchet was on hand to show them the way back to the entrance hall.

Grant waited for Urton to come and find him. There was more to it than the auction, he was sure. Urton would never have dragged him halfway across the country for this. Beside him, the Doctor also sat unmoving, as if waiting for more. As he glanced round the room, Grant saw that several other men were also lingering.

It was Nepath who approached them. He stared at the Doctor for a moment, and received a wry smile in return. Nepath turned to Grant. 'Sir William, how good of you to come,' he said quietly, reaching down to shake the man's hand. His huge grip was firm. 'Your journey will not be wasted, I assure you.' He glanced again at the Doctor, frowning.

'I am glad to hear it, sir,' Grant told him. 'So far it has been interesting, but hardly my sort of event I admit.' He tried to inject the right amount of anticipation and censure into his tone. Admonishing but not alienating, he hoped.

Nepath smiled thinly and turned to the Doctor. 'I apologise, Doctor,' he said. 'It seems that nothing here engaged your interest. A pity. But perhaps another time?' It was clear that the Doctor was not invited to stay behind.

Yet still the Doctor did not move. He made no effort to stand, let alone leave. 'Yes, a great pity,' he said smoothly. 'I'm sad to think I was invited here under false pretences.'

Nepath drew in his breath sharply. 'What do you mean?'

The Doctor stretched and yawned. 'You said there would be

artefacts here that were unusual, intriguing. Of interest to a specialist.'

Nepath was angry, but he struggled to hide it. 'I think the guests were well pleased with the occasion and with what they saw and purchased.'

'Oh I don't doubt it.' The Doctor leaped suddenly to his feet, his eyes level with Nepath's as he leaned slightly forward and returned his stare. 'But to those of us who have been there, who have seen the temples of living rock, drunk from the fountains of cascading white water, spoken with the wise men of the mountains.' He shrugged and sighed. 'Hardly enthralling.'

Before Nepath could respond the Doctor nodded towards another of the men who was waiting behind. Grant recognised him as the final buyer. He was holding the statuette of the man within his ring of fire.

'Shiva,' the Doctor said. 'A rare and beautiful piece. But hardly extraordinary.'

'Perhaps you are misinformed, Doctor,' Grant suggested. He could see that Nepath was annoyed, and wanted to help.

'Oh, I doubt it,' the Doctor said lightly. 'The god of dance and of music. His dancing keeps the universe moving, like the ring of fire. It supplies the raw cosmic energy that fuels all life. He beats the drum in his right-most hand to signify the pulse of creation itself. The fire simultaneously creates and destroys the universe as he constantly dances, isn't that right? And heaven help us, literally, if he should stop.'

'I see that you know your subject, Doctor,' Nepath said. There was a hint of appreciation in his tone.

'I know many subjects,' the Doctor responded. 'But I am surprised you were prepared to part with such a piece. After your comments on the fire theme.' He smiled widely. 'Unless you have another, or there is some flaw in this one.' He clicked his tongue. 'I hate to be kept in the dark, you know. Like the dwarf.'

'The dwarf?' Grant asked.

'The figure, Shiva, is standing on the head of a dwarf,' Nepath

96

said. His eyes were still on the Doctor. 'The dwarf represents ignorance.'

'Ah!' The Doctor had lifted his finger in the air, like a schoolboy with an urgent question. 'Got it!' His voice echoed round the room. He seemed oblivious to the stares of the few people left as he leaned close to Nepath and whispered, just loud enough for Grant to catch the words: 'It's a copy, isn't it? And you have the original.' He stepped back and clapped his hands together as if in congratulation. 'Well, I hope you've sold the right one.' He sighed loudly. 'Such a pity you had nothing of real interest. Such a disappointment.' He hesitated for a moment, his eyes locked with Nepath's before adding. 'Well, I must be on my way, no doubt you have some other bric-a-brac to offload.'

Nepath seemed to flinch at the word. His face crumpled round the eyes for an instant before he regained control. His voice was level and stern, drained of emotion. 'Perhaps you would like to stay and see exactly what sort of bric-a-brac, as you call it, I really have, Doctor.' It sounded more like a command than a question.

The Doctor had already turned away even as Nepath was speaking. 'Oh I doubt it's anything much,' he said. 'Baubles and trinkets.'

'I insist!' Nepath's voice was a thunderbolt of angry sound. Then, more restrained, more controlled. 'Please, Doctor.'

Slowly the Doctor turned. His face was grim, mouth taut. 'Well, in that case,' he said quietly, 'I should be honoured, of course.' Without another word he returned to the seat beside Grant.

There were five of them left behind, not counting Nepath and Lord Urton. When all the others had gone, Nepath led them through the house to Urton's drawing room. A fire was set in the grate, the flames roaring up in a brilliant display of orange and yellow. In front of the fire was a low table on which were arranged several items. Grant surveyed them as he took his place in an armchair close by.

There was what looked like a solid sphere of dark material,

rather like a cannonball. Beside this was a statue which stood about a foot tall, made of burnished, shining metal. It was a bird, its wings outstretched and its head turned sideways so that it was seen in profile. The detail of the feathers and the features was intricate and impressive. Further along the table were what looked like pebbles or small rocks, of the same dark material as the sphere. Next to these was a bowl, and Grant caught sight of dark liquid within it. At the end of the table was a pair of tongs taken it seemed from the fire irons that stood in a brass bucket beside the grate, and a large lump hammer.

'This is more like it,' a voice said quietly close to Grant.

He turned and saw that the Doctor had taken the chair closest to him. 'Why? What's going on?'

'I have no idea,' the Doctor confessed gleefully. 'But that's always more fun, don't you think?'

Grant did not agree. He liked to know exactly what was happening. He liked to understand and control the situation. He shuffled uneasily in his chair.

When they were all seated, Nepath strode to the front of the room and stood with his back to the fire. Lord Urton stood close by, hands behind his back, expression fixed and stony. Grant was again surprised at how reticent the man was. Quite unlike his usual self.

'I think,' Nepath said with obvious relish, 'that you will all find this session instructive.' He turned and nodded to Lord Urton, who took the rocks and pebbles from the table and passed them out to the assembled men.

Grant examined his pebble as Nepath waited. It was smooth and heavy. The material was warm to the touch, which made him suspect it was neither metal nor stone. He pressed at it to feel how hard it was, and felt the material squash under his thumb. He almost dropped it in surprise. He looked up quickly, hoping nobody had seen his reaction, and found his movement mirrored by most of the others as they too shared the discovery.

Only the Doctor seemed not to be looking to Nepath in

surprise. He was busily squeezing the material he had been given into a flat shape. The tip of his tongue was just visible at the corner of his mouth as he worked at it, folding and bending it. Slowly, everyone turned to watch. He seemed to realise the attention, and looked up, eyes wide and innocent. Slowly, like a guilty schoolboy he held up the material, to show he had squeezed and shaped it into a perfect sphere.

Nepath's voice recaptured their attention. 'The material you have been given to examine…' He paused and glanced pointedly at the Doctor. '…To play with,' he corrected himself, 'has some interesting properties. It is, in answer to what is probably your first question, rock.'

'You mean it occurs naturally?' a man at the back of the group asked.

'Yes,' Nepath replied. 'And no.' He waited a moment before continuing. 'The rock itself is unremarkable. In fact, it can be found in the mine workings close to here. What gives it its unique properties is the way it is refined. A technique known only to the Abritzi people of the Urdesh.'

'Never heard of them,' someone muttered.

'And,' Nepath continued without pause, 'to myself.'

A third man spoke, his voice quiet and reasonable. 'So we have squashable, compressible rock. Remarkable I grant you, but is it of practical use? Of value?'

'I suggest you save that thought, Mr Milton,' Nepath told him. 'I trust that in a few minutes you will not consider any need to repeat it.' He turned towards where the Doctor was sitting admiring his sphere. 'Doctor, may I?' He held out his hand.

The Doctor smiled. 'Of course.' He tossed the ball of material to Nepath, who caught it cleanly.

Nepath held up the ball for everyone to see. Then he turned and threw it into the fire.

'Not impressed?' the Doctor asked.

'We shall see who is impressed, shall we?' Nepath passed the tongs from the table to Lord Urton who took them to the fire. He reached into the flames with the tongs and carefully picked out the material. He held it up for them to see.

It was no longer a sphere. It had changed shape again, and was an amorphous lump of dark rock.

There was silence.

'It's melted,' Milton called from the back. 'Is that what you're showing us?'

Before Nepath could reply, the Doctor leaned forward in his seat, his eyes gleaming. 'No,' he said, 'no, that's not it at all. Is it, Mr Nepath?'

'At last, you are impressed, eh, Doctor?'

The Doctor returned Nepath's smile. 'I am,' he admitted. 'But do please continue with the parlour tricks. Do let's impress everyone else too.'

'Thank you, Doctor.' Nepath turned his attention back to the table and lifted the large sphere. It was obviously heavy and he needed both hands. 'This is a hardened version of the material. You may examine it later if you wish. It's characteristics are very similar to those of toughened steel. You will see in a moment the opportunities that offers.' He replaced it on the table. It dropped the final inch with a crack.

Next he turned to the statue of the bird. He held it up, examining it closely. 'An intermediate stage,' he explained. 'Not so malleable as the raw material you have, but not so unyielding as this.' He tapped the sphere. 'Mr Milton, would you join me for a moment, please?'

Milton made his way to the table. He was a tall, thin man with oiled hair brushed across the obvious baldness of his head. His nose was a flattened lump on his broad face.

'Your material?' Nepath asked. When Milton held it out, Nepath gestured for him to place it on the table. 'Press it flat, if you would. Good.' Nepath took what looked like a pen from his pocket, but it had no nib. It was merely a thin rod of metal that tapered to a blunt point. He handed it to Milton. 'Write something. Anything. Just scratch it on to the surface would you? Or draw something, it doesn't matter.'

Grant leaned forward to watch as Milton bent to scratch at the material. When he was finished, Urton stepped forward and took hold of the flat disc of material with the tongs. He carefully dipped it into the bowl of liquid, holding it there for several seconds before pulling it dripping out again. He held it out to Nepath.

Nepath had his handkerchief out and wrapped it around the disc, patting it dry. An inky blot appeared through the cotton. When he was done, Urton placed the disc back on the table before Milton.

'Now,' Nepath told him, 'I want you to pick up the material. Good. Now, squash it into another shape. Anything.'

Puzzled, Milton squeezed the disk into a blob.

'And throw it on to the fire.'

Milton tossed it into the flames. After several seconds, Urton stepped across and once again reached in with the tongs. He drew out a smoking disc of material and carried it to the table. He dropped it on to the table before Milton who stared down at it in disbelief.

'It's a trick.' He reached out, his fingers stopping shy of the surface.

'No trick,' Nepath said. 'And you can touch it. The heat is all absorbed in the process, it won't burn you. Not now.'

Milton picked up the disc and examined it. 'But, how could you know. My daughter's name. And a scratched pattern.' He gave a short sharp laugh and returned the disc to Nepath. 'How's it done?' he demanded.

Nepath smiled in reply. Realising his role was over, Milton returned to his seat.

'Perhaps, Mr Grant, you would assist me with the explanations?' Nepath said.

'Me?' Grant got to his feet and approached the table, negotiating the other chairs. He felt slightly nervous, though he did not know why. 'What do you wish me to do?' He tucked in his shirt. It always worked loose when he was seated. His waistcoat buttons were straining again, he noticed.

Lord Urton held out the lump hammer. Grant took it. The handle was smooth, pale wood. The business end was heavy, dark metal. He hefted it experimentally as he waited for Nepath to explain.

Nepath patted the bird's head. 'Let's see if you can hammer this flat,' he said.

Grant was amazed. 'You can't be serious?'

'Oh, I'm very serious,' Nepath assured him. 'Go on.'

Grant stared at him. Then at the statue of the bird. He took a deep breath. 'Very well.' He let the hammer fall on the ends of a wing, holding the base as he cautiously bent the wing tip. The hammer rang as if striking metal.

Nepath was shaking his head. 'Put some effort into it man,' he said. 'Hammer it flat. I mean it.'

Grant looked up, saw the determination in Nepath's face, and then set to with more vigour. The wings bent down with little effort. Then, at a further nod from Nepath, he set about the beak and the head. The audience watched transfixed as he worked. It seemed to take forever, but eventually all that was left of the intricate detail of the statue was a lump of bent and squashed metal.

'Thank you,' Nepath said taking the hammer.

Grant was breathing heavily, perspiring from the exertion. He watched Urton lift the results of his work in the tongs and carry the shapeless lump to the fire. He perched it carefully on top of the burning coals and stepped away.

'Once treated,' Nepath said as they watched and waited, 'the material, as I have said, has the characteristics of workable metal.'

Something was stirring within the flames. The material was moving, writhing within the fire.

'Another treatment, and the form is fixed. We can determine whether the substance remains malleable or becomes hardened. We can fix it at any intermediate state we wish.'

Within the fire, the lump seemed to be expanding. As Grant watched in amazement, what looked like a wing unfolded from the mass and stretched out.

'That second treatment imbues the material with memory. Memory of its form.'

A second wing curled outwards and upwards, artificial feathers reflecting the light.

'Whatever happens after that, whether the form is squashed or broken or dropped or moulded, it remembers how it was.'

The centre of the mass was lifting, thrusting upwards now. The head of the bird emerged within the fire, staring out accusingly at Grant before it slowly turned sideways into profile. The beak seemed to expand from the head. The flames licked round the bird's feet.

'We merely apply heat, and it gains the energy it needs to return to that form.'

Nepath nodded to Urton. As they watched, Lord Urton reached into the flames with his bare hands and took hold of the bird. He pulled it free of the fire and held it up for everyone to see.

'And thus is the phoenix reborn,' Nepath said.

For a moment there was silence. Then there was sudden applause and everyone started talking at once. The only still points were Nepath and Urton standing in front of the fire, the phoenix raised above them. And the Doctor, sitting absolutely still in his armchair, his elbows resting on the arms, his fingers steepled to his chin.

The guests seemed reluctant to leave after the demonstration. But Nepath assured them all that he would be in touch directly to discuss with them the opportunities the incredible material offered them in their own lines of business. Grant watched it all through a kind of mist. His mind was racing, trying to take in what he had seen and assimilate it, trying to assess the possibilities.

Finally, it seemed that only Grant was left with Nepath and Lord Urton. He realised they were waiting, expecting a comment.

Grant cleared his throat. 'Very impressive,' he conceded. 'I've, well – I've never seen anything like it. Though I have to confess...' His voice trailed away.

'Yes?' Nepath prompted.

'Well, I fail to see how this substance, remarkable though it is, can be relevant to my own field of interest. To military procurements.'

Nepath nodded slowly, as if the same idea had just struck him. 'Perhaps a more practical demonstration would help clear up that matter?'

'It would help,' Grant agreed, wondering what he had in mind.

'Good. Excellent.' Nepath clapped his hands together. He turned, almost in triumph, it seemed, to Lord Urton who stood stony-faced beside him. Then he leaned towards Grant, reaching over the ample stomach to place a hand on Grant's shoulder. 'Actually,' he confessed, 'I did anticipate your reservation. So I have taken the slight liberty of arranging such a demonstration. Tomorrow. On the moors. Colonel Wilson in command of the Engineers stationed at Ambleton has kindly agreed to help me organise it.'

'What a terrific idea. Is it open to anyone?'

Nepath gaped. For a moment he was frozen in surprise in front of Grant. It was obvious that he too had forgotten that they were not alone. Grant turned in time to see the Doctor rising from his armchair and grinning across the room at them.

'Doctor.' Nepath's voice was low, edged with anger and a hint of something darker. 'I regret that it will be a private demonstration. Military security, national interest. I'm sure you understand.'

'I think I'm beginning to.' The Doctor's voice was also low. 'Thank you for a fascinating time. I feel I have learned a lot.' Suddenly his manner brightened. 'Though I'm happy to report that you didn't quite manage to tempt me to part with any money.'

'No.' Nepath's voice was level, almost toneless. 'No I didn't, did I?' He took a step towards the Doctor. Somehow, Grant thought, the gesture seemed threatening. 'Goodbye, Doctor.'

'Au revoir,' the Doctor replied amiably. He gave a brief wave, and turned to leave.

'Oh, Doctor?' Nepath called after him, his tone lighter now.

'Yes?'

'Here. Catch.'

Nepath threw something to the Doctor, who caught it easily and held it up. It was the small piece of the dark material he had examined earlier. Grant could see that it was once again perfectly spherical, returned to the form the Doctor had moulded.

'A souvenir,' Nepath explained. 'I would hate you to depart empty handed.'

'How kind,' the Doctor said. He seemed genuinely grateful. 'Something to remember you by.' He gave a quick nod of his head by way of farewell, then he was gone.

Nepath watched the empty doorway for several moments before he returned his attention to Grant. 'Tomorrow then, Sir William,' he said. 'Colonel Wilson will call for you and bring you to the test area.'

'Thank you.'

Nepath glanced back towards the door. 'By then,' he said quietly, 'we should be ready to discuss business without further distractions or interruptions.'

Grant waited. But Nepath seemed to have finished. He strode from the room without another word, leaving Grant standing alone with Lord Urton.

'Robert,' Grant said, wondering how to phrase his question. 'Robert, is everything… you know? All right?'

Lord Urton met his concerned look. Grant could see the firelight reflected deep within Urton's eyes, flickering as if behind the irises. 'Everything's fine,' Urton said. His voice was empty and dead.

Grant hesitated. Suddenly he felt very hot. He slid a sweaty finger round his damp collar. 'Good,' he said. 'Good. And Eloise is well?'

Urton held out his hand. 'Everything's fine,' he repeated.

Grant took hold of Urton's hand and shook it. He felt Urton's grip tight on his own damp, pudgy hand. A grip like stone.

Chapter Ten
Firing Test

Professor Dobbs was tired after the long return journey. He gratefully accepted the cup of tea that Betty Stobbold gave him. There was a good fire burning in the drawing room of the Rectory and he sat for a while, alone and silent, watching the patterns the flames threw against the black of the chimney.

When Stobbold came in, he was good enough to sit quietly alongside the Professor, not disturbing his thoughts.

'It is kind of you to extend your hospitality to me once again,' Dobbs told him at last.

Stobbold smiled by way of reply. A sympathetic, understanding smile. 'You are always welcome. Though I am not certain I know why you would want to return.'

'Unfinished business. Isn't that so, Professor?' The Doctor was across the room in a moment, sinking himself into the sofa across from Dobbs. 'And I shall be glad of your help.'

Stobbold frowned at the Doctor, but Dobbs shook his head. 'The Doctor is right,' he said. 'Unfinished business. Like the Doctor, I believe there was more to poor Alistair's death than a freak lightning bolt, whatever the coroner may have decided.'

'Good for you.' The Doctor rubbed his hands together happily. Then, abruptly, his face fell and his expression hardened. 'I'm sorry,' he said quietly, 'how was the funeral?'

Dobbs turned back to the fire. For a while he watched the flames again dancing and flickering. 'Hardly the best way to say one's farewells,' he said. 'But an opportunity for friends and family to air their grief.'

Stobbold leaned across and put his hand on Dobbs's shoulder. 'The grief will pass. Treasure his memory, while it is fresh. He will always be with you, in your mind, but the pain will ease as he retreats and waits for you to search for him. When you need him.'

Dobbs drew a deep breath. 'I shall miss him. He was infuriating, he was so naive. He had such a lot still to learn.'

'As do we all,' the Doctor said.

Dobbs swallowed and pulled himself together. With an effort he swung round to face his friends. Stobbold let go of his shoulder and sat back. 'Unfinished business,' Dobbs said again. 'I too am learning. I am learning to keep a more open mind. To inquire and not to assume.'

The Doctor was nodding, his eyes bright and interested.

'I am open to the possibilities,' Dobbs said to the Doctor. 'All I ask is that we stop this... whatever it is. Before anyone else suffers. Or dies.'

Stobbold looked from Dobbs to the Doctor and back. 'What do you mean?' he asked quietly. 'What is going on here?'

'I wish I knew,' the Doctor said simply. 'But the Professor here is right. There are forces at work, evil afoot. Death is approaching.'

Stobbold snorted, a sudden laugh of surprise. 'You exaggerate, surely.'

'Do I?' The Doctor leaned forward, eyes wide and hard as rock. 'I don't know what it is, not yet. But we stand on the brink of the abyss. And while Professor Dobbs's sentiments are laudable, I fear it is already too late to prevent the death and the destruction. All we can hope to do is to stem the flow, to hold back the forces of darkness.'

'A powerful speech, Doctor,' Stobbold said quietly.

'Thank you.' He seemed pleased with the comment, nodding appreciatively.

'But by your own admission, you don't really know what is happening here. If anything.'

'True.' He seemed amused now.

'So how do we find out?' Dobbs asked.

'Ah!' The Doctor leaped to his feet. 'That is the question. And I believe I have a lead or two that might help to define the problem.' He stood directly in front of Stobbold, staring down at him with a sudden intensity. 'You know the moorland round here, Reverend.'

'Well…'

'Well, where would you hold a test? A secret test that you did not want anyone to oversee or overhear? There can't be many areas that are remote enough from the roads and distant enough from Middletown, Ambleton and Branscombe-sub-Edge yet still readily accessible for such an exercise.' He shuffled from foot to foot as he spoke, as if already impatient for the answer.

'There are a couple of possible areas,' Stobbold said thoughtfully. 'Let me get a map.'

Several minutes later the three of them were hunched over the maps spread across the dining room table. Stobbold pointed out several areas that he said were secluded yet accessible with equipment. Betty brought them a tray of tea, standing between the Doctor and her father as she watched their deliberations. She was quiet and withdrawn, offering no comment.

'Did I drop that?' the Doctor asked suddenly. 'How careless.' He reached out and Betty returned to him the shiny black cube that she was holding.

Her face creased into a frown as he put the cube back in his pocket.

'I've had it for years,' the Doctor said. 'A souvenir. Perhaps.' He smiled, tilting his head to one side. 'Thank you for the tea.'

'You're welcome, Doctor.' She returned his smile, then turned and left them to it.

'She seems a little…' Dobbs was not altogether sure what he wanted to say.

Stobbold nodded and gave a sigh. 'Since her birthday. She's growing up. Really growing up. She has had to cope with so much that I think maybe it's a bit of a shock to her to find she's still got a way to go.'

'A never-ending process,' the Doctor agreed. 'So you think this is the best spot?' He jabbed a finger at one of the points Stobbold had indicated on the map.

'I would say so,' he agreed. 'But what exactly have you in mind?'

The Doctor seemed surprised. He stood upright and slapped his palm across his chest. 'Me?'

'This test you spoke of,' Dobbs reminded him. 'I confess I am intrigued too.'

The Doctor gave a short laugh. He recovered his more serious composure immediately. 'Oh, it's not my test,' he admitted. 'I have no idea what's going on.'

'I beg your pardon?' Stobbold faced the Doctor, gripping his lapels.

'No, no, no. Nepath has arranged some sort of demonstration for tomorrow morning. With the army.'

'In secret?' Dobbs asked.

The Doctor nodded.

'And you intend to spy on them?' Stobbold's voice was as stern as his expression.

The Doctor smiled back at him. 'Of course. We have to know what's going on.'

'Jolly good, Doctor,' Dobbs agreed, clapping his hands together. 'That's the spirit, take the action to the enemy.' He paused and thought for a moment. 'I assume they *are* the enemy?'

'This is how we find out,' the Doctor told him.

Stobbold was shaking his head. 'I cannot allow this,' he said. 'I really cannot countenance such surreptitious means to obtain information.'

'What?' The Doctor seemed scandalised. 'You can't?' He stood absolutely still for a moment, then said: 'All right.'

'All right?' Stobbold repeated, disbelieving.

The Doctor nodded. 'All right,' he said again. 'We'll go without you. Won't we, Professor?'

'But, Doctor – Professor…' Stobbold objected.

Dobbs met his gaze. 'The Doctor is right,' he said. 'Any means are justified if we are to prevent this calamity that he describes.'

'Describes?' Stobbold was barely holding his anger in check. 'He describes nothing, nothing of substance. All we have are some suspicions that everything is not as it should be and a mysterious death.' He paused, making an obvious effort to control his emotion. 'I feel for your loss, Professor. But is this sort of underhand and dishonest action warranted? This prying into the private affairs of others, perhaps of the nation itself, justified?'

They both turned back to the Doctor for an answer. But he was once again leant over the map, his finger tapping thoughtfully on the location they had agreed.

Since the Doctor had no idea what time the demonstration was due to take place, they arrived just before dawn. As the light spread across the shallow dip of the secluded moorland, the Doctor pointed to a low ditch that ran across the ground at the edge of the concealed area. The angle of the ground was such that from beyond the ditch it would be difficult to see into the shallow basin where they hoped the demonstration might take place. A long, low ridge framed the far side of the area.

Dobbs drew his coat tightly about him in the frosty air and settled down beside the Doctor. It might, he knew, be a long wait. And that was assuming they were overlooking the correct location.

'Let's hope they aren't intending to watch their demonstration from this ditch,' the Doctor said brightly.

Dobbs grunted a reply. He was cold, and the ice in the bottom of the ditch was melting under his freezing feet to produce slippery mud. Everywhere he looked he saw snow. 'How long do we give it before we decide we're in the wrong place?' he asked.

'Not long,' the Doctor reassured him. 'Military men are early risers.'

'Are you sure?'

'Oh yes.' So saying, he lay back in the ditch and closed his eyes.

An hour later, the Doctor had not moved and Dobbs was getting cramp. He shuffled his position, trying to stretch out his leg and ease the building pain.

'Keep still,' the Doctor hissed. 'Here they come.' His eyes were still tight shut.

'How can you tell?' Dobbs whispered, trying to bend his toes within his boot.

'Can't you hear them?' The Doctor's eyes snapped open and he eased himself up on his elbows to peer over the top of the ditch.

Dobbs joined him and together they stared out across the low ground. There was nothing to be seen except the frosted grass and frozen land. But as he surveyed the ground, Dobbs could hear something, a jingling sound. As he watched, a team of horses crested the low ridge on the far side of the area. Instinctively, he ducked down slightly lower.

There were four horses harnessed together in pairs, controlled by a single rider on one of the front horses. They were pulling something that made tracks through the thin covering of snow. Dobbs could see the mist from their hot breath as they dragged the gun carriage down the embankment and into the middle of the concealed area. They were coming straight towards where the Doctor and Dobbs were hiding. He glanced at the Doctor, but he seemed intent on the scene before them, not at all discomfited by the horses now racing towards them.

The horses stopped two thirds of the way across the area. The rider leaped down and undid the harnesses so that the gun carriage stood free of the horses. Then he remounted and rode the horses back the way he had come. The field gun stood abandoned fifty yards from where the Doctor and Dobbs were hiding. The polished brass of the gun shone in the early morning sun. The wheels had made barely an impression on the hard ground.

On the ridge behind the gun, more horses were arriving. Their riders dismounted, and grouped together looking down at the field gun. Several of them had field glasses. A carriage drew up on the ridge and Dobbs saw a portly man clamber out and join the soldiers. Behind him were two other figures – Nepath and Lord Urton. The team of horses that had pulled the gun disappeared over the ridge. A moment later a similar team appeared, pulling another gun.

The second gun was positioned on the ridge, beside the observers. Its crew of five artillery men wheeled the gun forwards slightly, turning it so that it pointed across the basin of ground. Towards the ditch where the Doctor and Dobbs were hidden.

'Fascinating,' the Doctor breathed.

'Frightening,' Dobbs corrected him. 'They're going to fire on us.'

'No, no. They'll be aiming for that gun.' The Doctor pointed across the moorland. 'Antiquated muzzle-loading canon, probably left over from the Crimean. Anyway,' he went on, 'I think we've seen enough now.'

'Enough?' Dobbs was puzzled. 'We've seen nothing. Nothing at all.'

'Oh, I think it's obvious what's going on,' the Doctor said dismissively. He turned and looked out of the ditch the other way.

'Not to me it isn't.'

But the Doctor seemed not to be listening. 'The problem is that from the ridge there, with binoculars, they'll see us if we move. I'd rather that didn't happen.'

'Doctor,' Dobbs said with enforced patience, 'will you please tell me what is happening?'

'I think we'll have to wait here anyway,' the Doctor replied. 'So you'll see for yourself.'

As he finished speaking there was a whining sound. It seemed to come from above them, and Dobbs pulled himself up the side of the ditch to try to see what was happening. The Doctor immediately grabbed him by the shoulder and pulled him back again. A moment later the ground just beyond the lip of the ditch exploded with a thundercrack that deafened Dobbs and sent clumps of frozen mud and grass flying across him.

'Good God! I knew it – they're shooting at us!'

'Just getting the range. I think they overshot slightly, but they'll have it in a moment.' He cautiously leaned up and peered over the broken edge of the ditch. 'Here we go.'

Another whine, followed by another explosion. This time further back. Dobbs remained huddled in the bottom of the ditch, no longer concerned about the freezing mud round his ankles and shins.

'You really should watch this, you know,' the Doctor told him.

Reluctantly, Dobbs joined the Doctor and looked out across the moorland. Smoke from the previous explosion was drifting slowly in front of the field gun. The crater was within fifteen feet of the gun. The Doctor was right – the next shot would be a direct hit.

On the ridge, Dobbs saw the flash of light and puff of smoke from the muzzle of the field gun pointing across at them. He held his breath.

In the hollow before them, the target gun exploded in a loud fireball. The wheels were blown outwards off the axle, the gun barrel twisted in the air, broken and bent. The carriage itself was splintered into fragments. For several seconds after the explosion, the grass under the gun burned with a pale orange flame. The smoke drifted away to reveal the wreckage.

'A good shot, Colonel Wilson,' Grant congratulated him. 'Excellent work.'

'Thank you, sir. I will convey that to the men.' Wilson nodded to his sergeant who marched across to the gun team, still kneeling and standing in position round their weapon.

'But I fail to appreciate the significance of this demonstration,' Grant went on, this time addressing his comment to Nepath.

'Perhaps that is because the demonstration has not yet begun,' Nepath told him. He nodded down towards the wrecked field gun. 'Watch.'

Grant shrugged and turned back towards the hollow basin of ground. As he saw what was happening there, he began to understand why Nepath had brought him here.

'Good grief,' Wilson said beside him.

At first it was a twitching, a slight movement of the broken fragments of the gun. But before long, the distorted metal was bending and twisting back into shape. One of the wheels, bent almost back on itself by the blast was slowly unfolding. The other sprang back to a perfect circle. The broken pieces of the gun carriage seemed to flow back together like viscous liquid before reforming into their original shape. The pieces blown further out left dark trails through the covering of snow.

'The material uses the exothermic reaction of the explosion itself, draws on the generated heat of the blast,' Nepath explained. 'That provides the energy.'

'The gun was made of your memory material,' Grant realised.

'That's right. We took moulds from an actual Crimean weapon to which Colonel Wilson was good enough to provide us access.'

'I don't follow, sir,' Wilson said. 'You mean that was not our own artillery piece?'

'A copy. Made from a material mined not far from here in fact,' Nepath said. 'A material treated and refined according to the techniques of the Urdesh sorcerers and wise men.'

Nepath pointed down at the field gun. It was still in pieces, but the pieces were each complete and whole again, laid out across the blackened moorland. 'All you need to do is put it back together. Hardly a difficult task, I imagine.'

'Self-repairing equipment,' Grant said quietly. 'This could save a fortune in acquisitions.'

'Even the ammunition can be reclaimed, assuming it is made to my specifications, and with my materials,' Nepath said. He handed Grant an envelope. 'My terms,' he explained. 'For an initial exploratory contract, exclusive to Her Majesty's Ordnance.'

Grant immediately made to take the envelope. The importance of the deal was not lost on him. Nor was the kudos that would go to the man who arranged it. But Nepath pulled the envelope away.

'I would appreciate the initial payment immediately. I do have certain overheads that must be met in the short term.'

Grant licked his dry lips. 'I'm sure that won't be a problem,' he said. His voice was dry and hoarse. He was feeling hot again despite the cold of the morning.

'Lord Urton will accompany you back to Ambleton,' Nepath said. 'You have a train to catch.' He nodded to Urton, who gestured for Grant to lead the way back to the carriage.

'Do you need dropping off on the way?' Grant asked.

Nepath shook his head. 'I shall walk to the mine. It isn't far.'

Colonel Wilson was still staring down at the remains of the field gun. 'Incredible,' he said. 'Absolutely incredible. As an engineer, I...' He turned to Nepath. 'Well, I don't know what to say, really I don't. Remarkable.'

'Indeed,' Nepath agreed with a thin smile.

'It's just a shame you can't do the same thing with people,' Wilson added.

Nepath's smile froze. Grant just caught his reply as he followed Urton back to the carriage. 'Yes,' he said levelly. 'Isn't it.'

'I don't believe it, I really don't believe it,' Dobbs said for the third time. They were still in the ditch, waiting for the soldiers to finish clearing away the pieces of the field gun.

'I gathered,' the Doctor said.

'I just don't believe it,' Dobbs said. He shook his head. 'It's...'

'Unbelievable?' the Doctor suggested.

'Well, yes.' A thought occurred to him. 'Do you believe it?'

'I saw it,' the Doctor replied. He was evidently amused by Dobbs's incredulity.

'So did I. But I don't...' He broke off and smiled. 'Sorry. I suppose I'd better just get used to the notion.' He was silent for a minute. Another thought had come to him. 'I didn't believe in dowsing either,' he said slowly.

'But you do now?'

'I'm more inclined to,' Dobbs decided.

'That's good.'

'Is it?'

'Oh yes,' the Doctor told him. 'If you've seen something happen, however incredible it might seem, it's no great leap of faith to believe in it. But now you're really opening your mind.' He grinned and clapped Dobbs on the shoulder. 'Well done.'

'Thank you,' Dobbs replied automatically.

The Doctor looked out of the ditch. 'Right, they seem to be done and dusted. Let's go.' He clambered out of the ditch and reached back to help the Professor negotiate the steep side.

As they made their way back to the Rectory, the Doctor described to Dobbs the exhibition he had attended the previous day.

'So you had a good idea what was to happen?'

'Once I saw what they were preparing it was pretty evident,' the Doctor agreed.

'Is this why you came here?' Dobbs asked. 'Because of Nepath and the material he intends to mine?'

'Oh no.' The Doctor paused and reached into his jacket pocket. He pulled out a dull ball of dark material, similar to a large marble. He glanced at it briefly and replaced it. 'Wrong pocket,' he murmured. 'That was the free sample that Nepath gave me.'

'He gave you some of the material? Why?'

'I can't imagine,' the Doctor said. He was reaching into his other pocket. 'Well, actually I can imagine. But I think I'd rather not. Not for the moment anyway. Ah, here we are.' He pulled a small cube from his jacket with a flourish that would have befitted a stage magician. He held it out to Dobbs. 'Do you know what it is?' he asked. His voice was low and serious now.

Dobbs took the cube and examined it closely. It seemed solid and it was quite heavy. There was no apparent hinge or lid. The machining was perfect. The material it was made from was shiny black, so black that light seemed to be lost in it. The surface was so glossy that it seemed it should act as a mirror, but it reflected nothing other than indistinct shapes of light. It was slightly warm to the touch. He turned it over in his hands, then held it back out for the Doctor to take.

'No,' he said. 'I've never seen anything quite like this. What is it?'

The Doctor sucked in his cheeks. 'I was hoping you could tell me,' he said. It was the first time that Dobbs had heard real disappointment in his voice.

'You don't know?'

'I have no idea.'

'Where did you get it?'

The Doctor started walking again, so briskly that Dobbs had to make an effort to keep up. 'I can't remember,' he said. He seemed embarrassed at the admission.

'Yet you say it is why you are here.'

'That's correct.' The Doctor turned to him as they continued to walk, his pace slowing slightly. 'You noticed that the cube was warm?'

'I did.'

'It used to be cold. Like ice. Then one of the faces of the cube became hot. I felt it through the lining of my pocket.'

'Just one face?' Dobbs frowned. What did that say about the conductivity of the material it was fashioned from?

'But not the same face.'

'I beg your pardon?'

'If I turned the cube, a different face became hot and the previously hot side was instantly cold again.'

'But why? How?'

'I wondered that. Then it came to me. No matter which way I turned the cube, the side pointing in a particular direction was hot. If I angled it, then the edge or corner was hot. Always pointing me in the same direction.' His voice had become distant, almost wistful as he remembered.

'And so you followed that direction? And it brought you here?'

The Doctor nodded.

Dobbs was struggling to absorb this. On top of what he had seen, he could feel his whole scientific belief structure beginning to crumble. 'And you say the side of the cube pointing towards Middletown was always hot?'

The Doctor quickened his pace, striding across the moorland, his shadow stretching out across the snowy surface. 'Burning,' he said.

The faint sounds of the machinery that had already been installed were just audible at the mouth of the tunnel. Harry Devlin was supervising the unloading of a trepanner, a vast contraption built from oily steel, as Nepath arrived. The two horses that had pulled the trepanner on its cart were sweating heavily, stamping their cold hooves on the frozen ground and tossing their heads. They seemed unnerved by the attention of the silent mine workers.

Nepath spared a moment to sooth them, patting their damp flanks and talking quietly to them each as he held the halter and looked into their eyes.

'How is it going?' he asked Devlin when he had finished with the horses.

Devlin's voice was a monotone. 'The equipment is installed. Except for this trepanner, which has only just arrived.'

'So I see. And what progress?'

'Progress is slow,' Devlin admitted. His eyes were wide, unblinking as he spoke. 'We shall need more equipment if we are to reach the depth you require.'

'Equipment is expensive,' Nepath told him. His mouth twitched slightly as he stifled his smile. 'Bur fortunately I expect a large cash injection shortly. We shall arrange others when and if they become necessary. I have several possible customers lined up. But do what you can for now.'

'Yes, sir.'

Nepath stared into Devlin's eyes as he spoke. 'We shall need more material, of course. Much more.' If he looked closely he could see it inside the man. 'But we should dig that out in the process of our main objective.' Could see the fire that burned inside him.

Chapter Eleven
Night Callers

Though it was bitterly cold, it was a bright crisp day. Stobbold spent the daylight hours visiting. He never seemed to have enough time to get to everyone who needed his attention. He took sick communion to Mrs Olson, and he inquired after Jimmy Moorgate's gout; he called on Michael Grisham to ask why he had missed church that week and found him suffering from a fever. He listened attentively and sympathetically while Rosie Devlin poured out her worries about her husband, about how he had become introverted and quiet since the mine reopened. Ruffling his hand through little Annie's hair, he told Rosie not to worry. Harry would work things out, he was a good man.

It was dark by the time Stobbold returned to the Rectory. Betty was already preparing the dinner. He could hear the Doctor and Professor Dobbs talking in the drawing room as he took off his coat. At once he was reminded of the disagreement of the previous day, and again he felt annoyed by the Doctor's attitude. He tried to push his feelings to the back of his mind as he went up to remove his cassock.

By the time Stobbold joined them, dinner was almost ready. 'My apologies that I was not here when you returned from your expedition,' he told them, trying to keep his tone neutral.

'Your hospitality is more than generous as it is,' Dobbs replied. 'Please think nothing of it.' He glanced at the Doctor, as if for approval before adding. 'We have had a most remarkable morning, I must confess. Regardless of your misgivings, I believe you would have been fascinated by what has occurred.'

Despite his earlier feelings, Stobbold found himself intrigued, and before long he was sitting listening to Dobbs's account of the events of the morning.

'I still maintain that it was not polite or proper for you to eavesdrop on this demonstration,' Stobbold said when Dobbs had finished. 'But I do have to admit that this is indeed a remarkable story.' He turned to the Doctor. 'This material, these strange Eastern ceremonies… I have come across nothing of the kind before. Not in fact, or in the literature I have read on the subject.'

'Comparative religion?' the Doctor asked. 'I recall you said you had devoted time to the subject.'

'Indeed,' Stobbold admitted. 'In the study I have various volumes on the subject. Eastern mythology and beliefs in particular interest me. There are distinct parallels with our own religion, as well as many differences. But the underlying metaphors and teachings are I believe reconcilable.'

'We must talk more on the subject,' the Doctor said, taking something from his pocket. 'But for the moment, this intrigues me rather more.'

It was a dull, dark ball which looked to Stobbold like a children's marble, only larger. As he watched, the Doctor squeezed the ball in his palm. When he opened his fingers the material was squashed into an amorphous mass. Like clay.

'It gets warm in my pocket,' he explained. 'Warm enough to reform into my rather dreary and crude attempt at sculpture.' He tossed the material across to Stobbold.

It was soft, more malleable than Stobbold had expected. He squeezed it flat and rolled it between his palms. There seemed to be no discernible smell, and it left no residue on his hands. He was still examining the substance when Betty came in to tell them that dinner was ready.

She watched her father work the material as she spoke. 'I've already eaten,' Betty said. 'I was hungry. I hope you will excuse me if I don't join you for dinner, but I am rather tired.'

'Of course, my dear.'

'What is that?' She reached out tentatively and Stobbold handed her the lump of dark material. She held it for a moment between her forefinger and thumb before giving it back to the Doctor. 'Please excuse me,' she said again.

* * *

As he washed his hands at the small basin in his room, the Doctor could feel the warmth in his jacket. At first he thought it was the glossy cube that had led him here. Was it time, perhaps to move on?

But what he drew from his pocket was the dull material that Nepath had given him. It had once again refashioned itself into a small sphere. It was warm, almost hot. He held it up, examining the material with interest. Was that the hint of a crack, a hairline mark anywhere?

'Are you coming, Doctor?' Dobbs called from outside his door.

'I'll be right with you.' He considered for a moment, then he dropped the ball into the basin, watching it sink below the soapy surface of the cold water. 'If you're a sphere when you're warm,' he murmured, 'what are you when you're cold?'

He did not wait to see. He closed and locked the door behind him on his way to dinner.

It was over the port after the meal that Stobbold raised the issue of predestination. He had been mulling over the subject throughout the meal as Dobbs again described the events he and the Doctor had witnessed that morning.

They were back in the drawing room, each of them in his accustomed armchair. Stobbold felt warm and comfortable, enjoying the company. 'We spoke before, Doctor, of what you called a clockwork universe, I recall.'

The Doctor nodded. 'We did indeed. We discussed the idea that it is possible with Newton's laws to predict the behaviour and path of every particle in the universe and how it reacts with and to every other particle,' he explained to Dobbs.

'I see,' the Professor replied. 'An intriguing notion. You subscribe, I assume then, to the prevalent theory that everything is indeed "particulate" in structure and composition?'

'We had some debate about the soul of Man,' Stobbold told him. 'Everything physical, then.'

'It occurs to me,' Stobbold went on, 'that there is something of that same argument in the singular behaviour of the material you have described to me. It is as if the atoms within it know their appointed paths and places and return to them, if that is possible.'

'All atoms are in perpetual motion,' Dobbs agreed. 'That is well known. There is only the atoms and the spaces between them. Relatively large spaces in the case of a gas, less space in a liquid, hardly any in a closely-knit solid. But still motion.'

'Leave an ingot of gold on top of another soft metal like lead, and you will find that the two begin to merge,' the Doctor added. 'Over a period years, you will begin to find grains of the one embedded within the other.'

'I didn't know that,' Stobbold said. 'So does this mean that we admit a possible solution?'

'Doctor?' Dobbs prompted.

The Doctor was silent for several moments. 'I am loathe to ascribe so simple an explanation to so strange a phenomenon,' he said at last. 'If it were that straightforward, why has such a thing not be observed or demonstrated before?' He stood up and went over to the fire, turning so that he faced back to his friends. 'I am inclined to believe, partly because of my reluctance to give up free will, that there are more things in Heaven and Earth than are dreamed of in Newton's philosophy.'

'What a piece of work is a man?' Stobbold asked, amused.

The Doctor's reply was as serious as it was passionate. 'Exactly,' he declaimed, arm raised. 'Exactly so. There is something in this more than physical, more than explicable. The ancient Greeks had atomic theory of a sort. But they found it too boring, I'm sure that was why they never pursued the idea seriously. No, they saw more value – more intellectual if not scientific value – in the Platonic notion that everything is a flawed copy of the actual, perfect object. Or in Aristotle's theory.'

'Forgive me,' Dobbs interrupted. 'I am no philosopher.'

'Aristotle,' Stobbold said, 'inclined to the belief that the universe is constructed of natural elements. Is that not so, Doctor? I assume that is your point.'

The Doctor was nodding enthusiastically. 'For two thousand years we have preferred Aristotle's romantic suggestion to Democritus's more accurate diagnosis of the nature of the world. And Aristotle said that everything devolved from, was created in some part from the four elements.' He counted them off on his fingers. 'Earth, air, water.' He paused, glanced at the dancing flames behind him. 'And fire.'

'And what does that tell us about the nature of this material? How does it help?' Dobbs wondered.

'Maybe it doesn't,' the Doctor admitted. 'But the solution is, as ever, within the problem itself. Understand the problem, and we shall find the answer.'

'The answer to what, though?' Stobbold wondered. He was feeling weary from his long day walking. He stifled a yawn.

'There is evil here, all around us.' The Doctor leaned forward, hands thrust deep into his trouser pockets like a lecturer admonishing an inattentive student. 'Can't you sense it? Doesn't it eat into your bones, your very being?'

'I am not sure that it does,' Stobbold said. 'I am not sure that I understand at all, Doctor. But allow me a few hours sleep and, rested, I may be better able to follow your reasoning.'

As Stobbold left the room, Dobbs was also rising, also yawning.

'Professor,' Stobbold heard the Doctor's low voice behind him. He paused in the doorway just long enough to catch the rest of what the Doctor said: 'A moment, if you would.'

Stobbold hesitated. Perhaps the Doctor wished to offer his condolences for the loss of Alistair Gaddis alone and in private. He stepped out of the room.

'I have a suggestion.' The Doctor's voice floated back to him as Stobbold closed the door.

Stobbold did not linger further. He might not be able within his heart of hearts to condemn the Doctor's cavalier and unwarranted behaviour, but neither could he bring himself to condone it.

* * *

123

Although he was filled with both excitement and trepidation at the pending adventure, Dobbs drifted off into a light sleep. He was awakened by the Doctor's insistent knock at his door. Dobbs pulled on his coat over the clothes he was still wearing and joined the Doctor on the landing.

'What time is it?'

'A shade before three. Won't be light for a few hours yet.'

They made their silent way down through the house, pausing only when there was a creak from above them. Dobbs held his breath, feeling a prick of guilty conscience that they had not involved their host in their plans. But the Doctor's argument that Stobbold would rather not know of their intentions had seemed persuasive at the time.

Hearing no further sounds from above, they continued on their furtive way. The Doctor managed to draw back the bolts and undo the lock on the front door without making much noise, and he carefully closed the door behind them. Still without a word, they made their way down the Rectory drive and up the hill towards the Grange.

Getting into the house was rather easier than Dobbs had anticipated. He imagined the Doctor had some devious and convoluted plan to pick the lock of the door and deal with the heavy bolts and chain. In the event, the Doctor's strategy was to walk all round the Grange in the hope that they would find a ground floor window that was unlatched.

'That's a bit of luck,' Dobbs hissed as the Doctor led him round to a window that was indeed slightly open.

'Luck? I don't believe in luck.' The Doctor gestured for Dobbs to lace his fingers together to make a cradle for his foot. 'I unlatched it when I was here for Nepath's coffee morning.'

'Coffee morning?' Dobbs asked. But the weight was gone from his hands, and the Doctor's feet were disappearing through the window. Moments later, the Doctor was at the window, reaching down to help the Professor through.

The house was in darkness. Only the light of the pale crescent moon shone at intervals through open curtains to illuminate their progress. The Doctor led Dobbs through the night silence, up a flight of stairs and off into a wing of the large house. At every point where they might be overlooked, or where there was a door within sight, they paused, and Dobbs caught his breath. His stomach was churning and he was sure that anyone asleep nearby would be wakened by the beating of his nervous heart.

'Here we are,' the Doctor murmured as he opened a door and stepped into another darkened room.

Dobbs followed him inside and the Doctor closed the door behind them. They were in a room that was about twenty feet square. As Dobbs's eyes adjusted to the gloom he could make out cabinets arranged round the walls. A table stood at the front of the room, chairs set out in front of it and he realised this was the room where the Doctor had attended Nepath's auction.

The Doctor seemed not to have needed to let his eyes adjust. He was already at a display cabinet, examining the contents through the glass doors.

'Anything of interest?' Dobbs inquired, making his careful way over to join the Doctor.

'Not in here, I'm afraid.' The Doctor's eyes gleamed in the faint light. 'But he'd hardly put it on display. We must extend our search. Leave no stone unturned, no nook or cranny unexamined.' With that, he was gone.

It took Dobbs a moment to work out quite where he had gone. It was when the door opened again that he realised the Doctor was leaving the room, and he hastened to catch up.

'Let's try this one,' the Doctor whispered as he opened the next door along the corridor. He opened the door, and immediately closed it again, moving on to the next one. 'Small bedroom,' he explained. 'Empty.'

About half way along the corridor the Doctor gave a quiet exclamation of delight and stepped inside a room. Dobbs followed, expecting to find himself once more negotiating a gloomy half-darkness. But in fact there was more than enough light to see. There were no curtains at the high windows and so the moonlight streamed into the room unhindered. It cast its pale light over the display cases and cabinets, the packing crates and tea chests, the bare floorboards and the door at the far end of the room.

Dobbs lost track of the time they spent rummaging about in the gloom. Before long he was bored with the process despite the inherent danger of the situation. 'What are we looking for?' he asked.

'I really don't know,' the Doctor admitted. 'I just hope I know when I find it.'

'So do I,' Dobbs said. He pulled another carefully-wrapped bundle from the packing case he was searching. A few tugs at the tissue paper covering the item was enough to satisfy him it was nothing out of the ordinary or sinister. It was a statue of a bird, its wings spread. It looked vaguely familiar, but he pushed the wrapping back into place nonetheless.

'What was that?' the Doctor demanded close beside him.

Dobbs froze. 'I heard nothing.'

'No, no, no. What was it you just wrapped up again?'

'Oh. A bird.' It came to him then. 'Same as one in the case you were looking at in that first room.'

'The Phoenix,' the Doctor said, his voice an urgent whisper.

Dobbs shrugged, handing the package to the Doctor. 'If you say so.'

The Doctor pulled the tissue paper from the statue, ripping it away. 'The display case in the other room was labelled *Urdesh*,' he said as he freed the bird. 'It contained the items that Nepath claims have the memory ability, can reform themselves in the heat. Here, hold this.' He thrust the metal bird back at Dobbs and dropped to the floor.

'What are you doing?' Dobbs demanded as the Doctor crawled round the crate on all fours examining the sides.

'Aha!' With a harsh whisper of triumph the Doctor pointed to dark writing stencilled on one of the sides. It read 'Urdesh

Province'. Then he started rummaging in the newspaper packing and pulling items out of the crate and unwrapping them frantically. As he unrolled each item he dropped the tissue paper to the floor and handed the artefact to Dobbs. Before long his arms were full.

'Doctor,' Dobbs said, 'all these items were in the cabinet. Or copies of them anyway.'

'Copies, yes,' the Doctor agreed with delight. 'And these seem normal enough. Just genuine valuable antique exotica.' He started to retrieve the items from Dobbs, re-wrapping each one carefully and rapidly then returning it to the packing case.

'You mentioned copies earlier,' Dobbs said slowly as he thought back to their after-dinner conversation. 'Plato, was it?'

'You think these are the originals from which the others imperfectly derive?' The Doctor took the final artefact – the phoenix – from Dobbs and smothered it efficiently in tissue paper. 'You may be right. But it isn't any celestial mechanism at work here.'

'No?'

'No. It's a con.'

'What?'

'A confidence trick.' The Doctor started across the room. He was making for the door on the far side. 'A deception. This property that Nepath says comes from the secret techniques and ceremonies of the Urdesh, this quasi-religious expertise is nothing of the sort.' He paused in front of the door, turning to face Dobbs. 'He's making the things himself. There is no refining, no magic, no distillation or manufacturing process. It's a property inherent in the material itself.'

He did not wait for Dobbs to comment. He opened the door. Beyond was a black void, an impenetrable darkness. The Doctor stepped into it.

Dobbs stood for what seemed a life time at the edge of the darkness. The Doctor seemed to have been swallowed up. For a few seconds Dobbs had heard his muffled footsteps fading deeper into the void. Now there was nothing. Just as he was deciding that perhaps the easiest and safest thing would be to turn and leave, to abandon the Doctor to whatever fate had befallen him, he heard the scrape of a match and saw the sudden flare of light across the room.

The Doctor had found a gas lamp on the far wall and was lighting it. The light as the mantel caught cast angular shadows across his face as he leaned across to replace the cover, and the soft glow seemed to permeate the room. There were curtains at the windows here, heavy and dull drawn across to blot out any trace of natural light.

Beneath the light, beside the Doctor, stood a single large, upright display case. It reminded Dobbs of the animal cases in the Natural History Museum.

'There.' The Doctor stepped back, evidently pleased with himself. He shook the match to extinguish it. A dark trickle of smoke continued to rise from the blackened stump of wood. 'Oh dear.' As he spoke, the Doctor was standing between Dobbs and the display case, obscuring his view. 'Oh dear, oh me.'

Dobbs walked across to join the Doctor, to see what was in the case.

The Doctor was shaking his head, lips pursed tightly together. 'I don't like the look of that at all.'

Dobbs looked at the Doctor, unsettled by his manner. The Doctor turned, and their eyes locked. Then the Doctor turned back to the case, and Dobbs mirrored his action.

The case contained what looked to Dobbs like a hideous, twisted statue. It was composed of tarnished and scorched material that looked suspiciously like bone. Blackened remnants of clothing hung in places from the distorted shape. The whole form seemed disjointed, hideous and monstrous.

But the face was the worst. Dobbs could feel his gorge rising as he stared with horrid fascination at the charred skull. Slivers of dark skin and flesh still adhered to it like crumpled parchment. Whatever it was, and whyever Nepath had seen fit to preserve it, this grotesque creature, Dobbs realised with horror, was no statue. It had once been alive.

'I think,' the Doctor said, his voice a dry rasp, 'that it was time we were leaving.'

The darkness that returned when the Doctor extinguished the light was merciful. Dobbs backed carefully out of the inner room, waiting for the Doctor to join him and close the door. Together they picked their way across the larger room, through the sea of artefacts and packing materials.

The figure at the end of the corridor was so still that Dobbs almost failed to notice it. He saw the eyes first. Lady Urton seemed to be waiting for them to emerge from the room. The Doctor was closing the door quietly behind them as Dobbs tapped him urgently on the shoulder. His face was an unspoken question as he turned.

Dobbs nodded down the corridor, and the Doctor stiffened as he too saw her.

She seemed almost to glow in the shadows. She wore a long pale night gown which seemed lit from within, like an alabaster lantern. Until Dobbs realised that it was not the gown but her skin, her whole form, which was glowing. Her eyes flickered and danced with inner fire, yellow, orange and red mingling as she approached them.

They were backing away now. Dobbs knew instinctively that there was something wrong here, very wrong indeed. There was a smell in the air, like cooking meat. A faint hissing with each step she took. A curl of smoke seemed expelled from each bare foot as she walked along the corridor, leaving a smoking, blackened trail across the floorboards behind her.

The Doctor and Dobbs both turned at the same moment, both started to run back towards the stairs. And both saw the figure approaching them from the other direction – a mirror of the woman behind them.

Except that the housekeeper was holding an oil lamp. Her hatchet-features cast sharp shadows across her face as she stepped forwards. She seemed surprised.

Dobbs looked from Mrs Webber to Lady Urton, noted the difference in their expressions – Lady Urton's face was blank, staring; Mrs Webber's was a mask of astonishment and indignation as she saw them. Dobbs decided to take his chances with Mrs Webber. The Doctor must have thought the same.

'Excuse us!' the Doctor shouted as he pushed past her, Dobbs close on his heels. Mrs Webber spun and gasped and shouted something incoherent after them. Dobbs did not wait to hear what it was.

There was an angle in the stairway, a dog-leg half landing. As he turned the corner, Dobbs could see the two women frozen above him. Lady Urton's pale hand was extended, touching Mrs Webber's angular cheek. Steam was erupting from the blistered skin, and the housekeeper's mouth was gaping in agony. Whatever sound she was making was lost beneath the hissing and spitting of the burning flesh.

'Come on!' The Doctor grabbed Dobbs by the shoulder and fairly threw him down the next flight of stairs.

Dobbs staggered and stumbled his way into the hall. He reached the bottom of the stairs and turned back to wait for the Doctor. As he turned he caught sight of Lady Urton standing at the top banister, staring down through firelight eyes; and of Mrs Webber as she came screeching towards him. Her whole body was a blackened mass of charred bone and tissue as she fell. Only her gaping, screaming mouth seemed to remain her own.

Dobbs leaped aside as the blackened corpse crashed to the floor beside him, crumpled and broken. Again, the Doctor grabbed him, pulled him away.

'Back to the window, come on.'

'But, Doctor…' He was wheezing – breathless from exertion, from fear, from realisation. 'That's what happened to Alistair,' he managed to gasp out.

'I know,' the Doctor hissed through gritted teeth. He hurled the Professor down the passageway ahead of him. 'I know!'

The Doctor reached the window where they had climbed in,

and flung it open. Dobbs caught up with him, but before he could say a word the Doctor lifted him bodily and pushed him into the gap. He twisted and struggled, pulling himself through, out of the nightmare house. As he tumbled into the moonlit snow, he caught a confused, spinning glimpse of the Doctor climbing after him. And of Lord Urton, his eyes blazing – literally blazing – reaching out for him from behind.

'Doctor!' Dobbs screamed out as he fell. 'Behind you!' Then he was rolling and tumbling and cold.

The Doctor was half out of the window when Dobbs recovered himself. He was on his back, pivoted on the sill, kicking out furiously with his feet. Dobbs could see the pale, glowing form of Lord Urton reaching back at the Doctor. Sparks were flying from Urton's hands as he make to grab the Doctor's feet. Flames were licking out of the window, though Dobbs could not see what was burning. Oily black smoke poured out over the Doctor, making him choke.

Dobbs pulled himself to his feet. He grabbed the Doctor under the arms and heaved with all his strength. He could see now that it was the Doctor himself who was on fire; or at least, the bottom of his jacket, where Urton had tried to drag him back through the window. At the same moment the Doctor gave a final frantic kick, striking Urton full in the chest and propelling himself backwards. He exploded from the window like a cork from a champagne bottle, and the two of them were rolling and tumbling in the drifts of snow. All that Dobbs could see was the fire, all he could smell was the burning fabric, all he could breath was the choking fumes.

Dobbs fell still, watching with incredulous fascination as the Doctor continued to roll and tumble in the snow. The bottom of his jacket was still on fire, but the snow was smothering the flames, slowly but surely the fire was dying away.

At the window, Lord Urton stood watching them. He was utterly still. The only movement was the flickering, dancing, light of the fire behind his eyes.

Chapter Twelve
Lines of Inquiry

Once back in his room, the Doctor shrugged off his crumpled velvet jacket. The back of it was still steaming slightly and there was a smell of burnt cloth. He lifted it up to inspect the damage, sighed, gave it a quick shake and then put it back on. He thrust his hands into the jacket pockets as he stared into the distance.

Immediately he whipped his right hand out again with a cry, and sucked at his fingers. More carefully, almost gingerly, he reached back into the pocket and pulled out the glossy black cube. It was hot. So hot that it was glowing with an inner brilliance. So hot that he dropped it at once. It fell to the floor, bounced once, and came to rest.

If he screwed up his eyes he could see that one side of the cube was brighter – and presumably hotter – than the others. He knelt down on the floor and rested his head on the boards close to the cube. He could feel its heat on his face as he turned slightly to see where the hottest face of the cube was pointing.

There was nothing there. Just a blank wall where the sink was mounted. The sink.

Slowly, cautiously, the Doctor got to his feet. He went to the sink and looked down into the soapy water. Inside, beneath the scummed surface he could see something else glowing, giving out a faint light. Pushing back his sleeve, he reached in and retrieved the sample of the substance that Nepath had given him. It was warm.

As it came clear of the water, he felt it get hotter, felt it tremble with inner life. Quickly, the Doctor set it down on a low table close to the basin. The material was a shapeless mass now. He could see the shape changing, bulging, the top coming to a point almost like…

…a volcano.

With a stifled cry of realisation, the Doctor leaped backwards – just as the top of the thing erupted. Fiery, viscous liquid bubbled up from inside, forced out of the mass. Impossibly, it kept coming, a glowing orange trail of the stuff poured to the floor, started to run across the boards towards where the Doctor was standing. The surface of the liquefied material was crusted as the air cooled it. The crust seemed to burst with every surge of fresh material forced out of the small volcano. A rolling, steaming, scorching river of liquid fire inched its way towards the Doctor leaving a blackened trail in its wake.

He took another step backwards. The lava, whatever it was, blocked his escape. It was between him and the door. He stumbled, almost fell. At his feet, the cube he had carried for so very long, was glowing white hot. And he realised that it was not himself that the liquid was drawn towards at all. Heat to heat, like to like. The cube was somehow attracting the substance. Was this what had brought him here? Was this what it had wanted all along?

Fascinated, the Doctor climbed on to the bed. He lay on his stomach, elbows supporting his arms supporting his chin as he watched the molten river close on the glowing cube.

There was a flash of light as they met. A sound like the scraping of metal on tearing metal. When the light faded, the Doctor could see the whole body of material sucked rapidly into the small cube. How could something that size hold so much?

As if in answer to his unspoken question, the light in the cube faded. And the cube began to grow. It was getting taller, elongating, becoming a rectangular rather than a square box. Featureless, reaching almost to the ceiling of the room, four feet wide at least. The inner light died away, and the box's exterior faded to a dark colour.

He approached it carefully, reached out cautiously, let his fingertips graze the uneven surface. Like wood, yet not like wood. It tingled, trembled slightly. An upright, featureless box. Completely sealed, for he walked all round it to check. It was dark blue.

* * *

133

When the visitor arrived for the Doctor, Stobbold made up his mind. Neither the Doctor nor Professor Dobbs had risen for breakfast, and Stobbold was certain they had engaged in some nefarious nocturnal endeavour. He was torn between his curiosity and his moral conscience. So an excuse to waken the Doctor was welcome.

He left Betty to look after his distinguished if taciturn visitor, and went upstairs. There was no response to his knocking at the Doctor's door, so he tried the handle.

The door opened easily. 'Doctor?' Stobbold inquired as he stepped inside.

Two things struck him at once. First, the bed looked unslept in. Second was the smell. It was a hot, close smell. Like you got on the moors in the height of summer, but mingled with it was the sense of something burning. 'Doctor?'

'Hmm?'

He was sitting cross-legged on the floor. And now Stobbold noticed what he was looking at. He was facing away from the door, staring apparently at a large blue box that was in the corner of the room, just out from the walls and reaching almost to the high ceiling.

'Good gracious!' Stobbold stared.

'Hmm,' the Doctor agreed.

'How on earth did that get in here?' It was far too large to have been brought in through the door or the window. It looked solid, but perhaps it could be dismantled in some way.

'Well,' the Doctor said slowly as he rose to his feet, 'it certainly didn't materialise out of… ' He paused, half turned towards Stobbold, a sudden look of perplexity and confusion on his face as if he had forgotten what he was going to say.

'Are you all right?' Stobbold asked. The Doctor seemed pale, drawn.

'There's something… ' His face cleared as suddenly as it had clouded over and he shook his head. 'No,' he decided, 'it's gone. Never mind. Is there something I can do for you, Reverend?'

134

'What?' He was still looking at the box. 'Oh, yes. You have a visitor. I'm sorry to disturb you. Downstairs.'

The Doctor was already on his way. 'Hardly unexpected,' he announced as he passed Stobbold. 'Which one of them is it?'

Stobbold turned to follow. On the low table by the wash basin he noticed a dark lump, about the size of a billiard ball. It looked like something that had been burned – was this the source of the strange aroma, he wondered? It was a husk, an empty shell. He reached out a tentative finger and touched it gently. At once the husk disintegrated. Charred slivers and fragments floated away on the draught from the open door, like burned paper escaping from a bonfire.

He was only half way down the stairs when he heard Lord Urton's raised voice.

'You, sir,' he was saying with considerable anger, 'yes, *you* sir. I demand an explanation, sir, for your wholly unacceptable behaviour.'

Stobbold arrived in the hall to see Urton standing in the doorway from the drawing room where he had been waiting with Betty. The Doctor was at the bottom of the stairs, his hand on his chest in an innocent 'who, me?' gesture.

Urton barely paused for an answer before continuing. 'What, may I ask, is the meaning of your behaviour, sir? Tell me that.'

Still the Doctor said nothing. Stobbold hesitated, then decided it was best to join them and try to mediate. 'Can I help?' he asked, keeping his voice quiet and calm. 'Is there perhaps a misunderstanding I can assist in explaining?'

'No misunderstanding, sir,' Urton said. His voice was shaking with anger, though his whole body was absolutely still as he spoke. Again he addressed the Doctor. 'You break into my house in the middle of the night and scare my poor wife half to death –'

The Doctor spoke for the first time, interrupting Urton's angry tirade with a tone that was almost mocking. 'Got her fingers burned, did she?' he asked, eyes wide, still playing the innocent.

At once Urton was silent. When he spoke again it was to

Stobbold. 'I see that there is no explanation or apology to be had here. May I ask that you reconsider in the strongest and most urgent manner the sort of house guests that you allow under your roof? As a man of God, you should hardly be playing the host to sinners.'

Again the Doctor's tone was light, as if engaging in after dinner banter with an old friend. 'Oh but surely that's exactly what he should be doing.' He raised a finger, in an instant becoming a theatrical preacher. 'There is more joy in heaven over one sinner who repents –' he began.

'I see no repentance here, sir,' Urton told him abruptly.

'Redemption, perhaps?' the Doctor said, his voice sterner now. 'Or is it to be the fires of hell and damnation for us all?'

Urton did not reply immediately. When he did, he was already on his way to the door, pushing past the Doctor who sprang back out of his way, as if afraid of touching the man. 'I see that I am wasting my time. Good day to you, sir.' This last was aimed squarely at Stobbold.

He waited until Urton was well on his way down the drive, visible through the open front door. A light breeze blew a flurry of powdery snow across the threshold. Betty appeared in the door to the drawing room, her expression neutral, and Stobbold gestured for his daughter to leave them. She stepped back into the room and closed the door.

'I think you owe me an explanation, Doctor,' he said, trying to keep his tone neutral.

The Doctor was watching Urton's receding figure. 'I wish I had one,' he said absently.

'I think I am entitled, sir. You are a guest under my roof, as Lord Urton points out.' he was angry now, this man seemed to have no idea of civility, or social behaviour or, it now seemed, of the laws of the land.

'Yes. I do rather think that was the point, don't you?' The Doctor beamed at Stobbold as he waited for his reply. 'He wanted to ensure I was no longer welcome here. He and Nepath hope I'll just give up and leave.'

Stobbold fought to keep his voice level and calm. 'Doctor, I have asked for – demanded – an explanation. Yet you offer no excuse for your behaviour. Since you do not even deny it, I assume that Lord Urton is correct in his accusations?'

'Oh yes,' the Doctor agreed. 'Quite correct. Everything he said was true. As far as it goes.'

Stobbold breathed deeply as he considered his words. 'I am not given to evicting guests,' he said. 'I do not intend to change that habit now, Doctor. But let me be clear, unless and until you can reasonably explain yourself or offer an adequate apology I cannot say you are welcome.'

As he listened to Stobbold's words, the Doctor's face darkened and his features hardened. 'I have told you as best I can what is happening here. I have said time and again that there are forces that must be opposed if we are to survive the horrors that are almost upon us. I cannot be more specific, and for that – for that alone – I apologise.'

'I'm afraid that just isn't good enough,' Stobbold said. He could feel his face colouring as he spoke, could feel the anger in him growing.

'Then perhaps Lord Urton is right,' the Doctor snapped back.

'Ah, so you admit –' Stobbold began.

But the Doctor shouted him down. 'Perhaps it would be best if I gave up and left. Left you all to your fate.'

He did not wait for Stobbold's reaction. Instead he turned on his heels and stamped out of the house.

Stobbold watched the figure following in Urton's dark footsteps until he was out of sight.

'Was that the Doctor?' Dobbs's voice startled Stobbold. The Professor was on the stairs behind him.

'Yes.'

'I thought I heard Lord Urton too.' Dobbs continued down the stairs and joined Stobbold in the hall. He seemed oblivious to Stobbold's anger. 'Yes,' Dobbs was nodding. He pointed out into the snow. 'You can see his tracks.'

Stobbold had been about to ask Dobbs what if any involvement or knowledge he had of the Doctor's visit to the Grange. But there was something in Dobbs's tone that made him follow the old man's gaze out across the drive. He had not noticed before, in his anger, but now it seemed suddenly odd. Where the Doctor had walked, the snow was compacted, leaving indentations for footmarks.

But where Urton had trod – both on his way to the Rectory and back down the drive again, the snow had melted away to leave a dark shoe-shaped hole down to the gravel beneath.

'Professor,' Stobbold's voice was hoarse and dry. 'Professor, would you please enlighten me as to what happened last night?'

Dobbs was aghast. 'The Doctor hasn't told you?'

Stobbold shook his head. 'He was not in the mood for explanations.' A thought struck him and he looked away. 'I think he was asking me to believe in him, to take it on faith.'

But Dobbs missed this. 'You mentioned you have a collection of books on comparative religion,' he said. 'Myths and legends?'

'That is true. In the study.' Stobbold found himself leading the way, smiling at Betty as she opened the drawing room door once more and watched them.

'I think,' Dobbs was saying, 'that we should do some research. Find out everything we can about fire demons.'

He was standing beside a gap in the hedge, looking through at the view of the moors beyond. The road was on a rise here, so it served as a vantage point. As Matthew Stobbold approached, he could see the dark slash of the fissure cutting through the snow visible over the Doctor's shoulder.

The snow was falling again, quite heavily now, and Lord Urton's footprints were slowly filling up.

They stood together, shoulder to shoulder, silent, looking out at the fissure for a long while before Stobbold spoke. 'Doctor,' he said falteringly, 'I… well, that is –'

The Doctor raised his hand. 'Never mind.'

'I should not have lost my temper. What I said was, I believe, justified, Doctor.'

The Doctor did not reply. He chewed at his bottom lip and continued to stare out through the gap in the hedge.

'But the manner in which I expressed it was not warranted. I apologise.'

Still the Doctor did not reply. He frowned, looked up at the sky, blinked, and then pointed out at the fissure. 'You see that dark line?' he asked, putting his hand on Stobbold's shoulder and bending him to follow his own line of sight. 'It's perfectly straight. There's another over there.' He swung his pointing hand, pulling Stobbold round as well.

'Yes, I think I see.' Stobbold straightened up again. 'Are you leaving, Doctor?' he asked hesitantly. 'Only, your box...'

'My box,' the Doctor echoed quietly. He seemed to come to a decision, drawing himself to his full height and pushing his hands into his jacket pockets. 'Do you suppose,' he asked with a sudden brilliant smile, 'that you could show me the view from the top of the church tower?'

It took a moment for Stobbold to work out what the Doctor was saying. As olive branches went, an interest in his church was subtle and considerate. He could feel that he was smiling too. 'Of course, Doctor. It would be my pleasure.'

The snow had eased off by the time they reached the top, but the wind was biting. Stobbold drew his coat tight about him, amazed at the Doctor's apparent indifference to the climate. The top of the tower was a lead roof, sloping up to a flagpole. There was no flag flying. The stonework rose above the level of the roof, forming a wall.

The dam was a grey smudge in the distance. Away on the other side of the church was the huddle of buildings and the gaping maw of the tunnel that was the mine. But it was towards the ragged fissure cutting across the snow-covered moor that the Doctor was pointing.

Not for the first time as he surveyed the landscape, it struck Stobbold that the shape of the top of the church tower was extremely similar to that of the tower of a castle. Not for the first time as he looked out across the moorland, he found himself thinking he was looking out over the church's battlements, and he mentioned this lightly to the Doctor.

The Doctor's reply was less humoured. 'This is St Michael's church,' he said as if that explained it. When Stobbold made no comment, he went on: 'When they were looking for places to build their churches, the early Christians adopted, took over, many sites of ancient power.'

'Power?'

'Often the church built on such a site was consecrated to St Michael.'

'The traditional enemy of Lucifer, of the devil,' Stobbold realised. It made sense.

'The sun god, in most of the old religions,' the Doctor said. 'In those days it really *was* seen as a battle.' He clapped his hand on the solid stone wall in front of them. 'Fortifications of the soul,' he said with a wry smile. 'Very useful in such times.'

'I suppose so.'

'Yes,' the Doctor said in a tone that suggested he was about to change the subject. He pointed out at the fissure. 'You get a much better view from up here than from the dam. You see that dark line we observed earlier?'

Stobbold looked where the Doctor was pointing. 'Yes.'

'That's where we found the body of poor Gaddis.'

It was the first time Stobbold could recall the Doctor saying anything that suggested sympathy or regret. 'It's a dead straight line,' Stobbold said. 'The snow seems not to have settled there. I wonder why.'

'Why would you think? Why is there no snow where Lord Urton has stepped?'

'Heat?'

'Exactly.'

Stobbold swallowed. 'Professor Dobbs gave me a brief account of your adventures last night, Doctor,' he said. 'He is now researching fire demons.' He gave a half laugh that failed to dispel his unease at the thought.

'As are we,' the Doctor said. 'And what have we discovered?'

'That there is a line where the ground is warm. Too warm for the snow to settle?'

The Doctor nodded. 'But not just one line.'

The sun was in his eyes, so Stobbold had to squint to see where the Doctor was now pointing. As he made out the dark line across the moors, the Doctor's hand moved and he squinted after it again.

'But there are… several,' Stobbold said in surprise.

'One line of hot ground might be accounted a coincidence or a natural feature,' the Doctor said quietly. 'But I count more than seven, and that smacks of purpose.'

'All dead straight,' Stobbold observed.

'"Lines of power," Gaddis called them. And while you may still be uncertain whether to believe Professor Dobbs's account of our encounter with Lord Urton last night,' the Doctor said, 'while you may not agree with my implied diagnosis of his behaviour, while you may scoff at stories of fire demons, you will notice that all the lines run from some point on the edge of the fissure…' He turned and walked to the adjacent side of the tower, Stobbold following, watching as he pointed again. '…directly to the mine.'

He spent several minutes tracing each of the dark lines with his eyes. But however he looked at them, there was no denying it. They focused on, met at, led to the mine.

'Doctor,' Stobbold said slowly, 'I think perhaps I do owe you an apology. Whatever is going on here, I have to confess it is outside my sphere of experience.' The Doctor was standing between Stobbold and the sun, a dark shape against the brilliant snow. 'You have the manner and knowledge of one who has come across such things before.'

'Perhaps,' the Doctor admitted.

'Tell me, Doctor,' Stobbold said quietly, 'what brings you here? Who exactly are you?'

The Doctor's voice came from the black void that was his silhouette. It was at once distant and quiet. 'I'm afraid you will have to believe me, my friend, when I tell you that I do not know. Who I am, who I was... A blank.'

'A blank?'

The Doctor sighed. 'Apart from the last few years,
   His voice was almost unnaturally quiet.
Apart from the time since I suppose you might say I "awoke"
   Barely a whisper...
I have no memory of my past.
   ...Lost in a sudden flurry of fresh snow.
No memory at all.'

Chapter Thirteen
Into the Depths

Stobbold stood in the doorway, agape in astonishment. His small study was strewn with books and papers. However meticulous his mind might be, Professor Dobbs was not a tidy worker. A pile of books stood precariously high on the side of the desk, leaves of writing paper marking various places in each. On the shelves, other books had lurched sideways into the spaces left by their absent neighbours. The floor was largely hidden beneath books and papers.

'Having fun, I see,' the Doctor said lightly as he negotiated a path towards where Dobbs was standing by a bookcase looking along the spines. 'Found anything of interest?'

It was evidently a rhetorical question. But Dobbs responded anyway. 'Indeed, Doctor, indeed I have.' He gestured to the pile of perched books on the desk. There are all sorts of references to fire gods and demons in classical mythology as well as the religions and legends of the Far East, of the Incas and Myans, and countless others.'

Dobbs sat at the desk and started to pull the books enthusiastically towards him. The Doctor leaned over, his face already a mask of concentration.

'I'll see if Betty can make us some tea,' Stobbold said weakly. He left them to it.

The Rectory was too big for the two of them really. If he had been able to afford it, Stobbold would have employed a maid or a housekeeper and a cook. As it was, he and Betty were lost in the large house and it took almost all of Betty's time to keep it. It was a refreshing change, he thought, to have guests. It meant more work for Betty, but she had not complained so he assumed that she was also grateful for the additional company.

Such a shame – a tragedy – about poor Gaddis, he reflected as he walked with Betty to the kitchen.

She said nothing. She had been quiet of late. Perhaps it came with getting older, Stobbold thought. She was growing up, he knew. She was a woman now, not a child. Some day – maybe some day soon – he would lose her. He shied away from the thought. He had no idea what he would do, how he would cope without her, and he had no intention of addressing the problem before he had to.

'Are you quite happy?' he asked as she put the water on to boil. 'With the Doctor and the Professor staying, I mean. It's… all right?'

'Thank you,' she said, watching the water begin to steam on the stove. 'It's lovely.' Her reply was level, toneless, automatic.

'Good,' Stobbold said, not quite sure if it was. 'Because, Betty – you would tell me, wouldn't you if… Well…' he shrugged. 'If, you know…' He was standing behind her, could not see her face. He reached out a hand, made to put it on her shoulder, to reassure her. He could imagine her reaching up, covering his hand with her own, turning and smiling at him and telling him that everything was fine. Really fine.

But his hand was shaking, and he lowered it to his side.

'Thank you,' she said again, her voice distant and quiet. 'It's lovely.'

The study had been restored to something approaching a state of order by the time Stobbold took in the tea. He brought in another chair and sat at the desk beside Dobbs. The Doctor insisted on sitting cross-legged on the floor, the saucer balanced uncertainly on his out-turned knee.

They spoke for an hour, talking over what Dobbs's researches had brought to light. They spoke of fire demons, of Inca creation myths. They talked about Agni the Indian fire god, and of the elements of earth, air, fire and water. The Doctor spoke of volcanoes and described with impressive detail his understanding of the last hours of Pompeii.

'Imagine it,' he said as he finished, 'imagine the sky turned dark and the choking dust. Think of the scorching river of molten rock that rolled towards them, the ash blown at them, the very air turning solid around them. Imagine the terrible speed of the catastrophe.' He shook his head, his eyes blinking back moisture. 'What must they have felt? What must they have thought. Their gods had turned against them in an instant. Their world was ending. Oblivion. Armageddon.' Finally his voice sank to a throaty whisper: 'The Apocalypse.'

'That's the trouble with research,' Dobbs said into the silence that followed. 'You can get rather involved, caught up in it all.'

'But a worthwhile exercise, nonetheless,' the Doctor said. His tone was lighter now, and he leaped to his feet, cup in hand, saucer spinning away. 'Nothing concrete or specific that helps, but a good general impression of the subject.'

'So what do we do now, Doctor?' Stobbold asked, retrieving the Doctor's saucer and returning it to the tray.

'More research, I think. But a subject rather closer to home.' The Doctor smiled at Dobbs. 'The Professor here has been telling me of a friend he has in London who works at the British Library. A most useful contact, and someone who can, I think, furnish us with the information we need.'

'The Doctor proposes to send him a telegram,' Dobbs said, a hint of pride in his voice.

'Concerning...?' Stobbold asked. He anticipated it would be some arcane subject which was not covered by his own small collection of materials or likely to be catered for in the local libraries. So the Doctor's reply surprised him.

'Concerning Roger Nepath,' the Doctor said. 'Know thine enemy,' he added, tapping the side of his nose with his index finger and giving Stobbold a huge wink. He whirled round and snatched a paper from the table. 'Now then,' he said, thrusting the paper at Stobbold, 'here is the text of the telegram together with the name of the recipient and his address. Perhaps you can organise that while the Professor and I organise a quick tour of the mine.'

'The mine?' Both Dobbs and Stobbold spoke together. Both seemed equally surprised.

The Doctor, by contrast, seemed confused by their reaction. 'It is the centre of events here,' he pointed out. 'Everything that happens revolves about that mine. I think it's high time we took a look, don't you?'

'Doctor,' Stobbold said as he scanned the copperplate handwriting on the paper the Doctor had given him, 'I doubt very much that either Lord Urton or Mister Nepath will give you permission to go snooping about in the mine. Especially after last night. And,' he added, 'especially if there is any foundation for your suspicions and evidence to be uncovered.'

'Which is precisely why,' the Doctor rejoined with a wide grin, 'I do not intend to ask them.' He leaned forward and tapped on the paper that Stobbold held. 'You'll organise this?'

Stobbold nodded, unsure of whether to comment on the Doctor's proposed course of action. 'Betty is going into Middletown later to order the groceries,' he said. 'She can send this at the same time. I have a sermon to write, so I shall be in all afternoon if there is a reply.'

'Excellent,' the Doctor clapped his hands together. 'Then let us be on our way, Professor.'

The ground was freezing again, and there was a thin crust of frost over the snow. Their feet crunched through as they walked. As they approached the mine, Dobbs noticed that the snow seemed thinner. His feet sank less far into the moorland, left less of an impression.

'Perhaps the ground is a little warmer here?' he suggested to the Doctor. He got no reply.

The Doctor was walking with his hands thrust into his jacket pockets, his head down.

'What do you expect to find at the mine, Doctor?' Dobbs asked after a few more minutes of silent walking.

'The unexpected,' the Doctor told him.

Dobbs laughed thinly, assuming this was a joke. But when the Doctor looked at him, his expression was anything but humorous.

They finished their journey without another word. Only when the cluster of huts round the entrance to the mine was visible did the Doctor speak again. He put out his arm to stop Dobbs and turned to him. 'Let me do the talking,' he said. 'If we can, I suggest we just slip into the tunnel. But I suspect we shall have to bluff our way past several people.'

Dobbs nodded. He was more than happy to let the Doctor do the bluffing. Already he could feel the lightness of trepidation and excitement in his stomach. How on earth, he wondered briefly, had he ever got into this situation? He was dreading as well as relishing the coming hours.

As they approached, Dobbs could hear the sound of the heavy machinery that had been brought in. A huge iron contraption stood between the huts and the gaping entrance to the tunnel into the mine tended by men with grimy faces wearing stained boiler suits. Steam puffed out from various joints and funnels and pipes as pistons pounded and flywheels span. The noise was incredible, and the smell of engine oil and grease hung heavy in the air. As they grew closer, Dobbs could feel the warmth from the machine. He wanted to ask the Doctor what it was doing, but he would have to shout to make himself heard.

His assumption was that they would sneak up as unobtrusively as possible and attempt to enter the mine unobserved. He was wrong. The Doctor squared his shoulders, and marched straight towards the mine entrance in full view of the men working on the machinery outside the huts. Several of the men turned, saw them, then turned away again. It seemed that the Doctor's plan of acting as if they had every right to be there was working.

Until they were almost at the entrance. From the dark mouth of the tunnel, a line of men filed out. Their faces were as black as the tunnel, stained and dirty. Their clothes were torn and grimy. Over their shoulders they variously carried shovels, picks and other tools. The man in the lead was almost as broad as he was tall. His expression was set, and his eyes seemed almost to glitter from out of his dusty-dark face. He stopped directly in front of the Doctor and Dobbs. The other men waited behind him, shuffling and tired.

'Can I help you?' The man's voice was a low monotone, just audible above the sounds of the machine behind them and the clang of working that reached them from deep inside the mine.

'I'm sorry,' the Doctor called back, louder than was necessary, 'I can't hear you above the air pumping machinery behind us. We're just conducting a quick inspection. On Lord Urton's orders.'

He made to dodge round the big man, but the man moved with him, still blocking the Doctor's way. 'I've heard nothing,' he said.

'I'm not surprised with this racket.' The Doctor smiled good-naturedly and tried again to get past.

Again, the man blocked his way. He hefted the shovel from his shoulder, holding it upright, raised in his gloved hands, as if ready to strike at the Doctor. 'Lord Urton gives no orders here without me knowing,' he said.

The Doctor glanced at Dobbs. 'Well,' he said slowly, 'actually it was Mr Nepath. Things being what they are.'

The man's response was a hiss of anger. 'Why are you here?' he demanded.

'I told you –'

The man cut him off. 'I'm Devlin, I am foreman. I would know.'

'Communications breakdown?' the Doctor hazarded. But Dobbs could tell from his tone that he knew the game was up.

'Why are you here?' Devlin asked again. Behind him the other miners were fanning out, blocking any hope of getting into the tunnel.

The Doctor sighed. The sound of the machine behind seemed to have faded into the background as he spoke, addressing all the men and not just Devlin. 'I am here because I believe you are in great danger.'

The miners exchanged glances. They looked to Devlin.

'I don't know what danger exactly,' the Doctor admitted. 'But there is something terribly wrong here. Surely you see that?'

'See what?' shouted one of the miners. He was a shorter man, but almost as broad as Devlin. 'What are you talking about? We got our jobs back, our livelihood.'

'But at what cost? And for how long?'

'What do you mean?'

'This machinery.' The Doctor waved a hand at the engine behind him. 'All the other machinery Nepath and Lord Urton have brought in. And there will be more and more, until you – until people – are no longer needed. Don't you see that? Whatever he is after down there, whatever it is, people are not a part of his equation. As soon as he can, he'll be rid of you. If I'm right, he'll be rid of us all.'

There was a hubbub of general muttering amongst the men as the Doctor spoke.

'Most of the work's being done by machine now,' the short man conceded. 'But he still needs us. Machines can't do it all. And he needs people to work the machines.'

The Doctor was almost hopping from one foot to the other. Devlin stood impassive and silent between him and the miners. 'But don't you see, Nepath shouldn't be mining at all. There's nothing here, nothing good!'

'Not mining at all?' the man asked incredulously. 'Not mining at all?!' The miners looked at each other again.

'He wants to stop the mining,' one of them blurted out angrily. 'Lock us out.'

'Well,' the Doctor admitted, 'yes, but –'

'But nothing,' Devlin interrupted sharply. 'You have no business here. You want to take away these men's jobs, their lives when they have only just got them back.' He leaned forwards, his voice loud and angry. 'You are not welcome here.'

As he leaned forwards, Devlin's face fell into shadow. And as it did, Dobbs could see the faint flicker of firelight dancing within his eyes, floating behind the irises. Devlin let the shovel drop to the ground, and pulled the glove from his right hand. That too fell to the ground, and he reached out towards the Doctor. Dobbs could hear the hiss of cold air seared by the heat from the hand, could see the hazy hot air swirling round it.

The Doctor leaned back, arcing his body away from the hand as it neared him. As he moved close to Dobbs, he suddenly reached out and grabbed the Professor, pushing him behind as together they circled away from Devlin. Before long, Devlin had his back to the steam pump and was facing the tunnel. Only the ring of miners now stood between the Doctor and Dobbs and the mine itself. They watched intrigued as Devlin took a step towards the Doctor. They evidently did not realise the danger, had no inkling of the power that Devlin could unleash from his hand.

And they were not expecting the Doctor's sudden shout any more than Dobbs was. It took a hefty push as well as the cry of 'Run!' for him to realise what the Doctor intended. Then they were both running, pushing through the surprised ring of men, plunging headlong into the murky tunnel and still running.

'No!' Devlin's order was like a pistol shot behind them. 'Leave them to me.'

Dobbs kept running, his breath ragged and scraping as he followed the Doctor. They passed several side passages, knocked aside a couple of surprised miners who made half-hearted attempts to stop them. They kept running.

'Where are we going?' Dobbs managed to call out. Behind him he could hear the heavy slap of Devlin's feet as he ran after them.

'Deeper,' the Doctor called back. He seemed scarcely out of breath. 'Whatever it is must be deep in the ground for them to need the air pump.'

'To… breathe?' Dobbs assumed, catching at his own breaths.

'To fan the fire,' the Doctor's reply echoed back.

The race into the depths was a blur. There were men who tried to hold them, machines jammed into the narrow passages and tunnels that they negotiated, and always the heavy sound of Devlin's pursuit. The one time Dobbs risked slowing enough to look behind, he could see the man's eyes blazing after them in the near darkness.

At last, after what seemed forever, the Doctor pulled up, catching Dobbs as he stumbled into him. They stood for several moments, the Doctor alert and listening, Dobbs hunched over, gasping for air.

'I think we lost him,' the Doctor said. 'We're quite deep now.' He nodded at the wall of the tunnel. 'This is new work. They haven't even bothered to shore it up you see. Solid rock – which is why they needed mechanical help. It would take an age to dig this manually.'

'So have they already excavated what they were after, do you think?' Dobbs asked as soon as he had enough breath.

'I don't think so,' the Doctor said. 'They're still working, after all. Uncovering another section further round, perhaps.'

'Another section of what?'

The Doctor was examining the wall. 'Of whatever it is,' he said helpfully. He ran his hand over the ragged wall. 'Feel that.' He stood aside, looking round as Dobbs stepped up to the wall.

The Professor reached out a tentative hand and placed it flat against the rock, wondering what the Doctor expected him to deduce. He knew at once. 'It's warm,' he said in amazement. 'It should be damp and cold, surely, at this depth?'

'Indeed it should.' The Doctor peered at him through the gloom, his eyes wide. He knelt down and patted the ground. 'The floor is warm too,' he said quietly. 'And what's more, it should be dark.'

'Good Lord, so it should.' Dobbs looked all round. 'So where is the light coming from. There is no sign of phosphorescence…'

When he turned back, the Doctor was gone.

'Doctor?' Dobbs could feel his stomach churning, his face flushed with sudden fear. 'Doctor?!'

'Through here.' The Doctor's voice was calm, echoing slightly as it emerged from a crack in the rock wall.

Dobbs scrambled through the rock with some difficulty. He could see at once that this was where the light was coming from. A glow, an orange glow that suffused the air with a smoky texture.

There was a smell too, he realised as he emerged into the cavern beyond – sulphurous and heady. Hot.

The cavern was vast, a huge open area within the mine. The ceiling was perhaps twenty feet high, vaulted over them. Dobbs could barely see the far wall as he stepped cautiously after the Doctor.

The light came from everywhere. Everything seemed to glow with inner heat. The floor was a pale orange while stalactites and stalagmites were a dull yellow. The walls smoked and shimmered, their fiery innards crusted over here and there with carbon-black shadows.

'Is this what we were looking for?' Dobbs asked, his voice an awed whisper. 'What Nepath and Lord Urton are looking for?'

The Doctor had stopped about ten feet in front on him and was crouching down beside a pool of molten fire. It bubbled viscously, occasional bursts sending fiery trails through the smoky air. 'This is it,' the Doctor agreed. 'Or rather, a very small part of it.'

'Small?' Dobbs turned completely round as he reached the Doctor, peering into the far extremities of the cavern.

'Very small,' the Doctor said.

'And what is this… stuff?' Dobbs indicated the bubbling mass before them. Across the cavern he could see many pools of the liquid. Hundreds perhaps, all presumably fed by the same reservoir of material below the floor. He had a sudden frightening realisation that at any moment the floor might crack open and allow them to fall screaming into the boiling mass below.

'The fissure…' he realised.

The Doctor stood up, expression grave as he continued to stare down at the pool. 'Yes, the fissure. And Nepath's material.'

'This?'

'This,' the Doctor confirmed. 'Once cooled. If indeed it is ever cool.' He looked up at Dobbs. 'I think, Professor, that with your help I now understand the "what". The question now is: "Why?"'

As he finished speaking, the Doctor's mouth dropped open and his eyes widened. He was looking past Dobbs, over his shoulder.

And the expression on the Doctor's face, Dobbs realised with a sudden chill, was one of absolute horror.

Dobbs turned, to see what the Doctor was looking at. He wished he had not.

The whole of the wall behind them was bulging outwards. The dark crust that skimmed the surface peeled away as Dobbs watched and slid to the ground, shattering into charred fragments. All around the cavern the same was happening. Shapes were forming out of the walls, pushing their way through and into the space beyond. The air was heavy and hot, smoke billowed from the ruptures that split down the cavern's sides. With a lurch of horror, Dobbs realised that the shapes that were extruding from the walls were figures.

'Oh my God,' he breathed into the smoke-wreathed air.

Beside him the Doctor too surveyed the cavern. He turned slowly to check each wall. But all around them, Dobbs knew, the grotesque misshapen forms were stretching out of the glutinous material that formed the walls. Each figure was a swollen, viscous approximation of the human form, each was pulling itself bodily from the surrounding material, strings of it following in each of the creatures' wakes. Each was glowing red hot, smoke pouring from the ground as they took their first hesitant steps and the very rock beneath their feet melted and bubbled away.

'When I say "run,"' the Doctor murmured close in Dobbs's ear, 'then run.'

Dobbs nodded dumbly. But he could see nowhere to run to. The figures that ranged themselves between them and the opening to the cavern were a wall of fire. Flames jumped from one to the next as they advanced into the hissing smoke. A hand grabbed Dobbs's shoulder and he spun round with a cry.

It was the Doctor. He was pointing down at the boiling pool behind them, his face drawn and ashen through the smoky orange glow of the cavern.

The liquid in the pool was bubbling upwards, pushing, forcing its way out of the pool. As Dobbs watched in horrified fascination, the top of the shape that bulged upwards at them unfolded, into a head. There were no features, no eyes, but he knew it could see – could sense – him. Arms reached out, detaching themselves with a 'glop' from the sides of the nascent form which continued to rise upwards, pulling itself out of the pool, making way for the figure that was already forming behind it.

Dobbs stepped away from the figure, retching and coughing in the sulphur-laden atmosphere. The air was thickening, yellowing, hazy with the heat. Soon he would not be able to see at all. He blinked into the steamy mist between himself and the cavern's entrance, his eyes stinging with the heat and the fumes, his stomach heavy with fear.

'Run!' The Doctor's voice cut through the heavy atmosphere like a knife, and Dobbs ran. He had no idea where he was heading, which way he was facing, but he plunged forwards into a shuffling, stumbling run.

The Doctor's voice was distant through the haze, muffled. 'Over here! Professor, this way!' And he realised he was heading away from the voice. He staggered to a halt, tried to get his bearings, tottered on the brink of a lava pool as another of the creatures reared up in front of him, flames leaping from its outstretched hands as it lunged forwards.

He tumbled sideways, rolled on the hot ground, felt his coat ignite as one of the figures clutched at it. He was running again, he didn't care which way. Only the Doctor's voice mattered, only the reassuring sound, his bearings. But as he twisted and turned and ran at random to try to escape the fire that clutched at him from every side, the voice seemed to move too, seemed to spin round and back with no logic. In his mind's eye he saw the needle of his compass spinning erratically; he saw Alistair's body charred and broken on the moor; he saw the coffin disappearing into the cremation flames.

And he saw, through the closing ring of rising fire, the shadow of the back of the Doctor's jacket as it vanished through the dark crack at the edge of the cavern.

'Doctor!' he screamed after the disappearing figure. 'Doctor, come back!' Even to himself it sounded desperate, pathetic. 'Don't leave me.' A sob.

His coat was still burning. The flames stabbed at him from all around. The ground at his feet bubbled and burst, showering his legs with the white heat of molten rock. He could feel the flesh on his face blistering, his eyes bulging in the heat as his vision misted and ran. In front of him was another of the figures, lurching towards him, the flames running over and round its form, mirroring the fire that swirled round his own body.

'Don't leave me.' Even he could barely make out the words parched from his throat.

His legs gave way, buckled beneath his flaming weight, and he pitched forwards.

'Please…

Into the fire.

Doctor…'

Into the burning.

Chapter Fourteen
Fire Pattern

It was a long time before the Doctor said anything. He sat in front of the fire, shivering. Betty Stobbold had made tea, and the Doctor's hands were clasped round a steaming cup. His eyes were unblinking on the fire.

Stobbold sat with him. The clergyman asked nothing, said nothing. He was used to sitting with those who were not yet ready to speak.

When the teapot was long cold and the fire was dying, Betty removed the tray. She hesitated in front of the Doctor, but he showed no sign of having seen her. He continued to hold the bone china cup of tepid tea. She returned a few minutes later and stoked the fire, throwing on more coal. As she turned away, she seemed to throw something else into the rekindled flames. Just a gesture, Stobbold decided as she smiled at him.

'I think I'll go to my room,' she said. 'It's been a long day.'

'It has indeed.' He took her hand in his. It was hard and cold. He held it to his cheek a moment. 'Get some rest. I don't think either of us is in the mood for supper.'

She turned and they both looked at the Doctor. His expression was set, his eyes cold blue flints. Then as they watched, he blinked. Twice, rapidly.

'Has there been any reply to my telegram?' he asked. His voice sounded hoarse and dry.

'No,' Betty said at once. 'None. Not yet.'

He nodded thoughtfully and took a sip of tea. His frown changed to a grimace and he looked in disgust at the cup for a moment before holding it out to Betty. 'Thank you,' he said. 'It's... lovely.' His voice tailed off and his frown returned. He turned back towards the reinvigorated fire in the grate.

'Good night, my child,' Stobbold said quietly.

Betty nodded, half-smiling. He watched her cross the room and close the door behind her. He listened for the sound of her tread on the stairs, but the fire was cracking and popping and he heard nothing.

After what seemed a suitable interval, Stobbold said: 'I assume that Professor Dobbs will not be joining us for the moment?'

The Doctor nodded. 'Things are worse than I'd anticipated,' he said. Still he did not meet Stobbold's gaze. 'Much worse.'

'And the Professor…?'

'He's dead.' It was a whisper, barely audible above the sound of the fire.

Stobbold was no stranger to death, or to the idea of death. But it never failed to shock him, even knowing that Dobbs was now free of the trials and tribulations of this earthly life. 'Dead? Are you sure?'

The Doctor's look gave him his answer.

Stobbold sighed deeply. 'There will be arrangements to make,' he said. 'Next of kin. The funeral.'

'All that can wait.' The Doctor's voice was as hard as his expression. 'We have more important things to talk about.'

'More important…?' Stobbold could scarce believe his ears. 'Doctor, a man has died.'

'I know,' the Doctor snapped back. His voice was loud, his tone angry. 'I know!' He took a deep breath, and seemed to bring his anger back under control. 'But we must prevent the thousands, perhaps even millions of deaths that may follow.' He leaned forward, the firelight flickering across one half of his face, the other in shadow. 'There is nothing we can do for the Professor now.'

'Really, Doctor –' Stobbold began.

'Really.' He made it sound like an emphatic agreement. 'I'm surprised there's no reply yet,' he said as if continuing the same thought. 'But we must proceed as best we can without it. Now,' he said – and his eyes locked for the first time with Stobbold's, a piercing blue – 'tell me what you know about fire.'

'Fire? Is this…' he searched for a word that would not seem too trivial. 'Relevant?'

'Oh yes. Believe me, yes. Fire killed Gaddis. A creature of fire killed the housekeeper at the Grange. Some sort of molten lava moulded into the flames killed Dobbs.' His voice was like ice. 'It is very relevant.'

They both stared into the flames of the fire in the grate, watched them lick orange, yellow and blue round the coal that Betty had thrown on. Watched the sparks and the smoke rise and twist up the chimney and out of sight.

'It is only fairly recently that fire has been associated with hell,' Stobbold said. It seemed as good a place to begin as any. 'Dante, you will recall, saw hell – saw his Inferno – as a cold place. The lack of heat, lack of warmth was a part of the suffering engendered there.'

'Easy to see how fire became a more potent symbol of suffering,' the Doctor said. 'It has been associated with power ever since it was discovered. The power of Thor sending his lightning bolts down from the heavens; the breath of that most powerful of mythical creatures, the dragon.'

'But also of rebirth,' Stobbold said. 'The phoenix rises from the flames, is born out of them.'

'But it rises from the ashes of its own destruction wrought by that very fire,' the Doctor pointed out. 'Is that what he's doing?' His voice drifted, became quieter and more distant. 'Is he out to destroy or to recreate in another image? Is he an alchemist, using the fire to bind his essential elements together? But if so, into what form?'

'Who?' Stobbold asked.

'Nepath.'

'Not Lord Urton?'

The Doctor stared at him. 'Lord Urton is dead,' he said, his tone almost gentle, sad. 'Lady Urton is dead. Do you begin to understand now? The foreman at the mine is dead. We must destroy what they have become, what Nepath has made them.'

'Destroy them?' Stobbold shook his head, this was becoming ever more difficult to comprehend. 'And these fire creatures of which you spoke?'

The Doctor stood up. One hand waved in the air dismissively. A flame shot up within the fire, echoing his action. The coal hissed and crackled as he spoke. 'I don't know,' he said, sounding tired and impatient for the first time. 'It's to do with the mine. Something Nepath found there. The stuff that Dobbs and I saw. Bubbling, liquid fire. Magma or lava or somesuch. And Nepath has a way of controlling it. He can make these objects with it, objects that can refashion themselves.'

'Through some mystic process, you said.'

'There's nothing mystic about it,' the Doctor snapped. 'That's just sales talk. The material he uses does it. That is what it does.' He had been pacing up and down in front of the fire. Now he stopped and snapped his fingers – a rifle crack of sudden sound. One of the lumps of coal split in two, one half rolling down to the brass fire surround. 'Or is it using him?' he wondered aloud. 'What is Nepath after? What has it promised him?'

'You talk as if…' Stobbold's throat was suddenly dry, and he swallowed. 'As if this material, this magma, were a living thing.'

'Yes,' the Doctor said quietly, his expression blank, as if he were just realising the same thing. 'Yes, so I do.'

As he stood motionless in thought, the flames seemed almost to freeze over the glowing coals.

A good fire was laid in the grate. The flames seemed almost to freeze over the burning logs.

Roger Nepath leaned forwards to watch the fire more closely. Behind the chair, Lord Urton stood stiff and still and silent. The flames moved again, tracing the movements they conveyed. The logs crackled and spat. The effect was a staccato, halting approximation of the speech it relayed.

'Some sort of liquid creature? Liquid fire? Molten rock? A single entity. Is that possible?' The tall, yellow flames that approximated the form of a man resumed their dance back and forth across the grate.

'You tell me,' crackled a lower orange flame as it licked round a log. If you screwed up your eyes, Nepath thought, if you squinted at the patterns you could believe that you really were looking not at the fire but at a figure seated in a chair. The tip of the flames twisted, as if the figure's head were moving to watch the yellow flames' flickering progress.

'Not there yet, are you, Doctor,' Nepath said quietly. 'Nearly. But not quite.' He leaned back in the chair and steepled his fingers under his chin. 'And by the time you are, it will be too late. Far, far too late.'

Behind him he heard the door to the drawing room open. He did not need to turn to see who it was, he already knew.

'Come in, my dear.'

Lady Urton led the visitor over to stand beside Nepath's chair. They all stood, looking into the flames, watching the Doctor and Stobbold as they continued their discussions.

'What is Nepath after?' a semblance of the Doctor's voice crackled. 'What does he value more than anything else in the world?' Again, the flame-Doctor stopped his pacing, seemed to turn to speak directly to the four people in the room watching. 'More than the world itself, perhaps?'

The Doctor was looking directly into the fire, as if searching for an answer to his question within the heat and the flames.

Stobbold himself had no answer to offer. He stood up, stretching. The evening was drawing on. He went to the window and tugged aside the curtain, peering out into the dark. A smattering of water splashed against the other side of the glass. He could hear the rain outside now, could see a line of puddles forming amongst the slush of melting snow. Almost like a line of footprints, filling with water.

'It's raining,' he said.

'Temperature must be rising,' the Doctor replied absently.

'It is. The snow seems to be melting.' Stobbold let the curtain fall and turned back to the Doctor. 'Is this significant, do you think? This rise in temperature?'

'Well,' the Doctor said slowly as he turned away from the fire. Behind him a yellow flame twisted across the coals. 'It isn't what usually happens after dark in winter.'

'I suppose not. So what does it mean?'

'What does anything mean?' The Doctor sounded sulky, as if annoyed that the answers were still evading him. 'You're the theologian.'

'That may be.' Stobbold tried to keep his own tone light, hoping to lift the Doctor from his sudden gloom. 'But I think what we are missing is a meteorologist.'

'We're missing something, certainly.' He tapped his forefinger against his chin. 'Something obvious.'

'About Nepath? Some secret?'

'There is something about him, I'm sure. Some explanation, some clue. A key that will unlock the mystery for us.'

This seemed optimistic to Stobbold. He doubted that any one piece of information, however pertinent, could explain everything that was going on. So much had happened, so much that was extraordinary, and in so short a time. 'Perhaps,' he hazarded, 'when we receive a reply to your telegram...'

'Yes,' the Doctor said quietly. 'Perhaps...'

Nepath gave a snort of laughter at this and clapped his hands together. 'Perhaps not, I think,' he declared. Shaking his head in good humour he turned to the two women standing beside his chair.

Lady Urton took a step back respectfully as Nepath smiled at Betty Stobbold. She gave no indication that she was aware of him. She continued to stare fixedly into the fire. Her hand was at her neck, clutching the small pendant, the statuette of Agni the fire god. He could see it glowing faintly through the narrow gaps between her fingers, tiny flames licking the surface from within.

He reached out his hand towards her. 'May I?'

Now she did turn, did look at him, noted his outstretched hand. He beckoned with his fingers, encouraging. Her blank expression still fixed in place, Betty reached out with her free hand and gave him the screwed up paper.

The paper was rolled into a ball. She had clutched it so tightly and for so long that it was difficult to uncurl. Nepath carefully teased at the edges, unpicking the paper until he could smooth it out over his knee and read the immaculate handwriting.

Shaking his head, he read it again. 'Such presumption, Doctor,' he murmured. Then he looked up at Betty and smiled. 'Thank you, my dear. You have done so well, so very well. We are grateful.' He turned back to the fire. 'I am sorry that my sister cannot be with us. She would want to express her own gratitude I am sure.'

With a sudden, almost violent motion, Nepath crushed the paper back into a ball. His face scrunched with the effort and emotion as he squeezed it tight. Then he hurled it into the flames.

At once the fire roared up. It seemed to leap on the ball of paper, to flow into and through it. The edges uncurled again slightly, blackening under the onslaught. A thin line of charred paper detached itself from the edge and twisted and turned its way upwards, carried on a rising current of hot air before disintegrating. The paper continued to blacken and unfurl until the fire devoured it.

Chapter Fifteen
Torchlight

They had adjourned to the study by the time they heard the door. Neither the Doctor nor Stobbold was hungry, and neither mentioned the possibility of supper. It was getting on for midnight and the rain was clearly audible, blowing against the study windows.

Stobbold looked up at the sound of the front door opening. The Doctor was already alert, listening. He too had heard it. They exchanged glances as the sound of the door being quietly closed reached them through the night-still of the Rectory.

'Expecting callers?' the Doctor asked quietly.

Stobbold shook his head and went out into the hall. His whole body felt taut and alert, worried at who – or what – he might find. He relaxed immediately and let out a long sigh. 'Betty – where have you been?' He started down the hallway towards her. 'You must be freezing without your coat. And wet through.'

The Doctor caught Stobbold's arm, holding him back. 'I don't think so.'

'What?' He looked from Betty's neutral expression to the Doctor's grim face. 'What do you mean?' He shook his arm free.

'I don't think she felt the cold.' He raised his voice. 'Did you? And you don't seem to have got too wet.'

Now that he looked, her clothes and skin did seem remarkably dry. Yet he was sure it was pouring with rain outside.

'I avoided the rain,' she said.

'But where have you been?' Stobbold shook his head as she approached. 'I thought you were asleep.'

'Had a nice walk?' the Doctor asked. His voice was level, hard.

'Thank you,' she said. 'It's lovely.'

'Is it really.' It wasn't a question.

'Oh, come now, Doctor,' Stobbold retorted. He had no idea what was up with the man.'She must be exhausted. And freezing. Come into the warm.' He led his daughter into the drawing room. The Doctor followed them, keeping his distance.

Stobbold led Betty over to the chair nearest the dying fire. Once he had sat her in it, he took the poker and coaxed some life into the glowing coals. Flames licked out and the room immediately seemed warmer. When he turned back to check on Betty, he saw that the Doctor had sat himself in the chair opposite and was watching her closely.

'You know,' he said, and Stobbold knew at once he was speaking to him and not to Betty, 'something's been bothering me.'

'Just one thing, Doctor?' He tried to make light of it as he stood in front of the fire.

'How did Lady Urton know that the Professor and I were inside the Grange that night?'

'She heard you,' Stobbold said. 'Lord Urton too, from what you said.'

The Doctor was shaking his head. He wagged a finger in admonishment. 'I don't think so. No,' he decided. 'I think someone told them we were coming. Someone who saw us leave the Rectory, and either ran on ahead, or arrived soon after us.' He leaned forwards, staring intently at Betty's face. Or at her neck.

Her hand went instinctively to the pendant, and Stobbold fancied for a moment that he could see it glowing behind her hand. A trick of the light, he decided. A reflection from the fire.

'Or perhaps,' the Doctor was saying, 'she has some way of communicating from a distance. Firelight telegraph system.'

'What are you talking about?' Stobbold demanded. He was getting enough of the gist to be angry.

'Smoke signals perhaps?' the Doctor asked wryly.

'Doctor,' Stobbold said with enforced patience, 'I think we deserve an explanation for these ramblings. What exactly are you suggesting?'

'I am suggesting that there is a very good reason why we have had no reply to my telegram.'

That surprised Stobbold. 'What has that to do with Betty?'

The Doctor's voice was a charged whisper. 'Everything.' He leaped to his feet and thrust out his hand, close to Betty's head. Stobbold flinched. Betty did not move, she sat rock still as if not noticing.

'May I have the receipt?' the Doctor asked.

She did move now. Her head tilted and she looked up at him. 'Receipt?' A flash of puzzlement crossed her face, then was gone.

'The receipt for the telegram.'

'I…' She frowned and looked away, as if trying to remember. 'I lost it.' Her voice seemed to come from a long way away.

'What is this, Doctor?' Stobbold asked. He was surprised at how quiet and calm his own voice was. But even as he asked he knew the answer.

The Doctor shook his head and dropped back into his chair. 'I don't think you ever had a receipt, Betty,' he said. 'Because I don't think you ever sent the telegram.' His voice was quiet, almost a murmur, a contrast to his sudden shout of anger: 'Did you!' He was on his feet again, his movement punctuating, emphasising the words.

This time she did flinch. Her whole body convulsed at his thunder-crack voice. She blinked.

'Enough!' Stobbold shouted back. He struggled to control his voice. He caught the Doctor's elbow and drew him away, towards the door. 'Can't you see you're frightening her, Doctor?'

The Doctor stared at Stobbold, the amazement apparent in his eyes. 'You don't see it, do you?' he asked in a husky voice. 'You really don't.'

'See what?' Stobbold asked in a hushed whisper. 'You can tell she hasn't been herself lately, Doctor. Please have some respect for her feelings.'

He laughed at that, an explosion of mirthless noise. 'Feelings?' The Doctor stepped to one side of Stobbold and pointed back across the room, at the figure of the girl sitting absolutely still in front of the fire. 'It was you who chided me for my lack of feeling, you will recall. It was you who was so keen to mourn the people they have killed – *it* has killed.'

'Not in here,' Stobbold hissed. 'I have no idea what you are talking about,' he said angrily, 'but I will not discuss this in front of my daughter, do you hear?'

The Doctor nodded. Anger and contempt mixed in his voice. 'Oh yes, I hear.' He turned and strode from the room.

Stobbold watched him go, heard the sound of the front door, and looked back at his daughter. For a moment they were both still. Then she turned her head, and looked back at him.

And he could see nothing in her expression. Nothing at all.

'Am I to take it that you believe my daughter to be under some sort of unnatural influence?' Stobbold asked. He had to shout to make himself heard above the sound of the wind and the rain. It was the emptiness of her expression that had unsettled him and brought him chasing out after the Doctor. Her wide, dead eyes.

The Doctor seemed not to notice the inclement weather. He was standing in the middle of the driveway, amongst the diminishing islands of grey slush that were even now washing away. He was already drenched. 'Don't you?' he shouted back.

There was a fierce storm coming, Stobbold could feel the heady atmosphere that often preceded the worst of them. He staggered through the rain towards the Doctor, holding his jacket closed, fumbling for the button. He was soaked through before he had taken five steps. 'No,' he retorted. 'No, of course I don't. The idea is absurd.'

'Yet you were willing to entertain the notion that Lord Urton – that your friend – might be possessed.'

Stobbold slipped on the wet gravel, stumbled, caught his balance by clutching at the Doctor's arm. 'Yes, but that… That was different.'

'Oh? How?'

'You saw – you said. And Dobbs,' Stobbold blustered. 'But Betty has done nothing.'

'Really?' Still the Doctor ignored the rain, though it was running in streams down his face, dripping from the end of his nose.

'Really.' Stobbold stepped back. 'She is seventeen, Doctor. Adolescent. Alone.'

He said nothing.

'Her mother is long dead, God rest her soul. She's had nobody but her old father most of her life. She looks after me, keeps house, does the cooking, all the work I cannot afford to have anyone else do for us.' His mouth was racing ahead of his brain. He had never thought it through before. He had never had to.

He had never wanted to.

'So of course she's quiet, withdrawn,' Stobbold shouted. 'Of course she is introspective and saturnine. She has nobody to talk to, nobody to confide in, nobody to trust. Nobody but me.' He looked down at his feet, at the rain splashing into the deepening puddles. 'She is scared of growing up, of becoming a woman. She is scared of leaving me, and she is terrified of *never* leaving me.'

He looked back up, and saw genuine sympathy in the Doctor's expression, though his gaze seemed focused beyond Stobbold, on the doorway.

'I must make time to speak to her, to be with her,' he said as he turned to look. 'I should have done so long ago.'

He felt the Doctor's hand on his shoulder as he turned and stared back at Betty, standing in the doorway. Her long hair was untied, hanging down almost to her waist. She was under the light in the porch, so that even through the driving rain he could see her freckles, her mouth slightly open, her face devoid of expression.

'Yes,' the Doctor said quietly, close to his ear. 'You should have. It's too late now.'

She started towards them, taking quick, confident steps. The rain spat and hissed round her. He stood, unable to move, unwilling to believe.

'Oh Matthew, Matthew, Matthew,' the Doctor said. 'Can't you see what is so obvious? Won't you admit to yourself what is happening?'

For an instant, Stobbold felt like Jephthah, the Old Testament judge of Israel. He would give anything to be spared this. Like Jephthah, he would willingly sacrifice the first thing he saw on his return if only he was brought home safely.

The Doctor stepped round him and approached her. 'Nice weather for the time of year, don't you think?' the Doctor called into the rain.

'Thank you. It's lovely.' Her words seemed to carry despite the quietness of her voice.

'Yes,' the Doctor said, keeping his distance. 'I've been thinking about that. It's become a favourite phrase of yours hasn't it. An automatic response, something to say. Just being polite.'

He took a step back again, and turned quickly to see where Stobbold was. 'It also happens to be what you said when you put on the pendant, the statuette of the fire god, of Agni.'

Her hand was immediately at her throat. Still she stepped towards them through the steaming rain. The pendant was glowing deep red, casting a diffuse light across her throat and illuminating her face eerily from below.

'Your final words, I'm sorry to say. No wonder they come back so easily, so often. To haunt you.'

The Doctor was standing beside Stobbold once more.

Betty halted several steps in front of them. And now Stobbold could see the drops of rain hissing and evaporating as they struck her hot form. He could see how she had walked through the rain without getting wet. He could hear the spitting and hissing of the water boiling away the instant it touched her, and a sob of anger and pity and grief broke from him.

'Betty,' he sobbed. 'Oh Betty, tell me it isn't true. Tell me it's still you.'

She smiled then. Her mouth widened, her cheek bones and eyebrows lifted.

'I don't think she has been consumed, like Urton,' the Doctor murmured. 'It's more in the nature of a possession.'

She raised her hand, bringing her other hand underneath as if reaching out for the sacrament.

'Not that it makes much difference now,' the Doctor added.

Cradled in her palm was a glowing coal plucked from the fire. Red and orange flickered within the dusty black lump. Her hand was a blackened, scorched mess beneath. As the Doctor and Stobbold stood watching, a mass of flame spouted violently from her hands towards them, erupting from the glowing coal. A moment later, her forearms erupted, the fire spreading out from her palms, over her entire torso. Only her legs were still visible beneath the roaring, rolling sea of flame. She stepped towards them.

Stobbold stood his ground, shouting at her, pleading, begging. He was thinking again of Jephthah, of how he must have felt when the first thing he saw on his safe return home, running to greet him, was his own daughter.

Until the Doctor dragged him back.

'It's no use, can't you see?'

They continued to back away. Stobbold could feel the heat from the flames as Betty continued to advance towards him. He could feel the difference in texture beneath his feet as they stepped from the gravel of the drive on to the sodden grass of the front lawn. The roaring of the fire blotted out the sound of the gathering storm.

His foot slipped from under him and Stobbold fell backwards. He pushed himself away from her on his back. The Doctor had his hands under Stobbold's shoulders and lifted him, dragged him away. The ground was awash, a mass of slippery mud. Stobbold's feet sank into it as they had in the snow, except that they stuck. It was an effort to lift them, to move, to back away. And if they went much further they would reach the bank at the end of the lawn, rising to the boundary wall. They might slip and slide and climb the one, but never the other. Not in time.

He fell again, and this time found himself sitting at the base of the embankment. He could feel the ground squirming, running, washing away behind his back as the rainwater poured off it. Again the Doctor dragged him up.

For the first time he took his eyes off the fiery swirling pillar that was his daughter, and he glanced behind him. The rain was blowing so that it hit the wall. Narrow rivers were forming on the stone and running down to the ground with such force that they were eating into the top of the bank. As he looked, a section of the wall sagged towards them, the ground around its foundations washed away in the torrent.

A glance. Then he looked back at Betty. He saw the flames running, pouring out of her as she increased speed, racing towards them now, sensing that she had them.

The Doctor was dragging him up the steep slope. They slipped and fell. Tried again, scrabbling desperately at the liquid ground. Somehow they were at the top of the bank.

She was coming up after them. The mud exploded round her feet. The fire engulfed her legs now, dried and cracked the ground as she walked. The flames seemed to gather themselves, then the whole blazing mass hurled itself at them. Stobbold had his back to the wall, felt his feet slipping from under him, could only watch the fire growing until it filled his vision, his world, his life.

Suddenly he was tumbling down the muddy slope – the Doctor had knocked him sideways, winding him. The clergyman rasped in great gulps of rain-filled air as he fell. He landed on his back, saw the Doctor disappear past him. And he saw the ball of fire that had pitched towards him strike the wall with such force that he heard the explosion of heat-cracked stone.

Sparks flew from the centre of the fire. Acrid smoke billowed out. The wall was getting bigger as he watched. No – it was moving, coming towards him, falling forwards knocked off its crumbling, exposed foundations.

Stobbold rolled aside as the stonework shattered into the ground close by. The fiery shape of his daughter rolled molten towards him again, driven down the bank by the falling masonry. He saw her face coming at him, fire exploding from her mouth, her nostrils, the sockets of her eyes. Then she pitched downwards within the fire, a mass of stone and mortar crashing on top of her, crushing her into the sodden, muddy ground.

The mud exploded into smoke and steam. The sound of the hissing fire and of the falling wall almost blotted out the near-human screams. Then, the noise died. There was just the rain, and the bursting bubbles of boiling mud as the ground settled back down over her.

How long he stood there, watching the ground bubble and heave and eventually come to rest, he did not know. He was aware of the Doctor standing close by, hands folded in front of him, head bowed, like a graveside mourner. He was aware of the hot rain on his face mingling with the tears. He was aware of nothing else.

Until the eruption.

They both looked up at once. It was the loudest thing Stobbold had ever heard. A terrific explosion echoing across from the moors. At the same moment the ground beneath them shook with such force that Stobbold was sent staggering. He collided with the Doctor who was also struggling to stay upright. They held each other, braced themselves, feet apart until the tremor ceased.

'What the devil was that?' he breathed.

'The devil is perhaps right,' the Doctor answered as he stepped away. He pointed across Stobbold's shoulder, out on to the moor. Towards the fissure.

The whole sky was alight. A curtain of flame was shooting up towards a blood red moon. Sparks and dust spun and twisted out from it and they could feel the raw heat, the nascent power of the blast before the flames settled back and the sky began to clear.

'Hellfire, would you say?' the Doctor asked.

'Or a volcano.'

The rain was solid now. Hot particles of dust and ash that settled on their wet clothes and caked their faces like powder. There was a sulphurous, clammy stench to the acrid air.

The Doctor raised a hand to his face, and pinched at the bridge of his nose. 'I am so sorry,' he said. 'So very sorry.'

Stobbold looked down again at the patch of broken ground

where his daughter was buried. Entombed. It was already dusted with ash, like a sprinkling of grey snow.

'I should have realised long ago,' the Doctor went on, and it occurred to Stobbold that he was apologising for something quite different. When the Doctor looked across at him, his face seemed drained of colour. A late drop of rain traced a path through the dust and down his cheek. 'I should have seen it at once. As soon as I saw the fissure.'

'Seen what?'

'Even the place names are a clue.' He appeared not to have heard. 'Branscombe-sub-Edge, don't you see?'

Stobbold shook his head. His stomach was heaving and he ached all over. One side of his face felt stiff and sore.

'It's on the rim, lower than the old river bed. The whole of the moor is lower than the surrounding countryside. And Middletown is right in the centre, at the bottom of the basin.'

'The ground dips,' Stobbold agreed. His voice was calm and controlled, though his whole body was shaking. 'We all know that. It's to do with the water table, the moorland.' He shrugged. 'The composition of the rocks.'

But the Doctor was shaking his head. 'It's nothing of the sort. It's a caldera.'

'A what?' He was fighting to stop his teeth from chattering despite the heat of the air.

The Doctor turned back towards the fissure. The sky was no longer burning, but there was a glow, as if the ground beneath it were on fire. 'The basin formed by a volcanic eruption. By the flow of magma, of molten lava.'

Stobbold's mouth was open. But his brain was numb. He said nothing.

'Like a flood plain,' the Doctor went on. 'Only we know what it will soon be flooded with.'

They stared at each other in the firelit night. 'Oh my God in Heaven,' Stobbold breathed.

Chapter Sixteen
A Death in the Family

There was an abandoned warehouse at the edge of Middletown. Lord Urton had acquired it recently and now it contained the forge and machinery to produce Sir William Grant's field guns. The first batch of six was ready for collection, and Colonel Wilson watched as they were fastened to the teams of horses that stood patiently outside the huge warehouse doors.

They had been waiting since early evening for the final adjustments to be made, and he had considered more than once going back to Ambleton to return the next day. But every time he asked, the foreman assured him they were almost ready now. Just a few more minutes. Really.

Wilson was facing across town, towards the distant moorland, when the abyss erupted. He saw it before he heard it, glancing across at Captain Brookes, satisfying himself that Brookes had seen it too. Then the sound reached them. At first it was rumble, then it built rapidly to a roaring explosive thunderclap that made them cover their ears as they staggered to keep their balance. But they could not look away.

The dark sky was split by the rising column of flame. It rose slowly, majestically through the night before the top of the column began to tilt and bend as if buckling under its own weight. As it fell back, clouds of white hot steam rose to join the flames, racing across the sky behind the spreading fire, as if driven by the wind. Before long the whole of the night sky was a swirling mass of steam and fire. Then the ash began to fall.

The streets began to fill with people as well as ash and dust. They came out of their houses, mostly still in their nightclothes, staring up at the firelit sky. With the noise and the flickering orange glow in the heavens, many of them believed it was the end of the world.

The sound died back to a low roar. Wilson found he was running along the street, shouting for his men to follow, shouting for people to stay in their houses and not to worry. Brookes was close beside him, also shouting, though Wilson could not hear his voice. Whether this was because the noise was still too loud or because their ears were numbed by the initial blast, he could not tell.

The eruption lasted almost an hour. It faded far more slowly than it had begun, the sky glowing a deep orange that lit the smoky streets with a dull, diffuse light. The people seemed to calm as the noise dropped. Wilson and his men were able to reassure them, to guide them back to their homes.

Looking along the streets, Wilson saw that everything was once again coated, as it had been earlier. But this was not snow and slush, this was a powdery ash, fine and grey. It rose in puffs where you trod, it clogged the nostrils and the mouth and clung to the back of the throat. It smelled of sulphur and it dusted Wilson's uniform so that he was clothed in nondescript grey. His rank, his status, his profession were all masked by the fine powder. Everyone became the same, even their greyed faces looked similar. All individuality taken away by the ash.

As soon as he could spare someone, he sent a runner back to Ambleton to check on the situation there. They had no way of telling how far the eruption had reached, but if Ambleton was relatively unaffected, then he could get reinforcements. Or if not, then Ambleton would still need to know the situation in Middletown. Perhaps the whole of this part of the country was affected.

It was impossible to tell when dawn arrived. But the sun was visible now through the thick air, burning weakly above the horizon.

Other than keeping people calm, it was difficult to know quite what was to be done. Wilson and his men made their way through the streets, reassuring people and trying to seem knowledgeable about what was going on. It was not the Apocalypse, they told them; hell was not coming to Middletown; the end was nothing like nigh.

So it was with a sense of relief that Wilson saw a familiar figure emerge from the Post Office ahead of him. The Reverend Stobbold. With him was the Doctor, whom Wilson had met at the dam.

'Reverend, sir!' Wilson called as he run up. Clouds of dust erupted from his feet as he ran. 'We're trying to keep people calm, sir,' he said breathlessly as he reached them. 'But perhaps some words from yourself? A meeting of some sort to reassure people that this isn't the fires of hell breaking loose?'

Stobbold seemed drawn, old. He seemed grey even beneath the dust, Wilson saw. And there was a deep sadness in his eyes as he looked at the soldiers.

It was the Doctor who spoke. 'There isn't time to arrange a meeting,' he said. His voice was quiet but authoritative. 'If we're lucky, there may be time to evacuate the town.'

'Evacuate?' Brookes said in surprise.

'Explain please, Doctor,' Wilson said.

The Doctor took his jacket off and shook it. A dust storm swirled in the air, choking and dry. When he put his jacket back on, the Doctor was the only person in sight who was not uniformly grey – a splash of individual colour in the drab world of Middletown.

'That was a minor eruption,' he said.

'Minor?!'

'A precursor to the main event.'

'You mean,' Wilson asked slowly, 'that there is more to come?'

'Oh much more. This is just the beginning.' He turned to look at Stobbold, as if to get his agreement with what he was about to say. 'Colonel Wilson, despite your reassurances, it may well be that the fires of hell are indeed breaking loose. And I emphatically suggest that you get everyone you can away from here before they consume us all.'

'But, evacuate the whole town?' Brookes demanded. 'That's a huge undertaking, sir.'

'What do you suggest?' the Doctor's eyes were cold as he stared first at Captain Brookes, then at Colonel Wilson. 'Hang around for a bit to see if there really is a larger eruption? That will be too late.'

'We will need more evidence,' Wilson said. 'More than just your suspicions, Doctor.'

'Evidence?' The Doctor was incredulous. '*Evidence?*!' he shouted, spreading his arms and spinning in a full circle. 'What more evidence do you need?'

'Colonel, the Doctor may well be right.' Stobbold's voice was as drawn as his face. It cracked, as if he were holding his emotions in uncertain check.

'I'm sorry, sir. But I need more than that.'

'Then what do you propose?' Stobbold asked.

Wilson considered. 'We'll try to keep everyone indoors. Anyone who wants to leave, may. We will help organise transport. I've already send a runner to Ambleton for more men.'

'We should be getting people out, not bringing them in,' the Doctor complained.

'So you say, Doctor. And you may be right.'

'But you won't know until it's too late,' he pointed out.

'I said I needed more evidence, Doctor. I don't intend to wait for the evidence to present itself.'

'What will you do?'

'I shall inspect the fissure myself,' Wilson said. 'I am an engineer. What I see may enable us to form an opinion. In forming that opinion, Doctor you may rest assured I shall take your own views – your own emphatic views – into account.'

'And then?' Stobbold asked.

'If I believe it is necessary, I shall evacuate the town as you suggest.'

'You're wasting time,' the Doctor told him. He was shaking his head in a mixture of sadness and disbelief.

'I cannot act just on your say-so, Doctor. Whatever happens, or doesn't happen, I shall need to justify my decision to my superior officers. To do that, I need first hand evidence.'

'But –' the Doctor began.

Stobbold put his hand on the Doctor's arm and interrupted. 'Then make all speed, Colonel. And good luck.'

'Thank you, sir.' Wilson turned to go, then hesitated. 'Where will you be, gentlemen? If I need you?'

Stobbold looked at the Doctor. 'Are we finished here? Do you have what you need?'

The Doctor nodded. 'Oh yes. I have what I need now for our meeting with Mr Nepath.'

A yellow fog hung over the landscape. Everything seemed tinged with its effects. The grey of the dust had become a pallid amber as Stobbold and the Doctor made their way up the drive to the Grange.

Stobbold headed for the front door. He was still dazed, numbed by the experiences of the night before. Inside he felt empty, as if his stomach had dropped away to leave a gaping void where his heart, his emotions, his very soul sank without trace.

The Doctor drew him aside as they approached. 'Not that way,' he said. 'Let's try round the back.'

'You intend to break in? Again?' Stobbold tried to sound censorious, but somehow his words were flat and noncommittal.

'Just a little look round. I like to start off at an advantage. With all the information.'

Stobbold forced a smile. 'Some would say that was cheating,' he said.

'Well, I think it's about time we made some of the running. Even if it does mean cheating, as you put it.' The Doctor swung round suddenly, his eyes alive with anger. 'Look,' he demanded, 'do you have a problem with this? If so, then kindly return to the Rectory and leave it to me.'

'No,' Stobbold said quickly. 'No problem. Doctor?' he added hesitantly.

'Yes?' The Doctor was off again, striding through the yellow mist, not glancing back.

'Whatever it takes, whatever we have to do, we must stop Nepath. I know that. After last night, after what happened to Betty…' His voice tailed off.

The Doctor paused, slowly turning to regard Stobbold with large, yellow-stained eyes.

'You were right, Doctor,' Stobbold said quietly. 'This evil must be fought. There is always a cost, and we have already paid too much. No more, please. No more.'

The Doctor stepped back towards him and clapped him on the shoulder. 'It is almost over now,' he said quietly. 'I promise you that. One way or another, things are almost done.'

The tradesman's entrance was unlocked. They let themselves in and stood for a moment in the gloom. The sun struggled with limited success to illuminate the house through misted windows.

The Doctor led the way in silence to the back staircase. Stobbold recalled Dobbs's description of the events of several nights previously. He felt a pang of fear – but no twinge of conscience – as they made their way up to the landing. That was good, he decided. Feeling. He was feeling again.

And more than anything, he realised, he was feeling angry. He did not rile easily, rarely lost his temper, but inside he could feel the raw emotion swelling up, ready to burst once given an outlet.

'Let's start in here,' the Doctor whispered and led Stobbold into a room at the top of the stairs.

The room was lined with display cases and cabinets. The Doctor closed the door quietly behind them and led Stobbold to a case on the far side of the room.

'These are the copies,' he said keeping his voice low. 'Made from the reforming material, from the stuff Nepath and Urton have been mining.'

'This stuff is alive?' Stobbold hissed. He peered into the cabinet, saw the various ornaments and figures. Some he recognised as religious figures and icons from his studies of the Eastern religions. At the back of the case stood Kali, swords raised, fire dancing round the figure's head. He blinked as one of the arms seemed to move slightly – a trick of the misty light. Or of the moisture in his eyes.

'It is not life in the sense that you or I understand it,' the Doctor explained. 'Some sort of sentience, I'm sure. Nepath wants something from it and the substance is content to be used by him. For now. Until it gets what it wants.'

'Which is?

The Doctor shrugged, turning away from the cabinet. 'What does any living thing want?' he asked.

'Hope?' Stobbold suggested. 'Salvation? To believe in something, to have faith?'

'To survive,' the Doctor said.

Stobbold took a look back into the cabinet as he considered this. In that instant he saw the sword arm of Kali swipe down through the air as the figure took a lurching step forwards. Stobbold gave a cry of surprise and took a step backwards. The Doctor turned quickly at the sound.

The glass door of the cabinet shattered under the sword blow, sending a shower of glass slivers biting across Stobbold's face. He cried out again, hands raised to ward off the hailstorm.

When he looked, when he hesitantly lowered his hands, he saw that the statue was dissolving. The features were melting and running down the face, down the body. Like a candle burning away, rivulets of the materials were running down the sides and pooling at the feet. The other relics and artefacts were doing the same – melting into viscous steaming pools of liquid.

The Doctor took a step back, pulling Stobbold with him. The pools of liquid were linking up, running into each other, bubbling, hissing, boiling. Hot splashes spat across the cabinet as the pools joined, massed into a larger pool – a body of the glowing fiery liquid that seemed bigger than the parts that had formed it.

'Fascinating,' the Doctor said. There was real awe in his voice. 'Something is happening. It knows it is time... But time for what?'

The liquid seemed to bulge upwards and outwards, as if rearing up. It plunged out of the cabinet and splashed to the floor in front of them – between them and the door where they had come in. Slowly, inexorably, it rolled towards them. The air above it shimmered in the intense heat. Stobbold could feel it on his face as they backed away, towards the corner of the room.

'I think we're in trouble,' he managed to say to the Doctor as the shapeless mass before them expanded again, pushing upwards, sprouting limbs of fire, shuffling forwards. For a second he saw his daughter's fiery form reflected in the shape it was adopting.

The Doctor's face was grim, his features illuminated by the red hot glow from the creature that was gathering itself for the attack. 'It's frustrating that we never seem to keep the initiative,' he sighed. 'And if *we've* got trouble,' he went on, 'I wonder what's happening in the mine.'

The shape in front of them exploded into flames and hurled itself forwards.

Wilson had left Captain Brookes in charge in Middletown and taken Sergeant Griffiths with him to the fissure. He was reluctant to take any of the other men with him – there were few enough in any case. They could see no more than fifty yards in front of them through the misty gloom. It was worse than a London pea-souper.

They heard the sounds from the mine before they could see what was happening. Cries and screams broke through the fog. Both Wilson and Griffiths had seen active service. Both knew immediately that it was the sound of men in fear for their lives. Dying.

The first figures struggled through the mist in front of them, stumbling onwards as fast as their exhausted legs would carry them. One man fell close by and Griffiths ran to help him up. He was gibbering with fear, saliva speckling his dark beard. He said nothing, just tore free of the Sergeant and ran on.

'They're coming from the mine,' Wilson said as more men ran past. As he finished speaking another figure emerged into view, screaming, turning, twisting. His clothes were ablaze, the shape of his body hidden within the fiery mass. He collapsed before he reached the two soldiers. For several seconds the body writhed and convulsed on the ground. Then it was still and the flames continued to consume it.

Another figure was in sight now. A large, broad man. He approached them steadily, seemingly in less of a hurry than his work mates. Wilson recognised him as he drew closer, had seen him several times at church.

'My God, Devlin,' Wilson called to the mine foreman. 'What in Heaven's name is happening? Has there been an accident? Something caused by the eruption?'

'Can we help?' Griffiths asked, stepping closer.

Devlin's eyes seemed to burn through the fog as he regarded them. He was almost within reach of Griffiths now. There was something disconcerting about the man's measured gait, about the way he reached out, about the way his eyes seemed to shine with inner fire.

Too late, Wilson shouted at Griffiths to get away from Devlin. Too late, he ran forward to grab the sergeant and drag him back. Too late, he felt the explosive heat on his face as Devlin's hands erupted into flames and closed on Griffiths's neck.

The steam and smoke mingled with the fog. The smell of burning vied with the sulphurous fumes and Wilson watched transfixed as Griffiths's body blackened and burned. His screams and shouts choked off and he dropped, a charred amorphous mass, to the ground.

Devlin turned towards Wilson. His arms were ablaze. His face was illuminated by the light burning in his eyes. Behind him glowing, misformed figures of fire were lurching forwards to join him. The heat was indescribable, even before Devlin's face ignited and his whole body flared up into a huge flame. In moments he was the same glowing, molten mass. The vaguely human shapes rolled across the moorland leaving blackened trails and small fires behind them.

Wilson turned at last and ran for his life.

* * *

181

The Doctor shoved Stobbold aside as the ball of flame hurtled towards them. It splashed, liquid fire, against the wall where they had been.

But neither Stobbold nor the Doctor waited to see the creature reform and gather itself for another blistering charge. They were already running for the door. The Doctor ripped it open and again hurled Stobbold through into the passage outside. He slammed the door shut behind him, only for it to explode immediately into a mass of fire.

'So much for caution,' the Doctor shouted above the crackling of the burning wood. 'This way.'

'Where are we going?' Stobbold asked as he let himself be led at a run down the corridor, away from the stairs. His chest was heaving and his breath ragged. He was too old to run far. 'I thought we wanted to see Nepath.'

'He'll find us,' the Doctor snapped back and he pulled open a door and charged inside.

Stobbold was close behind him. The room was lit by the same misty yellow as the rest of the house. It was a very large room, apparently used for storage rather than display. There were tea chests and screwed up balls of newspaper between the wooden display cabinets. 'God's truth!' Stobbold exclaimed as he looked round. 'This is a tinderbox, Doctor.'

The Doctor skidded to a halt amongst the packing crates and looked around himself in apparent surprise. 'Yes, I suppose it is.' He glared across at Stobbold. 'So best not to hang around, wouldn't you agree, Reverend?'

'What?' He realised what the Doctor was saying and hurried across to join him. 'Oh yes.'

There was a door on the other side of the room, and the Doctor was waiting for Stobbold in front of it. 'This is it,' he said, raising his eyebrows, as if asking Stobbold if he was sure he wanted to continue.

Not that Stobbold had a lot of choice. He could hear the crackling of the fire along the corridor. How long before it came looking for them? How long before it found them? 'Best to take the bull by the horns, don't you think, Doctor?' His voice trembled as he spoke.

The Doctor smiled thinly. 'That's the spirit.' So saying, he opened the door and stepped through.

It was a small room by comparison. A single wall lamp was burning, but it was enough to illuminate the room. The curtains were drawn shut so that the air seemed clearer, without its yellowish tinge. The main furniture in the room was a tall, upright glass display cabinet. Despite the fact that the light was directly over it, was shining down into the cabinet, Stobbold could not see what was inside.

Roger Nepath and Lady Urton were standing in front of the cabinet.

Lady Urton's expression was fixed and staring – a face of stone. Nepath, by contrast, seemed in good humour. He smiled broadly and extended his hand. 'Why Doctor, and the Reverend Stobbold. What a very pleasant surprise.'

Neither the Doctor nor Stobbold made any move to take his hand. Nepath lowered it.

'Actually, not such a surprise at all. Not even unexpected in fact.' Nepath's voice was hardening. He blinked, one side of his face convulsing suddenly and sharply with the movement.

Still neither of them spoke.

'So impolite,' Nepath said sternly. 'Hardly correct behaviour. Not when I have a deal to offer you. A bargain.'

'The sort of deal you have made with the creature in the mine?' the Doctor asked. His voice was low. But his expression was stern. 'You really think you can bargain with it?'

'Oh but I have. I am.' Nepath laughed and flung out his arms. 'I do.'

'You *think* you do. It's an elemental force, Nepath. It doesn't distinguish between us, it doesn't think in any way we understand. All it does is burn. It consumes matter to sustain itself.'

'Oh, Doctor,' Nepath replied with a sigh. 'I had not thought you so naive. You do it a disservice, you know.'

'Do I?'

'Oh yes. Yes, indeed.' Nepath considered. He stroked his chin. 'You are so alike you know. You and the *creature* as you rather quaintly call it.'

'Alike?' The Doctor was scandalised. His lip curled. 'I hardly think so.'

'I know so much about you, Doctor,' Nepath said thoughtfully. 'So much that Betty told me, that she overheard or had relayed to me. God rest her soul.' He smiled thinly at Stobbold, who fought back his emotions. 'And you are right, the creature does not think as you and I. It just "is". It has no past that it is aware of. No memory of who or what it really is.' He was watching the Doctor intently.

Stobbold turned to watch the Doctor too. His face was a blank, as stony as Lady Urton's features.

Nepath continued: 'But what it does, as you have seen, Doctor, is to mimic. It can take on the characteristics and attitudes of whatever it chooses. It conforms to the expectations of others in order to survive. Perhaps in order to try to define itself.' He smiled again, teeth glinting in the gaslight. 'Does that ring any bells, Doctor?' He gave a short, sharp laugh. 'Am I getting *warm*?'

'Not even tepid,' the Doctor replied. But his voice was quiet, hard-edged. Stobbold could tell he was unsettled, thrown off balance by Nepath's observations.

'Why do you need the Doctor?' Stobbold demanded. 'If you and this thing are so friendly, surely you don't need anyone else.'

'No,' Nepath admitted easily. 'But the more help I have – we have – the simpler things become. It needs to expand, to feed in order to live. It has consumed all the earth and rock and stone that it can find beneath the moorland. It has been starved for too long now. It needs an outlet, a new feeding ground.' He nodded, as if to emphasise the accuracy of his statement. 'It won't be satisfied with Middletown. Or even Ambleton, not for long. Not now it has a taste for the matter above the earth. I will need to seed other

184

areas for it, hence my rather theatrical demonstrations. And in the wake of the fire trail it leaves, I will help re-establish order.'

'Seed other areas?' the Doctor echoed. 'So you can take over the world one village at a time with your amazing re-forming artefacts?' He gave a derisory snort.

'I think we shall progress rather more quickly and efficiently than you suggest,' Nepath said. He seemed unperturbed by the Doctor's attitude. 'I shall need ambassadors, salesmen, people to take the artefacts all over the world.'

'So that this thing can erupt from anywhere and feed itself?' the Doctor asked. His voice was getting louder, angry. 'Until it consumes the whole of the Earth?' he demanded.

'Oh I don't think it will come to that.'

'You don't?' The Doctor was visibly shaking with anger now. 'How do you know?' he shouted at Nepath. 'How can you possibly know?'

Nepath returned the Doctor's stare. He too was getting angry now. 'I can see that I am wasting my time attempting to save you, Doctor, attempting to enlighten you.' He turned to Stobbold. 'But what about you, Reverend?'

'Me?'

'Why not?' He smiled thinly. 'One of the thieves was saved, you know. But of course you do. You are a man of learning, after all.' He shot a glance at the Doctor before going on: 'Like me, I think you have searched for many years – for truth and enlightenment. But your choice is easier than the Doctor's,' he said, his voice quiet, compulsive. 'The Doctor's problem is that he doesn't know what he is searching for. And neither did you. Until now.'

'I – I don't understand,' Stobbold said. But at the back of his mind an idea was forming, an idea he scarcely dared contemplate.

'I can have whatever I want,' Nepath said. 'Whatever my heart desires. And there is one thing. One thing that has spurred my search across the world, one thing that drove me on, compelled me to travel to the most God-forsaken of places.' He smiled suddenly. 'I use the term advisedly.'

'And have you found it?' The Doctor asked. His voice was a sneer, but underneath was an undercurrent of genuine interest.

'Yes,' whispered Nepath. 'I believe I have. Here. Thanks to the creature, I have back what I have sought all my life to recover.' he turned back to Stobbold. 'And what would you seek to recover? More than anything else in the world? What, Reverend, would you ask for if you could have your heart's desire? We do not ask for much in return – just a little co-operation, a little help.'

Stobbold said nothing. Felt nothing.

'So little to ask,' Nepath breathed, leaning close to him. 'Considering that you would sell your very soul for the safe return of your daughter.'

Colonel Wilson found Captain Brookes outside the *Pig and Trumpet*, telling Arthur Melstead that he could open up as soon as he liked.

'No you can't,' Wilson gasped, overhearing the tail end of the conversation.

'Sir?' Brookes reached out to support him. Wilson was exhausted from running. 'Are you all right, sir?'

'I'm fine,' he managed to say between rasps of sulphurous air. 'But he's not opening up, he's getting out. Get everyone out, do you understand?'

'Yes, sir. Of course, sir. We've been assembling some transport, best we can.' Brookes looked round. 'Where's the sergeant?'

'He's dead, Michael,' Wilson said, drawing the captain aside. 'Have the men organise the evacuation, best they can. And get the field guns set up at the end of the street.'

'Field guns? Are we expecting some action, sir?'

'Yes, Captain. God help us, yes we are.'

'Doctor?'

The Doctor did not return Stobbold's look. He stared directly ahead, at Nepath. 'It is your decision,' he said. 'You must decide for yourself where your loyalties, where your priorities lie. Nobody 'can do that for you.'

'Indeed they cannot,' Nepath agreed. He licked his bloodless lips. 'But perhaps I can help.' He stepped aside, allowing Lady Urton to move in front of Stobbold.

As she did, she seemed to shimmer, as if in a heat haze. Her face blurred before his moist eyes. She became shorter, slimmer, younger. Her grey hair was dark now, lengthening. Her nose broadened slightly, a smattering of freckles appearing across her face.

'Betty?' He hardly dared to believe it. Yet here she was in front of him. Perfect. Exactly as she had been.

'Father?' Her voice trembled with emotion as she reached out towards him. 'Oh father,' she sobbed as she folded her arms around him.

He lifted his own arms, encircled her with them, desperate to hold her close. But he hesitated, a tear washing down his dusty cheek as he murmured, close to her ear: 'O Jephthah, what a treasure hadst thou.' His voice became a sob.

He felt her stiffen at the words. She turned her face up to look at him. He could see the detail in every freckle as it blurred beneath his tears. So young. So very young.

'Who?' she asked, amused and intrigued.

And he stepped away as his world collapsed again, as once more he felt voided and empty.

'One fair daughter, and no more,' the Doctor said quietly. 'The which he loved passing well.'

'Indeed I did.' Stobbold wiped the tears from his eyes with the back of his hand, drawing himself upright, fighting back the emotion. He stepped away from the thing that looked like his daughter, and stood beside the Doctor. Together they faced Nepath.

'I think you have your answer,' the Doctor said. 'A shame your creature is not more widely read.' He leaned forward. 'Or is it simply that the thing doesn't appreciate the value of the individual's knowledge?'

'What do you mean?' Nepath demanded. His anger was barely controlled, his voice loud.

The Doctor shrugged. 'It does not distinguish between people, any more than the different parts of itself have any individuality. Everything is spread so thin that it disappears.' His voice hardened again. 'You are making people into parts of a single huge machine. Tiny flames dancing in one huge fire.'

'And that is a disadvantage?' Nepath seemed amused at the comment. 'We stand in the workshop of the world, Doctor, the country where mechanisation has been taken to its limits. The machinery and manpower that helped us to release the creature is proof positive of the power of mechanisation, of working together.'

'There is a difference,' the Doctor told him, 'between being a willing part of a group and losing your individuality. As you, I think, will learn.'

'Is that what you think?' Nepath's eyes narrowed. There was no humour in his tone now. 'Let me tell you what I think Doctor, before you die. I think that you fail to see the significance of what we shall achieve. You fail to appreciate the wonder and beauty of the firestorm that we shall unleash. I think you would do well to consider how Britain could have established her Empire if she did not have armed forces that act like a well-tuned machine. I think it is time you realised that the power of the many is far greater than the sum of the powers of its parts.' His voice grew louder as he spoke until he was almost shouting. 'I think it is time you realised just how out of date – how anachronistic – your very *individual* views really are.' He gave a short nod to punctuate his point.

'Perhaps,' the Doctor replied, his voice quiet by contrast with Nepath's, 'I am ahead of my time.'

Nepath gave a snort of derision.

'Zebras,' the Doctor retorted angrily.

Nepath was taken aback by the comment. He blinked convulsively.

Stobbold had been staring at the frozen image of his daughter standing like a statue beside Nepath. 'What do you mean?' He turned to watch the Doctor explain.

'They have stripes,' the Doctor said.

'Spare us the zoology lesson,' Nepath sneered.

'Oh, so you know *why* they have stripes, do you?' The Doctor was shaking with pent-up emotion, his voice rising to match the volume of Nepath's. 'It's a collective defence. It's so that predators see only the whole herd. The stripes of one zebra blend into the next so it is difficult to see where one animal stops and the next begins. It's camouflage, it masks their form.'

Nepath took a deep breath. 'What exactly is your point, Doctor?' he asked with mock patience. 'I assume you *are* making a point?'

The Doctor stared back at him, unintimidated. 'The point is,' he said, mimicking Nepath's forced patience, 'that the Zebras understand the advantages of acting collectively. That's *why* they have stripes.' He raised a finger, like a school teacher explaining to the class, or a preacher sermonising from the pulpit. 'But no two zebras have identical stripes.'

'Is that so?' Stobbold asked, intrigued despite the situation.

The Doctor nodded. 'Oh yes. You see, zebras value their individuality. Each zebra knows it is different from the herd, even though it's a part of it. There is a time and a space for both the individual and the collective – the human and the mechanical.'

For a moment there was silence. Then Nepath slowly clapped his hands in feigned appreciation.

The Doctor turned to Stobbold. 'You will notice that Mr Nepath has not sacrificed his own individuality. Not yet.' He looked back at Nepath. 'But he will. He thinks he can control the forces he has unleashed, but he can't. He'll discover that soon enough.' He took a step towards Nepath. 'You do need our help,' the Doctor told Nepath. 'You need us to help you stop this thing, before it destroys us all.'

'I don't think so, Doctor.'

'You don't think at all,' the Doctor said.

'Enough discussion,' Nepath shouted angrily.

'Oh I quite agree,' the Doctor said lightly. 'But it is interesting to hear your views on the subject.' His voice hardened. 'Especially as your whole life has revolved round the quest for one particular *individual.*'

Nepath's mouth dropped open. 'What do you mean?' he hissed. For the first time he really seemed concerned. A frown creased his face. 'Explain yourself.'

In answer the Doctor pulled a flimsy sheet of paper from his pocket. 'I'd had my doubts about Betty for some time – so I sent a telegram too,' he said, nodding to the thing that looked like Stobbold's daughter. 'I'm sure you've seen the text, so you know that I was inquiring into your background. Checking newspaper reports, journals, society lists. Anything really. For some clue as to why you came here, what drove you on. We are all driven by something you know, as we twist and turn our firefly way through life.' As he spoke he waved the folded, flimsy paper in the air, just out of Nepath's reach. 'We gleam for an instant here, shed some light there, settle a moment along the way before we eventually burn ourselves out.'

Nepath seemed transfixed, unable to take his eyes from the paper as the Doctor slowly unfolded it.

'It is fairly obvious really what you have been searching for. Your heart's desire, I think you said. I understand your quest, really I do.' There was a hint of sympathy in the Doctor's tone now. 'Just as you and I both understand Matthew's yearning for his daughter.' More than a hint. For a moment the Doctor's eyes gazed off into space. Then he blinked quickly and shook his head. 'But I am forgetting my manners,' he said slowly, deliberately. 'I should have inquired earlier. How is your dear sister?'

At once Nepath's eyes flicked upwards, locking with the Doctor's.

The fire was a living thing. Burning. Roaring its way through the roof timbers and running liquid down the front of the

190

building. It licked its way out of the eye-windows of the house, crackling and cackling in the doorway.

The glow was hot on the boy's face as he watched. His eyes were wide, his mouth an open 'o' of rapture. He sat immobile, letting the firelight dance and flicker in his eyes and across his reddened cheeks. The blur of movement, of people running, buckets passed, hoses unwound, hands at the pump, was lost to him. Only the flames mattered, the heat. The burning.

'There you are.' There was relief mixed in with the annoyance in her voice. 'Mum was worried. We all were.'

He did not reply. He leaned slightly to the side, to watch the flames past her. They seemed to erupt from the black silhouette of her body in the autumn dusk.

'Supper's been on the table for an hour,' she said. 'Don't you know what time it is?' More anger now. 'What do you think you're doing?'
'Watching.' His voice was barely more than a whisper. 'I'm watching the fire, aren't I?'

She raised her hand, ready to cuff him for his insolence. 'I can see that,' she hissed. 'But it's time to come home. Long past time. Mum'll learn you to be late when we get back.'

There was a crack from across the street as a wooden beam gave way under the onslaught of the fire. It crashed through the weakened first floor joists sending cascades of sparks flying out of the ruptured roof and through the sightless windows. The girl turned to watch.

For a moment, the briefest of instants, her expression mirrored her brother's – awe, excitement, rapture. For an instant she too seemed to see the beauty and life in the dance of the flames. Her hand rested on her young brother's shoulder, holding it affectionately, protectively.

Then a fireman ran across in front of her, oilskin jacket glistening as the water from the steam pump dried in the heat. Behind him a horse whinnied and trod the air in fright and surprise at the sparks and the flames. The steam pump lurched

191

as the horses moved. Firelight gleamed off the brass of the boiler mounted on its carriage. Black smoke rose from the funnel, mingling with that from the house fire. The people encircling the burning house stepped back, as if part of the dance, as the fire jumped and raced to the adjacent house and started to rip into its roof with a dry throaty cackle.

'Mum says you're to come now,' the girl said. Her voice was husky and dry, barely audible above the cracking and popping of the fire and the cry of the horses and the people. Somewhere down the street a baby cried. At the front of the house the flames balled and gathered, as if preparing for an attack on the house opposite. It was gathering itself.

The boy licked his lips.

The girl shook her head. 'Come now,' she said again. 'I mean it. Now, or you're in big trouble.' She waited only a few seconds longer, long enough to see that the boy was not listening, that he was still watching the flames. Enthralled. She shook her head, and started to back away across the street.

The boy's attention flickered from the flames to his sister as she backed away. He watched her as she prepared to turn and walk off into the gathering dusk. Behind her the crack and rustle of the fire was reaching a crescendo.

A sudden eruption of spark and light, a thunderclap of exploding flames and the boy blinked. He leaped to his feet, his hand reaching out suddenly towards the burning house as it crashed forwards. The front of the house, the facade, was peeling away, toppling forwards towards him. He stood, motionless, transfixed as the frontage crashed down, trailing smoke and flame in its wake. His shouts and cries were lost in the mêlée of sound and light. But for a moment he could hear his sister above and through it all. Screaming.

The tears dried in his eyes, unshed.

'See for yourself, Doctor.' Nepath's hand went to his head. He rubbed at his forehead as he stepped aside. Betty mirrored his movement.

And framed between them, Stobbold saw for the first time into the glass cabinet. He stepped back in surprise and revulsion.

The Doctor took several steps forward. He stuffed the telegram into his pocket and stared with interest at the blackened husk that stood before him, his nose almost to the glass.

'You were fourteen at the time,' he said softly. 'A formative age. Impressionable, even before you'd stolen the body from the morgue. I can't imagine that was easy – for you, or for the family that lost her again. Especially your mother. She died within the year, of course... You've been through so much,' the Doctor said softly. 'Suffered so much already.'

'You don't need to tell me,' Nepath replied. His expression was neutral, distant.

'But there is *something* I need to tell you. To help you see that the suffering must end.' The sympathy was clear in the Doctor's tone as he turned away from the cabinet and faced Nepath. 'I don't know what promises you think you've been made, what sort of Faustian bargain you have entered into. But I do know this: The creature you have unearthed can never bring your sister back to you. I'm sorry, but that's the way it is.'

It was as if he had slapped Nepath. The man blanched, took a step backwards. Then he raised his hand as if to strike the Doctor. 'You know nothing,' he roared. 'Don't dare tell me what is possible or impossible. The fire took her, and it can bring her back. It consumes and creates, Doctor. Remember the Phoenix,' he roared.

'The *myth* of the Phoenix,' the Doctor shouted back. 'It's a story, no more.'

Nepath shook his head. His hands were clenched, shaking at his sides. His eyes were moist. 'Have you any idea how long or how far I have sought for this? Any idea what it means to me?'

'More than anything else in the world,' Stobbold murmured, remembering the Doctor's words. Knowing how he himself felt. 'More, perhaps, than the world itself.'

If either the Doctor or Nepath heard him, they took no notice.

'But can't you see?' the Doctor demanded. 'You can't change the past. What's done is done. "*Iacta alea est*", though Caesar actually said it in Greek as I recall.' Stobbold thought he saw a flicker of puzzlement cross the Doctor's face then, but he barely paused in his attack on Nepath. 'For your own sake you have to accept that. Accept it and live with it or banish it to the hidden depths of your memory where you never dare venture. One or the other.'

'No!' shrieked Nepath. 'Never.'

'Is it guilt? Is that it?' The Doctor was shaking his heard as he tried to understand, grey dust flying from his long salt and pepper hair. 'You shouldn't blame yourself for what happened.'

'Do not presume to know what happened, Doctor,' Nepath yelled at him. 'You weren't there. You did not see or hear her.'

'No,' the Doctor admitted. Then he jabbed his finger towards Nepath. 'But I'll tell you again, whatever you've been promised, she can never come back. Not ever. It may look like your sister, it may even sound like your sister. But it will never *be* her. Whoever or whatever is returned to you, Patience Nepath will still be dead.' He turned back to the cabinet. 'Whoever is to blame, this is how she will remain.'

He reached out and tapped his forefinger on the glass. 'For ever.'

Stobbold thought it was an effect of the glass moving slightly as the Doctor tapped on it. The grotesque, contorted shape within the cabinet seemed to move slightly. But then the Doctor froze, staring at the charred figure within. He too had seen something.

And Nepath was suddenly laughing. He threw his head back and bellowed with laughter that echoed round the room.

The blackened husk raised a skeletal arm, dark bone fingers stretching out in a bizarre parody of the Doctor's gesture, reaching for the glass. Then the whole figure seemed to lurch forwards, falling towards the front of the cabinet.

The glass exploded outwards, showering ice-like shards and splinters across the Doctor and Nepath. Stobbold felt blood on his cheek where a sharp fragment caught him. Clumsily, with jerky movements, the hideous stick-like figure lurched out of the broken cabinet towards them.

Chapter Seventeen
Moving Mountains

The figure stood for a moment in the middle of the sea of broken glass. It tottered on its spindly, brittle legs.

Seeing what was about to happen, Nepath reached out. But he was too late. The fragile legs shattered under the weight of the body and the figure crashed to the ground. Bone fractured and exploded as it hit the floor, a mass of broken black amongst the shining splinters of glass. The upper torso and the remains of the head remained intact, as if emerging through a hole in the floor. With a creaking of bone rubbing on bone, the head slowly turned towards the shape of Betty Stobbold.

Betty was already shimmering, blurring, changing. Stobbold gave an involuntary gasp as he watched. He knew it was not really her, but even so it was a shock to see his daughter's form again disappearing from him. In a moment she was a featureless blank of a figure. Like an unfinished sculpture – the form and shape but none of the detail. He swallowed drily.

The faceless woman stepped into the mess of shattered bone and glass. At once she seemed to become liquid. Her whole pale form clouded over with a dark crust, and the molten rock inside flowed out in a puddle over the floor.

The Doctor leaped aside as the hot magma rolled towards his feet. But already it was flowing back inwards, drawn up into the charred and broken remains of Patience Nepath.

Stobbold watched in horror as the fragile blackened corpse began to fill out. The liquid flowed into it, making the whole body glow with fire and life. The thin arms fleshed out; the sunken parchment features of the face puffed outwards. Slowly, painfully, the figure was getting to its feet, standing on legs that had been broken fragments of bone and now seemed to be restored to flesh and blood.

She was a tall girl, as tall as Stobbold. Blond hair erupted from her pale head, framing her youthful face. She looked about eighteen as she smiled at them, her eyes tight shut. Her chest heaved suddenly, a spasm of movement as she drew her first breath.

Then she opened her eyes, and Stobbold could see the firelight that danced within them. At that moment he knew - really knew - that whatever the consequences, he had made the right decision.

The guns were set up across the main street. There was room for three of them. The other three were positioned at the sides of the road further back to cover a retreat if it became necessary.

A gust of wind blew dust and ash into Wilson's face as he waited. The gun crews were crouched in position. The weapons were loaded and ready to fire. The runners from the edge of the town kept him informed of the progress of the creatures of fire as they approached. It would not be long now.

So far there had not been too many deaths reported. But unless they could slow the advance of the creatures, the more densely populated area of Middletown would become a graveyard. A crematorium. The evacuation was in full progress, but it was slow work to persuade people to leave their homes - at the point of a bayonet if necessary. There was a dearth of suitable transport, and more had not yet arrived from Ambleton, though it was promised, along with reinforcements. The soldier Wilson had sent had returned with the personal assurances of Sir William Grant - more troops would come.

But for the moment, Wilson and his men were on their own.

Just as he reassured himself that whatever happened now, things could scarcely get worse, there was an unearthly percussive crack in the distance. Beneath Wilson's feet, the ground heaved, throwing grey dust back into the air. Even before it had settled, it was joined by more. A lump of glowing rock shot past Wilson's head, exploding into flames as it hit the building behind him.

The sky glowed an angry red, the lines of smoke tracing across through the mist of dust and ash as more rocks were hurled upwards from the fissure. In seconds the air was alive with the firestorm.

'At last,' Nepath breathed. 'At last we are together again.'

His sister reached out her hand and brushed his cheek. 'For ever,' she said. Her voice was soft, innocent.

The Doctor shook his head, shuffled his feet and sighed loudly. 'I suppose it's too much to hope that you'll give my advice careful and close consideration?'

Nepath's face was a mask of emotion as he drew her to him, held her close, buried his face in her hair.

'That's what I thought,' the Doctor said. 'Still,' he said to Stobbold, 'actions speak louder than words.'

'Meaning?' Stobbold asked.

'Meaning it's time we were leaving.' He strode over to the door and flung it open.

Nepath's laughter was barely audible above the sound of the crackling flames that immediately leapt up in the doorway. A formless burning mass oozed into the room and the Doctor jumped back.

'I'd forgotten about that,' he said. 'Any suggestions?' he asked Stobbold.

'Yes, Doctor,' Nepath said. 'Die.'

The Doctor seemed to consider this. He nodded thoughtfully, biting his bottom lip. He raised his hand towards Nepath in a gesture that suggested he would answer him in a moment, then took Stobbold by the arm and led him across the room away from the rolling fire.

'There do seem to be few alternatives available to us,' Stobbold admitted. He looked from the fire to Nepath and his sister standing in front of the shattered remains of the cabinet, then turned to see the Doctor's reaction.

The Doctor was looking across the room, away from the fire.

Towards the heavy curtains that were closed over the window. 'Jump,' he said in a loud, clear voice.

Even so, Stobbold was not sure he had heard correctly. 'I beg your pardon?'

But the Doctor was gone. He was running across the room at full tilt. Seeming to sense his intentions, the fire leaped after him, a ball of orange flame trailing black smoke in its wake. Stobbold hesitated only a split second, then he was racing after the Doctor, desperate to keep ahead of the flames.

The Doctor leaped first, taking off several feet in front of the curtain, throwing his arms up in front of his face, turning slightly sideways, legs still working. He crashed into the heavy curtain, forcing it into the window behind, crashing through.

Stobbold was already in the air, flinging himself after the Doctor when it occurred to him that he was jumping through an upper storey window. And he had no idea what was beneath it. The billowing curtain rushed towards him, and he barely caught sight of the Doctor clinging to it as he swung back. Stobbold grabbed at the other curtain as the one bearing the Doctor began to tear, to rip, to fall.

The Doctor disappeared from sight with a wave of the arm that might have been intentional. His weight was tearing the curtain slowly along a seam, unravelling it, lowering him gently towards the ground.

In the same moment that Stobbold marvelled at the audacity and inventiveness of the Doctor's escape, he felt his own curtain move. He glanced up, and saw that it was not tearing slowly like the Doctor's. The material was ripping from the curtain rings, sending them rattling on the pole as it tore down.

He gave a cry of surprise and fright as he was pitched headlong towards the ground, still holding the curtain. Then the fire exploded out of the broken window frame above him, catching the end of the material as it was whipped free. The curtain burst into flames.

He let go. It fell away from him, blazing, and they both plunged towards the ground.

The Doctor was waiting for him ten feet below, arms outstretched in an attempt to catch him, or at least break his fall. They met in a sudden whirling maelstrom of arms and legs. The Doctor dropped him, of course, but on to the bundled, burning curtain which was itself cushioned on a pile of ash.

'I'm relieved that you aren't a large person,' the Doctor remarked as they both staggered to their feet.

Stobbold was bruised, singed and frightened, but he was alive and all his bones seemed to have survived the impact. He looked back at the window above them. The fire seemed to have disappeared, but as he watched, Nepath's face appeared, looking down at them.

'Time to go?' Stobbold suggested.

'Time to go,' the Doctor agreed.

They were at the side of the Grange, close to the back. Stobbold led the way round towards the drive. They walked briskly. The sky was alive with trails of fire; the air was thick like drifting smoke.

'Another eruption,' the Doctor mused. 'Not long now, I fear.' He looked round. 'What's that noise?'

Stobbold strained to hear. He could just make out a rushing sound, like the wind only stronger, louder, more regular. He turned to try to work out where it was coming from.

'It's the river,' he realised. 'There's a weir just upstream from here.'

'River?'

'Well,' Stobbold admitted, 'more of a brook. Over there.' He pointed into the gloom. 'About twenty yards. Doctor,' he went on as they continued on their way, 'you said there wasn't long. Until what, do you think?'

'Until a molten mass of red hot magma rolls across the moors and through Middletown devouring everything in its way.'

'Unless we can stop it somehow,' Stobbold said gloomily.

The Doctor stopped, putting out his hand to stay Stobbold. 'I'm afraid we have other things to deal with,' he said.

Ahead of them, from out of the smoky air, Lord Urton emerged, his eyes blazing like burning coals.

They had encouraged her, then cajoled her. They had threatened her with a rifle, but still she refused to go with them. Eventually a large corporal had lifted Rosie Devlin bodily and carried her kicking and shouting to the cart. He dumped her into it, and pushed her back when she tried to climb out.

The children sat at her feet, sullen, weary, too tired now to cry.

'He'll be here soon,' she reassured them through her tears. 'He just had some work at the mine to finish.'

Little Annie climbed on to her mother's lap and put her thin arms round her neck, clinging on and crying into her chest. Lawrence and James watched. Lawrence choked back a sob.

'You should have let us wait for him,' James told the soldier as the cart pulled away unsteadily.

'He'll come, you'll see,' Rosie shouted into the smog as they bumped along. Her words dissolved into tears. 'You'll see. He'll show you, Harry Devlin will. Show you all.'

The corporal watched the cart disappear into the ash-filled sky. He wiped the grime from his face on his sleeve, smearing it across with the moisture from his smarting eyes. He knew as well as she did that Harry Devlin was not coming home.

The air seemed to crackle and spark around him as Lord Urton stepped towards them. The Doctor and Stobbold backed slowly away, matching him step for step.

'I'll try to distract him, Doctor,' Stobbold said quietly. 'You should be able to get past him while he's… while he's busy with me.'

Urton circled round them, forcing them to change direction as they continued to back away.

'Very noble of you,' the Doctor said, keeping his eyes on Urton. 'But I imagine he'd go for me before you. Without undue modesty, I think they believe me to be more of a threat than your good self.' He grinned suddenly. 'And anyway, I don't intend to lose you.'

'Thank you,' Stobbold responded automatically. He could hear the sound of the weir again, and realised they were close to the brook.

Too close. He took another step backwards and almost slipped down the bank. He reached out to stop the Doctor. 'Look out.'

'Ah,' the Doctor exclaimed as he glanced back at the steep bank and the murky water below. He turned back as Lord Urton once more stepped out of the thickening air. His hands were stretched out in front of him like a sleepwalker. The firelight sparkled behind his eyes.

'Oh,' the Doctor said. 'How deep is it?'

'I don't know,' Stobbold replied. He risked a look backwards. 'Very,' he decided. 'Ten feet or more, what with the melting snow. And it's too wide to jump. I –' he paused, embarrassed. 'I can't actually swim, you know, Doctor.'

'I didn't,' the Doctor said. 'But I hope it won't be necessary. It's a thought, though,' he added with a frown. 'I wonder...'

'They're right to think you more dangerous than I,' Stobbold said slowly. 'Which is why you have to get away, Doctor.' It was not actually a difficult decision to come to, he thought as he stooped down and scooped up a handful of the dry ash. Now that Betty was gone, there was little to make him reconsider. He had lived his life preaching a code that put others before himself. Now, it was time to live up to that code.

Stobbold held the ash tight in his fist, afraid it would slip out between his fingers. With his other hand he pushed the Doctor roughly away. At the same moment he stepped up to face Urton, standing inches from his outstretched hands.

He could feel the heat from the twitching fingers, could see deep into the fire within his old friend's eyes. He leaned away as the hands clutched for him, and thrust the ash into Urton's face.

He had hoped that it might blind Urton, or at least distract him long enough for Stobbold to run past. He had seen the Doctor head off along the bank of the river, continuing in the direction that Stobbold had pushed him. But the ash had no effect. It seemed to explode into a myriad firefly sparks as it touched

Urton. Stobbold stepped back, knowing he had nowhere to go. Urton reached for him, the heat from his body singeing the air as he moved.

'Get down!' The shout reached Stobbold at the same moment as he saw the Doctor emerge from the smoke behind Urton. He was in mid-air, his feet in front of him.

The Doctor's jump-kick connected as Stobbold dived aside. Stobbold rolled on to his back in time to see the Doctor's feet slam into Urton's back, sending Urton spinning forwards, arms flailing. Urton staggered to the top of the bank, teetered on the edge where the ground dropped away, his arms windmilling, sending flames shooting into the air.

Just as he regained his balance, just as he began to stumble forwards again, just as he turned to look down at Stobbold lying defenceless before him on the ground, the Doctor stepped forwards. He leaned back, lifted his leg almost to the height of his waist and kicked out violently.

The Doctor's foot caught Urton full in the chest, sending him spinning over the edge. Steam hissed from the sole of the Doctor's shoe.

Stobbold pulled himself to his feet and joined the Doctor at the edge of the bank. He was in time to see Urton splash into the river. A great cloud of steam hissed up, obscuring their view. A high-pitched scream, shrill and loud reached them. The steam thinned, and Stobbold could see Urton clawing at the bank, his hands scrabbling to gain a purchase. But the rest of his body seemed to be dragging him back down, still and lifeless. His head remained clear of the water, his eyes flickering as he stared up at them, his mouth twisted into a scream of anger and fear.

Then he lost his grip completely, and sank slowly into the water. Steam erupted from his hands as they flopped into the river. His head remained visible a moment longer before it too was submerged.

'Let's get away from here,' Stobbold said. His throat was dry and he felt sick to his stomach.

'You're right.' The Doctor nodded thoughtfully. 'There's something... something in the research, the books and papers that Professor Dobbs was looking at.'

The water below them was still hissing and steaming. Occasionally the view cleared enough for them to see the water bubbling.

'What's that, Doctor?' For the first time in a long while, Stobbold felt there was a glimmer of hope.

'I'm not sure,' the Doctor replied. 'Confirmation, I hope.' He was still looking down at the thinning steam which clung to the river below. 'Confirmation of the nature of the world. The nature of the beast.'

When the steam had cleared, Stobbold saw that Urton was lying on the river bed. Through the deep, bubbling, murky water he could see that the man was stiff, his body angled awkwardly like an ungainly statue. One of Urton's legs was bent almost at right angles beneath him. His eyes were wide open, staring lifelessly up at them – cold and grey and empty. As they stood on the bank, staring down, the body shifted with the current flowing quickly from the nearby weir. The angled leg snapped away, drifted downstream a little way before scraping to a halt. Like brittle stone.

The first of the burning figures lumbered out of the gloom and started down the street towards them. Behind it, others broke through the foggy air until the street was ablaze with walking fire.

Wilson was tempted to order his men to wait until they saw the red of their eyes. But he was not sure they would appreciate the bleak humour. Even if they could hear him above the percussive impacts of the molten rock that fell like shooting stars around them and the crackling laughter of the approaching fire. Instead he raised his bayonet, hoping the faded light of the sun would catch on the blade and make it easier to see his gesture.

When he was confident that the figures were close enough to be sure of a direct hit, he brought his hand down.

The sound was deafening – an explosive roar. Wilson's attention was fixed on the wall of fire that rolled towards them. It was as if the creatures had blended together and it was almost impossible to tell where one ended and the next began. But nothing happened.

He turned to the gunners, to see what had gone wrong. The crews were looking at each other, mystified and bemused. There had been an explosion in each of the chambers, but nothing had emerged. It was as if the energy was bottled up inside the new guns.

A moment before the explosions, Wilson's blood ran cold. New guns. Fashioned from the material that Nepath and Lord Urton had demonstrated. Then the field guns exploded.

They went off in series, one after another. The closest to Wilson erupted in a blistering fireball, sending flame shooting across the street. Smoke drifted and mingled with the misty ash that again filled the air. Through it he saw the brilliant flashes of the other explosions. Wilson staggered back, driven by the intense heat.

When the smoke cleared enough for Wilson to see what was happening, he realised how lucky he had been. Several of the crews had been killed outright. A couple of men were staggering across the street, their clothes on fire. Colleagues ran to throw their jackets over them, roll them on the floor, try to smother the flames. Perhaps half a dozen men seemed uninjured.

But it was the remains of the field guns that held Wilson's attention. They lay abandoned and burning. The barrels had been ripped open by the explosions, the whole of each gun lying in a disintegrated heap – bent and broken. They reminded Wilson of the gun that had been blown apart on the moor.

As he watched, the shattered field guns seemed to melt. The heavy, dark material became glutinous, like melting jelly. The barrel of one of them sagged into a puddle of viscous liquid, the muzzle sticking out for a moment like the prow of a sinking ship. Then slowly the liquid flowed together, formed bigger pools, and became solid again.

Shapes rose out of the pools, pushing their ponderous way through the viscous, glowing substance. But they were not reconstituted gun components.

They were amorphous, malformed figures. Their surfaces were glowing a dull red beneath the blackened crust that had formed over them, that seemed to hold them together. As they stretched and grew and took their first faltering steps, they exploded into flames.

The wall of fire that was advancing down the street met the newly formed figures, and they seemed to merge. A single, reinforced line of blazing creatures continued down the street.

'Fall back!' Wilson shouted, desperate to make himself heard above the horrendous noise of the fire. He had no idea how many men he had left here, or how the evacuation was proceeding. But he had to save whoever he could.

One of the figures was almost on him, the ground at its feet smoking and exploding as it lurched forwards. Wilson lunged at it with his bayonet, gritting his teeth against the heat as his hand approached. He could feel the leather of his glove blistering. A short sharp stab. No effect.

He pulled back his hand, to find that the blade of the bayonet was gone. A stump of white hot metal sagged and broke from the smouldering hilt. Wilson dropped the useless weapon, turned, and ran.

'With me!' he screamed, barely aware of the soldiers running to join him. He drew his revolver and fired uselessly into the fire. Then he led them away at a run. He had no idea where he was going.

They ran for what seemed like an age, until the glow of the creatures was lost in the distance, swallowed up by the misty air. Brookes had joined them at some point, and he gestured for Wilson to stop.

It took Wilson a minute to catch his breath. He looked round. There were perhaps a dozen of them now, no more.

'We should abandon the town, sir,' Brookes said. 'We got out everyone we could.'

'And the reinforcements?'

Brookes shook his head. 'No sign of them.'

'Not that they would help much,' Wilson admitted. 'All right. We'll regroup outside the town. On the moor.'

'Away from the fissure, sir?' Brookes suggested.

Wilson nodded. 'And the mine. We need to find high ground. A vantage point. Near the reservoir perhaps.'

'Agreed, sir.' Brookes nodded. 'I'll get the men formed up.'

A river of molten rock flowed from the mouth of the tunnel that led into the mine. The huts clustered round the mine exploded into flame as the magma reached them. The burning shells of the buildings were crushed beneath the rolling torrent of lava.

The surface was a seething, bubbling mass of angry red. The air cooled the edges so that a thin dark crust formed, almost immediately to be melted away by the persistent heat of the body of gelatinous liquid that heaved itself forward.

A similar, but far larger, torrent was bubbling and streaming out of the fissure. It scorched its way across the moorland, a fiery sea. The air around it sizzled and shimmered with the heat.

Stobbold had thought his study a mess when Professor Dobbs was conducting his research. Now he realised that it had been a comparatively ordered and tidy procedure. The Doctor stood in the middle of an ankle-deep ocean of literature. He scooped books from off shelves and desk and chairs, flicking through each in turn before dropping it with an ever-more irritated grunt to the growing pile at his feet.

At first, Stobbold had retrieved the books and papers and made an attempt to return them to their proper place. But the Doctor read faster than Stobbold could file. He soon gave up, and instead watched the Doctor's increasingly exasperated progress.

'If you knew what we were looking for, I could help,' Stobbold said. Again.

The Doctor's reply was another grunt of annoyance, and a heavy book fell to the floor. It landed on its spine, the pages spilling over like a waterfall until its redistributed weight caused it to topple down the heap of discarded books and come to rest under the desk.

'No, wait!' The Doctor was suddenly on his hands and knees scrabbling through the pile. 'Where did it go?' he demanded. 'Where, where, where?'

Stobbold retrieved the book, smoothed out the bent pages and held it out to the Doctor who was still on his knees.

'Ah. Thank you.' He shuffled through the mess of paper on his knees, rifling through the book.

Stobbold knew the book, of course. He knew them all. It was a collection of creation myths from various cultures and geographies. The book was a limited edition published by a company based in Berlin.

'You understand German, Doctor?'

'Do I?' The Doctor glanced up, finger marking his place on the page. He seemed puzzled. 'Yes,' he said as he returned his attention to the print. 'Yes, I suppose I do.'

'What have you found? Anything useful?' Outside the study window, Stobbold could see that the whole sky was glowing a brilliant orange.

'Yes, yes I think so. Listen.' The Doctor raised his hand as he spoke, tapping the air to punctuate each sentence. 'This seems to be an Inca origin myth. From South America,' he explained, peering for a moment at Stobbold over the top of the page.

'Thank you, I know.'

'Excellent. Well this was recorded in the fifteen fifties by...' He flicked back a couple of pages and quickly scanned for the names. 'Cieza de Leon and Juan de Betanzos, whoever they might have been. Spanish presumably, so it's been through a few translations.' He turned back to where he had been. 'Now, they say that Viracocha, the Creator, banished the fire from the sky by giving it three strokes with his staff.' He sniffed. 'I imagine the fire in the sky was part of the creation process, I didn't actually bother with that bit too much.'

'This is fascinating, Doctor.' Stobbold was watching the sky darken from orange to blood red. 'But I can't say I am convinced it helps.'

'Hmm,' the Doctor said. 'No magic staff available, you think?' He nodded as if this was indeed a consideration. 'But,' he went on, eyes wide with enthusiasm, 'there is a related myth in which there is a fight between Pariacaca and Huallallo. That seems to replace the staff-banging stuff. Now we learn somewhere here…' He balanced the book on his forearm and started frantically flicking pages at lightning speed. '…That Huallallo is the personification of fire. Or god of fire. Or something.' He gave up searching and put the book down carefully on a free edge of the desk. It balanced for a moment before toppling sideways and falling to the floor. He continued undeterred. 'He represents fire, anyhow.'

'And Pariah-whoever?' Stobbold asked.

'Pariacaca. Yes. He represents water.'

'And they fought?'

The Doctor nodded, a huge grin spreading over his face. 'We're back to the essential elements. Fire and water don't mix.'

'We know that, Doctor,' Stobbold pointed out. 'Everyone knows that. But the rain, the snow – they've made no difference here.'

'That's because so far we've had the quantities wrong, the proportions.' The Doctor tapped a fingernail against his teeth as he considered. 'Remember Urton in the river,' he said. 'The rain, the snow – they're just not enough. Lots of hissing and spitting, but nowhere near enough to combat such a vast body of flame. Like using a hose pipe to try to calm Vesuvius.'

Stobbold blew out a long breath. He could see now why the Doctor had been interested. 'You're saying we need a sudden, vast body of water to douse the flames. To put out the fire.'

The Doctor beamed, nodding his head with furious excitement. 'That's exactly right.'

Stobbold found himself also nodding, caught up in the Doctor's sudden enthusiasm. 'Just one other thing, Doctor?' he said when they had both finished grinning and nodding. 'About the myth?'

'Yes?'

'Who actually won?'

The Doctor's face fell. 'Really,' he admonished. 'Have a little faith. It can move mountains, you know.'

'I did know that, actually, Doctor. Yes.'

'Then you won't be surprised to hear that Pariacaca, water, won the battle. The fire of Huallallo was quenched, and Pariacaca built a – presumably symbolic – dam and created a huge artificial lake. Again that's symbolic, I suppose.'

Stobbold nodded. That made sense. It also echoed similar myths and stories from other parts of the world. 'We have an artificial lake,' he said. 'The reservoir. But it's not very near the fissure. I still don't see how this helps, I'm afraid. I don't see us being able to lure this huge mass of –' He shrugged. 'Of whatever it is, I don't see us luring it into the lake. And even if we did, there's still Nepath to deal with. And his sister.'

'True,' the Doctor admitted. He tapped his fingers against his teeth as he considered. 'Very true. But this reminds us that we need a mass – a veritable torrent of water even to begin to deal with such a huge body of fire.'

'Faith may move mountains, Doctor. But I think we need something more worldly and physical to move this creature and deposit it in the reservoir.'

'Even assuming that would do the trick,' the Doctor said slowly. Then his face brightened. 'But there is another proverb about mountains which you should know.'

'Should I?'

'Well,' the Doctor said as he picked his way across the room, waving impatiently to Stobbold to follow, 'it does concern the prophet Mohamed. I assume you've heard of him.'

Chapter Eighteen
Doctor's Orders

It seemed as if the very ground was alive. It heaved and bubbled around them as the Doctor and Stobbold plunged through the choking air. Trees waved and dipped, not because of the wind, but because their roots were moving with the ground. When they reached it, the moor seemed to tremble beneath their feet. Steam escaped from splits and holes in the ground. Pools of molten rock were oozing their way up to the surface. The fumes and the smoke thickened the air still further.

'Where are we *going*, Doctor?' Stobbold choked out. It was not the first time he had asked.

'We need to get to higher ground, above this.'

'Smoke rises, surely?'

The Doctor shook his head. 'Not this smoke. It's heavier than air. It will roll along the ground. We might clear the top of it if we can rise high enough.'

They continued in silence for a while. The air was yellow and seemed to condense on Stobbold's skin and clothes. He pressed a handkerchief over his face, trying to keep the stench out of his nostrils and throat. He was completely lost. The Doctor seemed to be heading in a deliberate, specific direction, but Stobbold had no idea what it was or where they would eventually land up. 'We don't have any mountains, you know, Doctor,' he said through the handkerchief. But even as he said it he realised that they were walking uphill.

'Nearly there,' the Doctor assured him. 'I think.' He paused, licked his finger and held it up. Then he set off again, striding confidently into the swirling sulphur-laden fog.

There were figures approaching them. Stobbold could see their shapes, coalescing out of dark patches of mist. All walking in unison, all uniform in shape.

'Doctor,' he said, 'look.'

'We have company,' the Doctor agreed, his voice low and wary.

The nearest figure emerged into sight in front of them, the mist seeming to part as it marched towards them.

Stobbold recognised him at once. 'Captain Brookes – thank heavens.'

'Who is it?' a voice called from the gloom. A moment later Colonel Wilson appeared. 'Ah, Reverend. And Doctor. It's good to see you.'

'And you,' Stobbold assured them, though he was concerned at the state of both men. Their uniforms were scorched and torn. Their faces were almost black with soot and dirt and they looked exhausted. One side of Wilson's face was caked in dried blood.

'I fear we may have lost our way a little. We were making for the higher ground. By the reservoir.' Behind him a dozen other soldiers were now visible. They were in a similar state. Several of them were easing the straps of the large rucksacks on their backs.

'Then follow us,' the Doctor said and set off once more through the mist. 'I'm glad you found us, Colonel,' his voice floated back. 'It saves me having to come and find you. I have a little job you can help with.'

It was like emerging from a cloud. For several yards the air seemed to thin and become less noxious. Then, quite suddenly, they were out into milky sunlight. The air was cooler, and Stobbold felt the fresh breeze on his face. He looked around and saw that they were on the steep slope that led up the sides of the reservoir. The dam was only fifty yards away.

Below them, back the way they had come, the world was swathed in a blanket of yellow-orange mist. There were few features visible beneath or within it. Stobbold fancied he could make out the top of the church tower in the distance, but it was impossible to be sure.

The only feature that was definitely recognisable was the fissure. A ragged line of fire traced through the mist below them. Other pale, glowing lines stretched out from it. Even from a different vantage point and with no other references within the landscape, Stobbold could see that these lines traced the paths of the lines of melted snow the Doctor had shown him from the church tower.

'We should be safe here for a while,' Wilson said to his men. He turned to the Doctor. 'Shouldn't we?'

The Doctor nodded. He was standing looking out over the misty world. He turned slowly in an arc to survey the entire landscape, ending up facing the dam.

'Get some rest while you can,' Wilson continued. 'Captain Brookes, organise a watch rota.'

'No.' The Doctor's voice was firm. 'There's no time for that.' He swung round to face Wilson. 'Your men have work to do.'

'Really, Doctor?' Wilson sighed and looked round. 'What *can* we do?'

The Doctor's expression was grave. He fixed on Wilson with steely blue eyes. 'I want you to blow up the dam.'

Stobbold was shocked, and he had at least had some inkling of the Doctor's plan. Wilson and Brookes plainly could not believe their ears.

'You want us to what?' Wilson demanded.

'You heard correctly,' the Doctor said. 'I assume it is feasible.'

Wilson looked to Brookes.

'We've got some explosives with us,' the captain confirmed. 'You need demolition charges really, not grenades and ammunition salvaged from the field guns. But yes, it's possible.'

'Would you mind telling us why?' Wilson asked.

'Because I think water is the only way to stop that thing,' the Doctor told him. 'Vast quantities of icy cold water. In a sudden rush. It might just be a sufficient shock to put out the fire.'

'You think?' Wilson echoed. 'But you're not certain.'

The Doctor took a step towards him. His face was suddenly dark, his eyes deep with anger. 'Of course I'm not certain,' he shouted. 'How could I possibly be certain? But with every moment you delay I get less certain.'

212

Wilson's voice was more controlled, but it was still shaking with emotion. 'But if we blow the dam, the water in the reservoir will flood the entire area. It won't just be confined to the old river bed.'

'Exactly!' the Doctor shot back.

'Branscombe-sub-Edge is below the level of the river bed,' Brookes pointed out. 'Ambleton isn't much higher. The people there haven't been evacuated. You could cause untold damage. Even loss of life.'

The Doctor shook his head in astonishment. 'Listen to yourself,' he said emphatically. 'Cause damage?' He waved at the fiery trails blistered across the landscape beneath them. 'Just what exactly do you think is going on down there?' He stepped up to Brookes, apparently undeterred by the fact the man was a good head taller than him. 'This isn't some isolated incident in the darkest reaches of the Empire which we can ignore and it will go away. It doesn't stop here, you know.' He grabbed Brookes's arm and turned him suddenly so the captain was looking back towards the church. 'What's happening down there will not *stay* down there. Like the water, it will spill out and inundate the surrounding area. But the water will reach its limit and dissipate. *That* won't. It's hungry for more, and it's getting hungrier by the moment. It will expand and feed, in a never ending cycle until the blood-red map of the British Empire is a burning fire of destruction. And even then it won't stop. Not until this world is consumed and charred and burnt out.'

There was silence after this for several moments. 'The fact remains,' Wilson said eventually, 'that we could be making the situation worse.'

'Worse?' the Doctor screamed at him from point blank range. 'You said there might be some loss of life. Well, already people have been killed. They are *being* killed. They *will* be killed. How can it possibly get worse?'

Wilson looked away. 'You may be right, Doctor,' he admitted. 'But whatever action I take I shall need to justify to my superiors.'

'You know I was right about evacuating the place…' the Doctor reminded him.

Wilson nodded. 'But I really don't think I can take the sort of extreme measures you're suggesting now without orders.'

The Doctor snorted in derision, and turned to Stobbold. His tone was both sarcastic and at the same time sad. 'The military machine,' he said. 'No room for individual ideas, no room for initiative. No room for humanity.' He shook his head. 'I'm going to find Nepath,' he said abruptly.

'Nepath?' Stobbold was surprised. 'Why?'

'I may still be able to talk some sense into him. Perhaps there's another way to stop this. If so, then it seems I need to find it.'

Stobbold nodded. He could understand the Doctor's exasperation. But he also sympathised with Wilson's position. 'I shall stay here,' he told the Doctor. 'Perhaps I can persuade them.'

The Doctor nodded. One side of his mouth twitched upwards into a sad, almost pathetic expression. 'Thank you,' he said. 'And if there's nothing else you can do, you can least pray for them.'

Stobbold smiled weakly in reply. 'I shall do that anyway,' he said. 'And for you.'

The Doctor nodded thoughtfully at this. He seemed about to say something, but instead clapped his hand on Stobbold's shoulder, gripping it for a moment. Then he turned and walked away. Into the darkening smoke.

Nepath was in a dream world. A dream come true. Patience was at his side as he had always known she would be, leading him out into the fiery world. The smoke hung low in the sky, and beneath it the burning raged across the landscape.

The whole moor was alive with flame and steam. Pools of molten rock bubbled up around them, sending showers of fire into the air as the bubbles burst. Columns of smoke and flame seemed to hold up the very roof of the world. The sunlight was filtered, amber, diffuse, bathing the surreal world in unreal light.

His eyes were alive with the visions of the flames. He could feel the excitement of watching the fires dancing, the raw power, like never before. His whole body was tense with it. He could see the beauty of the flames, hear the joy of the fire, taste the sulphur. 'Now I have it all,' he breathed.

'No,' Patience Nepath replied. She took his arm in hers. 'This is only the start of it.'

Together they walked arm in arm across the blistering moor.

He had done as much as he could, though Stobbold was hardly pleased with the result. Colonel Wilson had agreed to send a runner to Ambleton with a recommendation that they blow the dam. He hoped, but did not seem to expect, that the runner would return with confirmation of the orders and demolition charges as well as reinforcements.

In the meantime, Wilson agreed they should make their way down to the dam and be ready to act as soon as the orders arrived. From the lack of enthusiasm in the tread of the soldiers, and the enforced high spirits of both Wilson and Captain Brookes it was obvious that they expected at best to get no reply at all. They were merely marking time; putting off making a final decision either way.

But as they neared the dam, Stobbold could see a figure standing at the end closest to them. He was holding on to the rail that ran along the top of the structure, watching them as they approached. He was a rotund man, not very tall. A distinctive shape, though Stobbold was sure that he had never seen the man before.

'What's he doing here?' Wilson wondered out loud. Evidently he did know the man.

'Brought the confirmation, sir?' Brookes suggested.

'There's not been time to get to Ambleton and back,' Wilson pointed out as they started down the slope towards the dam.

'Perhaps he met your man on the way?' Stobbold suggested. 'Who is it?' he asked.

They were almost at the man now. Wilson saluted, and the man raised a hand in reply. He was wearing black leather gloves that seemed to be struggling to contain his pudgy fingers. 'Sir William

Grant,' Wilson said both as reply to Stobbold and in greeting to the man. 'What brings you here, sir?'

'Can you confirm the orders, sir?' Captain Brookes immediately asked.

'Orders?'

Several of the men were unpacking their backpacks. They started to sort the contents on the ground. Most of them meant nothing to Stobbold, though he could see several grenades and pouches of gunpowder.

'What orders are those, Colonel?' Grant went on.

'The Doctor's orders,' Stobbold said. He had a feeling that confidence and determination might be key here. If Grant was in a position to give Wilson the go-ahead, then he needed to be convinced. 'To blow up the dam and put an end to this.'

Grant frowned. 'The Doctor. And just what makes you think that the Doctor is in any position to give orders?' His question was directed at Wilson.

'He does speak with authority, sir.' Wilson shifted uncomfortably.

'Not my authority,' he said. 'Nor her Majesty's.' He turned to Stobbold. 'The authority of the Church, perhaps?'

Stobbold met his gaze. The sun was shining directly at Grant, and it was difficult to make out his expression. 'The Doctor has my full support,' he said. 'My belief is that he knows what he is talking about.'

Grant gave a grunt of annoyance. 'A strange belief for a man of the cloth to put his faith in. But then the opinion of a second rate priest in a third rate parish in the back of beyond hardly counts as the full support of the Church, does it.' He returned his attention to Wilson. 'Your men will retire to barracks at Ambleton and await further orders.'

'With respect, sir,' Wilson said, 'I really think we should give the Doctor's suggestion some consideration.'

'Do you?' Grant was angry now. 'And since when does the army consider taking orders from civilians, Colonel?'

'I think –' Wilson started.

But Grant interrupted him. 'You *don't* think,' he said angrily. 'You are an officer in her Britannic Majesty's army. You obey orders. And on no account are you to interfere with this dam, do you hear? We can't afford to have millions of gallons of water destroying the countryside for miles around, to say nothing of the consequent loss of life and livelihood. At the moment this problem is extremely limited, take my word for it. If you go through with this mad plan of the Doctor's, the whole area would be devastated.'

'It is being devastated now,' Stobbold pointed out forcefully. 'Look at it.' He pointed out over the dam into the rising smoke. 'And in any case,' he added, 'what do you care about what happens to a third rate parish in the back of beyond?'

As Grant turned back, the sun dipped behind a cloud. His face was shadowed for a moment as he looked first at Stobbold then at Wilson. And in that moment the flames that flickered and danced behind his eyes were plain for them all to see.

'You will return to the barracks,' Grant said again to Wilson.

But Wilson shook his head. 'I am an officer in her Britannic Majesty's army, Sir William,' he said. 'I don't take orders from civilians.'

They faced each other for a moment, Grant's eyes burning with anger. He smiled. His face twisted into an approximation of amusement as he pulled off his gloves. When he raised his hands, when he started towards Wilson, his fingers were already outstretched, already smouldering.

Stobbold was fixed to the spot, staring, as Grant approached. Wilson too seemed unable to move. He was at the edge of the dam, Grant's hands closing on his neck.

Captain Brookes was a blur of motion. He launched himself in front of his superior officer, grabbing Grant's hands in both his own and forcing them away. There was a sudden loud hiss and steam erupted from their clasped hands. Brookes screamed with pain, but held on, pushing Grant back towards the railing along the top of the dam. As Stobbold watched, their locked hands exploded into flame. In a moment, the whole of Grant's body was an inferno. Brookes was leaning back, out of the fire. The side of his face closest was blistering, the skin melting and peeling away as he continued to scream.

Then slowly, deliberately, he seemed to lean back into the fire. His whole weight was brought to bear on the raging fire, forcing it back against the railing. Brookes's screams were lost in the roaring of the fire as it engulfed him. But still it was forced backwards.

With a sudden wrench of twisting metal, the railing gave way. One end flopped aside, dripping molten iron to the concrete surface of the walkway. Another section of the rail fell, clattering against the side of the dam as it bounced and rolled its way to the rocky ground far below.

A second after it, the burning fireball followed. An arm emerged for a moment as the fire spun and tumbled. A smouldering, blackened arm from which the uniform had been all but stripped away along with the flesh beneath.

Stobbold was at the edge, where the railing had been, leaning as far as he dared to see the flames spreading out along the bottom of the dam. Stobbold felt himself stumble as he felt the heat on his face, felt Wilson pull him back from the edge.

'Are you all right, sir?'

Stobbold nodded, his throat too dry to speak.

Wilson turned immediately to his men, standing behind them watching in silence. 'Place whatever charges we have,' he said. 'I want a concentrated blast at the weakest point, we'll let the water do the rest. And I want it done ten minutes ago, understand?'

When he joined Stobbold, his eyes were moist. 'I wish I *had* done it ten minutes ago,' he said quietly. 'Let's hope we're not already too late.'

At the base of the dam the fire thinned and spread. Like burning oil it ran liquid along the ground, discarding the charred and broken remains of Brookes's body. It raged and flared for a full minute. Then it seemed to draw back into itself. The flames died, to reveal a smouldering viscous mass at the centre of the fire. The edges were already black with a thin crust of solidifying rock.

Slowly, carefully, inexorably, the molten creature began to flow up the surface of the dam.

They worked almost in silence. Stobbold was impressed with the efficiency of Wilson's men. Despite being obviously tired they set to with enthusiasm and determination.

After several minutes, several of the soldiers had managed to create a demolition charge from the powder and grenades – a backpack full of the explosives with a fuse hanging out of the side. The problem now, Wilson told Stobbold, was how and where to place it.

After some discussion it was agreed that the weakest point of the dam would be in the very middle, where the strain was greatest. The curvature would also help once there was a hole, funnelling the water through. The sheer weight of water trying to escape would then finish the job. In theory.

'The problem is,' Wilson said, 'that blowing a hole in the top of the dam is no use at all. It has to be below the water line.'

'How do you get down far enough to place your charge?' Stobbold asked.

'How indeed?' Wilson shouted to one of the soldier: 'Carter – you got any rope? We'll need to lower a man down to position the charge.'

'Can't you just lower the charge?' Stobbold asked cautiously, worried he might be betraying his ignorance.

Wilson considered this. 'Provided the rope doesn't burn through before the full detonation. In that case the charge would simply drop down the side and make a nasty scratch. Ideally we want it fixed in place, tight against the wall.'

Carter was there with the rope. He caught the end of the conversation. 'We really need some way of focusing the blast into the masonry, sir,' he said. 'Otherwise it will just bounce off and do very little damage.'

This provoked another discussion. But it seemed that there was little available that would serve to focus the power of the explosion on to the dam.

'The best we can hope for then, sir, is that it's sufficient to weaken the structure and let the water start to leak through,' Carter said.

It did not, Stobbold thought, sound very promising. But he kept his thoughts to himself and left them to it. Looking out from the top of the dam it seemed to him that the smoke below was deepening. Yet the fire was just as visible, burning perhaps even more fiercely. And it seemed to stretch further than it had. On the other side of the dam he could see that the ice in the reservoir had melted. In several places the water was beginning to bubble.

He turned back towards Middletown, or rather where Middletown should be beneath the yellow-tinged glow of the smoke. He shook his head in disbelief and depression. He was tired, so very tired. He leaned down and rested his head on his hands as they gripped the railing. His eyes were closed. If only he could wake up back at the Rectory, wake up to a breakfast prepared by Betty.

Poor Betty. So young. So very young.

With a long sigh he opened his tired eyes, but he did not yet lift his head.

Something was moving. Down towards the base of the dam there was movement, a glow. He tried to focus on it. No – it was closer than he had thought, perhaps half way up. Not a single point, but a flowing, climbing mass spreading up over the dam. A river of glowing magma rolling upwards, towards him.

Stobbold straightened up abruptly. 'Colonel Wilson!' he shouted. 'I think your men should hurry!'

They did hurry. Wilson took one quick look over the side of the dam where Stobbold was pointing, then ordered the explosive pack to be lowered.

'We have to set it off before that stuff reaches the waterline,' he said urgently. 'Once it's above that, we have no chance. It's hot enough to burn through the rope and the backpack, the explosives will just fall out.'

The fuse was lit, and the backpack hastily lowered over the side.

'How long is the fuse?' Stobbold asked as he leaned over the rail to watch the package being lowered into position. The rail shifted slightly under his weight, the supports weakened from the break further along.

'Two minutes, more or less,' Wilson told him. He waved to the man lowering the rope to tell him to stop. 'Right, tie it off there.'

'Why so long? Why not set it off immediately?'

The soldiers were tying the rope to the railing, right in the centre of the dam.

'Because,' Wilson explained, 'we don't want to be standing on the dam when the charge goes off.'

'Ah.' Stobbold turned to gauge the distance to the side of the dam, to the ground beyond. They were almost in the middle. It was several hundred yards. 'Two minutes more or less, you said?'

The soldiers passed him at a run.

'That's what I said,' Wilson said as he pushed Stobbold into a stumbling run ahead of him. 'And it's been burning for a minute already.'

Neither of them looked back until they reached the high ground at the side of the dam. It rose slowly away from the structure, affording them a view back at the dam. Stobbold could see the diminutive backpack hanging by a fine thread. A tiny spark at the edge of the pack showed how close the fuse had burned. But below the charge, clawing its way slowly closer, was a glowing red stain. As they watched, it seemed to peel away from the wall of the dam, to reach up towards the explosives.

The spark disappeared, inside the top of the back.

'Any second now,' Wilson said.

There was utter silence from the soldiers as they stood in a rough semicircle watching. Stobbold held his breath.

The red mass curled inwards, pouncing in slow motion on the back pack.

There was a flash of light from the pack, just visible as the mass of glowing rock connected with it, smothering it entirely.

A rumble of sound, the start of a huge explosion.

Then nothing.

The smoke swirled about him like a yellow mist. The landscape was a hazy impression of jagged shapes; trees were skeletal lines of black as they emerged from the smoke; the ground was a mass of bubbling sulphurous pools that spat burning liquid through the thickening air.

He picked his way through the nightmare maze of fire. His expression was set, dark and impassive. His eyes were deep as faceted gemstones that absorbed rather than reflected the light, sucking it into their depths. His hair blew back from his head in a brown halo as he walked briskly onwards.

A splash of fire caught the sleeve of his jacket, glowing for a moment before burning itself out. The soles of his shoes trod smoke as he walked.

He paused only once. A dull rumble of sound penetrated the murky atmosphere, rolling in from behind him. The Doctor allowed his mouth to twitch momentarily into an approximation of a smile as he listened. He hoped to hear more, to hear the thunder-roar of the water pouring down into the old river bed, crashing towards the fissure, sweeping him off his feet perhaps in a sudden torrent. But there was nothing.

Ahead of him, through the gloom, two shapes were becoming visible, arms linked together so they seemed to form a single body. With a deep breath of the rancid air, the Doctor stepped towards them.

Chapter Nineteen
Solid State

They stood arm in arm, linked, together, and looked out over the fissure. They were on an area set back from the jagged tear across the moorland. Behind them the ground rose sharply, an outcrop of rock jutting up from the landscape. The air in front of them was thinner, the smoke drifting across the open mouth of the abyss driven by a strong breeze.

Nepath breathed in the acrid fumes, relishing the taste of the fire in his mouth. With Patience beside him he watched the bubbling rolling mass of fiery liquid that oozed over the edge of the fissure, spreading across the moorland. With each heaving, bubbling eruption of liquid, a wave rippled down the river of fire that flowed towards Middletown.

The glow was hot on Nepath's face as he watched. His eyes were wide, his mouth an open 'o' of rapture. He stood immobile, letting the firelight dance and flicker in his eyes and across his reddened cheeks. He licked his lips.

'Lord of all you survey?'

The words broke the spell and wiped the smile from Nepath's face. He turned slowly, Patience turning with him until they faced the Doctor.

'And what will you do,' the Doctor asked quietly, 'when there are no more worlds to conquer?'

'Let's cross that bridge when we come to it, shall we, Doctor?' Nepath said.

The Doctor was within ten feet of them now, coming down to their level from the rise. 'You make it sound like the Rubicon,' he said. 'But of course you crossed that long ago.'

'What do you mean?' In spite of himself, Nepath was intrigued.

The Doctor shrugged. 'Only that you made an irrevocable decision when you elected to deal with the creature that is now destroying our world.' He lowered his voice, eyes set hard on Nepath. 'Was it worth it, I wonder?'

'Any price!' Nepath retorted. He looked at his sister, drawing her close to him, feeling the warmth of her body close to him. 'I would have given anything to get her back.'

The Doctor took another step closer. Despite the circumstances, it was a strangely threatening gesture. 'It did not occur to you, I suppose, that what you were offering was not yours to give?'

Nepath met his gaze. 'But it is mine now,' he breathed. '"Lord of all I survey," that's what you said. But I shall have far more power than that.'

'Is that why you did it? For power?' He made the word *power* sound distasteful.

'Of course not. You know why I have done this. And I would do it again,' he said defiantly.

The Doctor gave a snort of feigned humour. 'How very odd,' he said. 'You'd make the same mistake twice? Sign in blood, on the dotted line, with no guarantees once again.' He shook his head, almost in pity it seemed. 'And all for nothing. For a dream, an illusion. A cheat.'

Nepath was silent, frowning as he tried to work out the Doctor's meaning.

'Talk all you like, Doctor.' Patience Nepath's voice was soft. 'You can't alter things now.' She smiled at him. 'After all, you are already dead.' She untwined her arm from her brother and advanced on the Doctor. The air around her began to hiss with the increased heat.

'Look who's talking,' the Doctor responded. He stood his ground, ignoring her for the moment, addressing his comments to Nepath. 'Can't you see that you've been cheated? You might have kept your side of the bargain, but you've got nothing for it. Nothing but misery, pain and death.'

'No,' he shook his head emphatically. 'No, that's not true. I have her back, just as she was. Everything is exactly as it should be.'

The Doctor did step back now, circling just out of reach of her as he spoke. 'Just as it should be? Look at her.' He pointed, careful to keep his hand away from her fingers as she stretched out towards him. 'Your *older* sister, just as you remember her. Despite the passage of time, the inexorable flow of the years, she remains unchanged.'

'She is restored,' he insisted. 'Brought back!'

'No she isn't!' the Doctor insisted. He jumped aside as she lunged at him. 'This is no more your sister than I am. She isn't even human. Look at her!' he shouted again. 'You can tell she isn't your sister, can't you? You must have some critical faculties, or are you completely blind to the truth?'

He was slightly slow avoiding her. With an almost balletic movement she whirled towards him, catching the edge of his jacket with her outstretched hand as she turned. The material smouldered, then burst into flames.

The Doctor stared at the fire, frantically patting it out with his hand. He tutted and sighed as he examined the damage, as if more concerned at this than the risk to his life or the devastation stretching out before them. 'This was something your sister used to do was it?' he asked, voice heavy with sarcasm. 'Parlour game perhaps? After dinner trick? I can well imagine that while the rest of you learnt recitations or played a musical instrument, she set fire to the soft furnishings.' He leaped aside as her hand swept back at him.

'As my sister said,' Nepath ground out through gritted teeth, 'you are already dead.'

'And as I said,' the Doctor replied, his voice level and his eyes hard, 'she is not your sister. No matter what you've been promised, no matter what you *think* you have been promised, no matter how much you give, you can never – *ever* – get her back. You know that.'

Nepath just stared at him, face drawn. He felt empty inside. He hardly heard the Doctor's words, they came to him as if through water as his anger swelled inside him.

'She's gone, Nepath. There is no way to bring her back. You must see that.' The Doctor circled past Patience's clutching hands until he was standing beside Nepath.

She smiled as she continued to stalk him, as if it were a game, as if she was letting him think he could escape when all the time…

'She's dead,' the Doctor shouted at Nepath. 'And she'll always be dead. I don't care what assurances you've been given. It doesn't matter what you do to me, *she is dead*.' His eyes locked with Nepath's, 'And you know that,' he said slowly, deliberately, clearly. 'And you know,' he said quietly, 'that it is your fault.'

Nepath just stared back. He could feel his lip quivering, could feel the emotion inside him about to burst out in a torrent, could feel his face creasing as he blinked back the tears. 'Patience,' he managed to sob. 'Oh, Patience.'

She was there at once. The Doctor jumped aside as she approached, as she took her brother in her arms and embraced him, as she kissed him.

The Doctor turned away.

Nepath ignored the Doctor. He concentrated on her touch, on her kiss, on her warmth, and he knew she was back. He knew he had done the right thing.

As the fuse reached the explosive charge fashioned from grenades and gunpowder, the glutinous, burning mass that had been in the shape of Sir William Grant smothered it. The charge detonated at the very moment the viscous liquid hardened rock solid around it, crushing it against the wall of the dam.

The substance was well able to absorb heat, absorb it and use it. But in its hardened state, the effect was somewhat different. So far as it had intentions and made decisions, it intended to stifle the blast, to render it ineffectual. What it could not know was that the explosives rigged within the backpack were nowhere near enough to make any impression on the solid masonry.

But as the charge detonated against the surface of the huge wall, the smothering, crushing mass of rock that closed over it had the effect of focusing the blast. The entire energy wave was directed at a single small area of the dam within the enclosing magma. The shockwave reverberated within the very structure of the dam.

Still it was not sufficient to break through the wall. But a single hairline crack erupted from the centre of the blast – a jagged black line breaking almost invisibly across the dam wall, a tiny fissure in the surface.

'Memories,' the Doctor said. 'The past.' He waited while Nepath and his sister drew apart. 'You should look to the future, you know. Not embrace the past.'

'Oh but I am.' Nepath seemed reinvigorated by his sister's embrace. 'We are.' He kept hold of her hand as he spoke. 'A future of flame, of conflagration. Of burning.' His eyes were deep wells of darkness. Behind him the fissure spat red hot trails of fire into the sky. 'Patience and I will hold dominion over the world, over the fire. Together, for ever, we shall rule the burned and burning land.'

'For whom?' the Doctor demanded. 'Not for yourselves, surely. Not for the people who are dying – burning – in the fires of the Apocalypse. No, you'll do it for an elemental force that had burned away what little was left of Patience Nepath.'

Nepath shook his head. 'You can't distract us now, Doctor. No matter what you say or believe, Patience and I are together once more. Nothing and nobody can tear us apart again.' He let go of his sister's hand, gesturing for her to approach the Doctor. 'Least of all you.'

On the high ground overlooking the dam, Stobbold stood beside Colonel Wilson. Across the misty ocean of smoke and fire they could see the red stain of the magma as it swelled and bubbled. It seemed to be spreading sideways, thinning to a line.

'The blast just wasn't concentrated enough,' Wilson said.

'What do we do now?'

He shrugged. 'Get back to Ambleton and collect some

demolition charges. Then hope we can get back here through the fire storm.'

'Have another go,' Stobbold said. 'Yes, I suppose so.'

There was a noise. A sudden snap of sound like a whip cracking, or a pistol shot.

'What was that?' Stobbold strained to see. It had come from the dam.

'I don't know,' Wilson said slowly. 'Unless…'

As they watched, a ragged tear was appearing from beneath the thinning red substance that adhered to the dam. A black line ripped out from under it, running across the wall.

'It's cracking,' Stobbold breathed. 'That stuff is trying to hold it together.'

Wilson was nodding. Behind him the soldiers were shuffling, trying to shoulder their way into better positions to see. 'Maybe we weakened the wall. Perhaps enough for the pressure of the reservoir to do the rest of the work.'

As he spoke, a trickle of water ran down from the top of the crack. It reached the edge of the hot liquid clinging to the dam and a sudden cloud of steam exploded from its surface. At once the viscous liquid seemed to flow back towards the point where the water was beginning now to run out in greater quantity. Tried to smother it, to seal the hole.

But the water was gushing out now. Pouring forth like a waterfall with enough force to spew out from the dam wall and cascade to the smoking ground below. The sound was incredible – a rumbling roar of exploding water forcing its way through the widening gap; the thud and crump of falling masonry colliding with the side of the dam and tumbling to the ground below; the percussive hiss of erupting steam and smoke as the water splashed across the molten rock that tried to force it back.

'Good God,' Wilson said as he watched.

Stobbold nodded. 'Very likely,' he murmured. 'Very likely.'

The liquid was gelling, forming into a shape. A huge almost human hand was pressing back against the rushing torrent, splashing it out and back against the dam as it tried to force itself into the hole, to plug it. At the end of the hand an arm was forming, a body. A glowing mass that might have been in the shape of Sir William Grant struggled to stem the flow.

But the figure was swamped, overwhelmed by the rushing tide. It seemed to shrink, its head thrown back screaming as it fought and struggled to cling to the dam. It was human-shaped, human-sized now, receding into itself, adopting a familiar shape. Perhaps using the only memory that remained to it.

Then the dam wall below the figure, below the rush of water, bulged suddenly outwards. Exterior brickwork peeled loose from the bulge, tumbling away as the wall exploded under the pressure. The tiny figure was left clinging to the broken brickwork at the top of the hole, arms working, hands clutching as it struggled to climb away from the roaring mass of steaming water.

Stobbold caught a flash of movement from beside him. He turned to see that Wilson was running – running towards the collapsing dam.

'Where are you going?' he shouted. 'Come back! You'll be swept away!'

Wilson kept running. He was twenty yards along the top of the dam now. Stobbold could see him stumble and stagger as the whole structure moved under his feet. But still he ran.

The figures formed three points of a roughly equilateral triangle. The Doctor; Nepath; his sister. The way that Nepath and his sister circled, the way the Doctor backed away and kept out of reach was like a dance.

'How can you believe there is anything of Patience Nepath left in that thing?' the Doctor asked as he backed away again. He was shouting to be heard. From somewhere in the distance was a rumbling, like approaching thunder.

'She is my sister, I can tell.' Nepath moved to cut off the Doctor's escape route. 'What does it matter to you anyway, Doctor?' he demanded. Now he was shouting too.

'What does it matter to her, more to the point?' The Doctor ducked under an arm as it was thrust at him. A lock of his hair recoiled as it was scorched by her clutching fingers. He staggered back, and ended up standing beside Nepath.

Nepath grabbed the Doctor by the arms, holding him tightly as he struggled. 'You were better off before,' the Doctor shouted at him as he tried to pull away. 'Better off with that blackened husk in the cabinet. At least that really was her. At least then you had your memories and your dreams.'

'What do you mean?' Nepath howled at him. He was pushing the Doctor slowly forwards, towards his sister's smoking, outstretched hands.

'I mean that now you have nothing. Nothing at all. There is none of Patience Nepath left inside that thing.' He twisted so that his face was close to Nepath's. 'Ask her – I dare you,' he challenged.

Nepath did not answer, but he stopped pushing the Doctor towards her, and held him still.

'Tell the creature to leave her, just for a moment. See for yourself what's left.'

She paused, watching Nepath, waiting for his response.

'Assuming you have any say in how that thing behaves, any authority at all – master of all you survey,' the Doctor sneered. 'Go on, ask it.'

Nepath snorted and pushed the Doctor forward another stumbling step. 'And what will that prove.'

The Doctor ripped his arm free, turned to face Nepath in a single blur of motion. His other arm came free too and they stood facing each other. Over the Doctor's shoulder Nepath could see his sister. Waiting.

'If that is truly a recreation of your sister, and not just some automaton,' the Doctor shouted, 'then when the creature, the substance that binds her together, leaves it we shall see inside the frame that it is built on. We'll see the charred and blackened corpse of your dead sister, Nepath. Just as she was, just as she died. Just as you left her.' He turned towards the figure of Patience

Nepath, her hands still extended, her fingers glowing red, her eyes on fire.

'But if not,' the Doctor said. 'You will be left with a shell, a statue, a shape. Or with nothing.' He twisted his head slightly, talking over his shoulder, throwing back an offhand comment. 'Or would you rather not know?' he said.

'That will prove nothing, Doctor,' Nepath shouted back.

'Then why not indulge me?' The Doctor gave a derisive snort. 'Or does it worry you what you might be forced to learn?'

'You're playing for time,' countered Nepath.

'But you have all the time in the world,' the Doctor shouted back. 'For ever, you said. That's long enough, isn't it?'

For a moment Nepath's eyes locked with the Doctor's. Then he turned slowly to face his sister. 'Do it,' Nepath hissed. His voice was barely audible above the roaring that seemed to be getting louder by the moment.

'Roger,' she said, shaking her head. 'Oh, Roger.'

'Do it.' Nepath said again, louder. His voice was shaking.

She shook her head, the fire brightening in her eyes.

'*Do it!*' he screamed at her.

The entire huge structure was buckling under him. He could feel the tremors shaking it to pieces as he ran. Colonel Wilson was breathing heavily, drawing in great breaths of the acid air as he raced towards the point where Grant was struggling to reach the top of the dam.

He was not sure why he was running, why he was risking his own life. Except that a man was in trouble, might die. Any life was worth a risk, he decided as he continued to run. If Grant was indeed alive... But so many people had died today – too many. If he could save just one more then that was one fewer death. One fewer family left to mourn. One fewer set of eyes to wipe dry, hearts to break, nightmares to scream awake from.

A hand was reaching up towards the railing as he leaned over. So close. He could see every detail of Grant's straining face, as if it was etched in stone. The wall below him was crumbling away under the strain. The rip running upwards, closing on the man clutching upwards for Wilson's own hand reaching down.

Wilson was lying on the buckling ground, stretching to reach. His fingers grazed the ends of Sir William's, fumbled, caught them. He managed to get a grip on the man's wrist just as the section of brickwork Grant was clinging to broke away and crashed down into the white water below.

Grant continued to stare up at Wilson, expression set, eyes dead and blank. The water splashed up over him, soaking him. But it seemed to stain him darker rather than soak into the man's clothes. And the weight...

Struggling to keep his own balance, to avoid being dragged over the edge, Wilson pulled. He managed to get both hands round Grant's wrist, braced his legs against the stanchion that held the iron railing in place and felt it creak and give.

Then the weight was gone. But he was still clinging on. His arms jerked upwards, and still he held on, rolling back from the edge as he clutched Grant's hand tightly.

He stared in disbelief at the severed forearm. It had broken away – snapped under the weight. Like brittle stone. Wilson struggled to his feet, dropping the hand in horror. It twisted, turned, fell to the ground at his feet. And exploded into a thousand slivers of cold, fragile rock. When he looked over the edge, leaning on the bent railing, he was in time to see the figure of Grant disappear under the water, shattered arm still outstretched. The body sank at once, carried away in the torrent, smashed to pieces by the pressure of the raging water. Like a statue.

The Doctor stepped aside as she approached.

'Roger.' She was shaking her head in sadness. 'Oh Roger, don't you know? Can't you tell?' She folded Nepath in her arms, holding him tight.

But despite the warmth, despite the proximity of her body, he remained rigid and cold. 'Do it,' he said to her. 'For me.' He held her slightly away from him, and looked deep into her eyes, into the flickering fires inside her. 'I have to know,' he told her. His whole body was shaking, racked with the sobs as he struggled to control his emotion. 'Please, I have to know before I can go on with this.'

Beside them the rolling river of molten rock had spread across the moorland. It was close enough for them to feel the heat, close enough for the glow to illuminate them in silhouette as they stood, holding each other, clinging to each other.

'Oh Roger,' she said again. 'Believe in me.'

He heard only her voice. Felt only her touch, her warmth. His heart was aching, burning as he ran his hands through her hair, held her face close to his. 'For me,' he repeated.

She shook her head, her arms coiled round him. 'No,' she breathed. 'You need me. I need you.'

'Is that why you won't do it?' the Doctor asked from behind them. 'Not because of any love or care for him. But because you need him. You need him to delude himself, to help you. Whatever the cost,' he snarled. 'Whatever the cost to *him*.'

'We don't need him,' she spat back, still holding Nepath tight. 'Not now.'

'We?' the Doctor challenged. 'That's a bit of an admission, isn't it?' There was a hint of satisfaction in his voice.

Nepath felt himself go cold, despite the warmth of her embrace. 'Is that it?' he demanded. 'Have you deceived me?' He was choking on the words. 'Tell me it's you, Patience.' He tried to pull free. 'I have to know.'

'Oh, Roger,' she said again, her voice honeyed and cloying. 'Don't make me do this.'

He pushed her away, held her at arm's length. 'I have to know,' he shouted.

She sighed. 'Very well. If that is truly what you want…' And she drew him close again, enfolding him in her warm embrace.

Over her shoulder, crying into her hair, through each delineated strand he saw the fire erupt from her feet. It leaped out from her heels, running as if following a trail of gunpowder across the broken bubbling ground. When it reached the river of magma, fire met fire and was absorbed by it, drawn in. He tried to push her away in dismay, anger and disgust.

But she held him close. Through the brittle broken threads that had been her hair he saw the smoke drift aside to reveal the Doctor standing, watching. Impassive.

Inscrutable.

And behind the Doctor, a white wall was rushing towards them. It broke and crashed down over the sea of burning rock that lay across the landscape. The sound was incredible. The white steam blotted out the yellow smoke.

Only when he tried to stand aside, to break free, to step away from what had been his sister, did Nepath realise that he was still held tight in her embrace. An embrace of cold, dead stone.

Stobbold reached the edge of the collapsing dam just as Wilson did. Wilson toppled backwards as the ground beneath his feet gave way. Stobbold lunged forwards and grabbed the exhausted soldier. He managed to drag him clear, up to the higher ground. Behind them the whole of the dam was crashing down into the water.

A cold breeze ruffled their hair, swept along by the mass of water as it spilled out across the moorland. The smoke was swept away before it, to reveal the unreal landscape beneath.

Solidified, bent and broken structures emerged from the water as it calmed. Like the trunks of long-dead trees or broken statues they thrust up through the land in tortured, twisted parodies of shapes. In the distance, they could see the steam thrown up as the water met the magma, rushing over it, leaving it solid and dead. The church tower was an island in the midst of the rising water.

At the bottom of the slope, making their way up towards where the soldiers were standing in jubilant awe, a line of the amorphous glowing figures was to be seen. They glowed with inner fire, arms of flame outstretched before them. As the water rose to their feet, they seemed to slow as if trudging through treacle. One of them staggered forwards, leaving its leg behind – a stump of broken stone that was soon submerged beneath the rising water.

Moments later, the water was over them, bubbling and glowing with the angry smothered fire. Then the glow faded, and the bubbles ceased, and the water continued to rise.

The water was round Nepath's feet, almost sweeping him off balance. He struggled and kicked and clawed to be free of her. But the stone cold arms held him in their tight embrace, wrapped around him, entwined, ungiving.

He saw the Doctor climb up on to the outcrop of rock, standing above the water, looking down at him. His expression was still unreadable.

The water was up to Nepath's knees. His braced his feet to try to stay upright. He managed to reach out past her shoulder, his hand brushing aside strands of hair, breaking them away so that they clattered down her back and splashed into the rising water at his waist. He reached upwards, towards the Doctor, fingers clutching.

'Doctor!' He had to shout, to scream above the tearing wrenching thunder of the water at his chest, pressing in at him. The stone dead weight of her held him down, kept him from climbing on to the rocky outcrop. 'Doctor, please!'

His hand was almost at the Doctor's feet, stretching, reaching, desperate.

The relief was palpable. He sobbed and cried with it as the Doctor stepped down, one foot splashing into the water. Nepath reached out round her, clutching, clawing towards him. The Doctor was standing on a ledge, his feet level with Nepath's shoulder. The water washed over the Doctor's shoes as he lifted one foot out of the water.

'Help me!' The water was in his mouth, making him gag and swallow as he screamed.

He saw through the spray that the Doctor had his foot on Patience's back, between her shoulder blades. Nepath clawed at it, grabbed it, scrabbled to get a grip.

The Doctor's foot pressed hard into her back. As if testing her balance.

'No – Doctor!' His words were a spray of bubbling acidic water.

The foot drew back. Nepath rocked forwards, head free of the water for a moment. A clear view for a second:

Of the Doctor giving a sudden, single, violent kick at the stone of Patience Nepath's back.

Then he was falling, her weight on top of him,

The view through the bubbling white water was a blur bearing him down,

The Doctor watching him as he sank slowly holding him tight,

Then turning and walking away so tight,

the bubbles of his own final breath misting out the image in an embrace of death.

never once looking back.

Chapter Twenty
From the Embers

It was as if, Stobbold thought, the whole of Middletown had been picked up and deposited somewhere else. The water had receded, but the ground floor of the Rectory still smelled of mud and mould. The church had fared better, with its stone floors and walls. There was little in the way of soft furnishings to absorb the water and retain and exude the smell of the damp.

The lower part of the west wing of the Grange had been washed away by the water as it raced past, so that the house slumped to one side – awkward and broken. It was convulsed down one side with the main windows collapsed in on themselves, into a bizarre approximation of a wink.

But the landscape was completely changed. Where the fissure had been, a narrow, jagged lake cut across the ground, fed by the river that now ran through the shattered remnants of the dam, retracing its previous course. The moorland was more like a marsh now, boggy and hazardous. All around, even in the streets of the main part of the town, weird rock formations jutted up from the broken ground, as if reaching up towards the sky to escape the receding waters.

The huts and machinery at the mouth of the mine had been swept away, leaving shattered driftwood and lumps of bent ironwork in their wake. The engineers had inspected the workings. They were worried about subsidence and collapse, though there was little above the old workings that could be damaged. Colonel Wilson had told Stobbold, in confidence, that most of the tunnels were under water now. But the changing landscape, the way the ground had moved had forced open new natural tunnels and crevices, and Wilson said he had seen shining rivulets of what might just be tin ore embedded in the walls of several of these newly exposed shafts and tunnels.

Stobbold's own sense of loss seemed emphasised, exaggerated by the imminent departure of his house guest. They had to remove the window of the Doctor's bedroom in order to get his large blue box out. Now it was strapped to a cart in the Rectory driveway. A horse – one of Urton's recaptured after his stables were washed away – stood ready to pull its load out of the driveway and away from Middletown.

'You know,' Stobbold said as he shook the Doctor's hand, 'when it catches the light, there seems to be some texture to it.' He nodded towards the box.

'I know what you mean,' the Doctor agreed. Together they stood and examined the box from a short distance. 'Almost like panelling of some sort. Just a hint, a shadow of a shadow.'

'Where will you go?'

'I have no idea.' He took the reins and led the horse slowly forwards. Its hooves crunched on the gravel. The wheels creaked into motion behind them. 'But it will be interesting finding out.' As they walked, the Doctor let go of the reins. The horse followed obediently beside him.

The Doctor pulled a tattered piece of paper from his pocket and opened it. Stobbold could see that there was writing on it. An even handwriting, almost mechanical it was so consistent, faded and smudged. It said:

Meet me in St. Louis', February 8th 2001.

It was signed with the same perfect writing. The name looked like *Fitz*.

'We're well into January now,' Stobbold said. 'Perhaps that means a minute past eight o'clock in the evening.' He tapped the *2001*.

The Doctor stopped. The horse stopped too. The Doctor folded the paper again and returned it to his pocket. 'Perhaps,' he said. 'But I don't think so.'

'Do you think the mine will open again?' Stobbold asked. The sun was shining in his eyes, so that the Doctor was a silhouette against the skyline.

'Who can say? The future is a closed book, I'm afraid.'

'I suppose so,' Stobbold agreed.'When we first met, we talked of predestination, I seem to recall. We debated whether our lives had any meaning, any individuality – whether they are there for us to shape as we will.'

'Or whether they are set in stone. Yes,' he said quietly. 'I remember.' He nodded thoughtfully. 'But so long as we don't know, perhaps it really doesn't matter.'

Stobbold hesitated before he spoke. 'Doctor,' he said, tentative and slightly nervous at his own words, 'there is one thing I should like to know very much.' His breath misted in the cold air.

'Yes?' The Doctor's tone suggested he knew already what it was.

'Who are you?' Stobbold asked.

'Ah,' he replied at once. Then he was silent for a while, and so still as he considered that he might have been a statue. 'That is something,' he eventually replied, 'that I must find out for myself.'

'Is it… is it something you really want to know?

'Yes. Yes it is.' He was walking again now, clicking his tongue to encourage the horse to follow. They turned the corner of the driveway and the empty moorland stretched out ahead of them beyond the gates. 'It's something I am burning to know.'

Before he could press the Doctor further, Stobbold was distracted by a noise. At first he thought it was the cartwheels scratching on the gravel of the drive. The gravel was thin, all but washed away by the flood. The wheels clattered on the frozen ground beneath. But the sound was more of a scraping, and it was coming from the other side of the cart, from the heap of stones and earth where the perimeter wall had collapsed, where Betty…

Betty

'Excuse me,' Stobbold heard himself mutter as he ran. He pushed past the Doctor, the horse, the cart. The stones in front of him were moving, shifting, falling. Something was emerging, something pale and delicate from amongst the heavy rock and stone, from out of the dead land.

Fingers

Clutching round a large stone, reaching for the cold air.

He grasped the hand in his own, felt it cool and fragile in his grip as with his other hand he rolled the stone away. He had to let go of her to clear the rubble, to dig with his nails into the frozen dirt, to drag her clear.

She collapsed at once, a tangled weeping mess at his feet. He fell beside her, pulling her to him, crying into her shoulder as he held her. Her face was smeared with her tears and the earth. Her clothes were torn, ragged, stained and in places charred by the fire. Her right hand was a blackened mass, the flesh peeled back like burned paper.

The fire, he thought, had consumed her. But she had been at its centre, in the eye of the flames, the burning.

They rocked back and forth, crying quietly. 'Oh Jephthah,' he wept into her scorched hair, 'what a treasure hadst thou?'

'One fair daughter,' she wept back. 'Oh Father… Father.' She held him tight in her embrace, their tears mingling where their cheeks met.

Eventually they climbed to their hesitant feet. Eventually he led her gently back to the drive. Eventually he realised they were alone.

A single line of cart wheel tracks led out of the gates and across the sodden moorland. Into the distance.

Disappearing into the empty wilderness.

Acknowledgements

Any novel is a collaborative effort. In the case of *The Burning* I am more than usually indebted.

I owe thanks to Ian Smith for advice on all things military pertaining to the era (and the loan of a nice red jacket – just like Michael Caine had in Zulu), though if there are any mistakes they are of my own devising.

In formulating an approach to the 'evolving' character of the Doctor I have to thank Ben Dunn, Dave Owen, Rebecca Levene, Paul Leonard, Lance Parkin, Terrance Dicks, Gary Russell and Peter Anghelides for their help, confidence, endorsement and support.

I thank both Jac Rayner and Steve Cole for their help there too. And for far more than that.

About the Author

JUSTIN RICHARDS is the pseudonym of an international conglomerate of writers and researchers. Seventeen of these trained, dedicated people were employed for three weeks to put together this carefully-crafted 'About the Author' blurb.

Back in the Real World, Justin lives and works in Warwick. He has written extensively for various media, with over a dozen published novels as well as non-fiction and a joke book (clue: this isn't it!). Justin acts as Consultant to BBC Worldwide's ranges of *Doctor Who* books.

PRESENTING

DOCTOR WHO

AN ALL-NEW AUDIO DRAMA –
FEATURING THE DALEKS!

Big Finish Productions is proud to present all-new *Doctor Who* adventures on audio! Featuring original music and sound-effects, these full-cast plays are available on double cassette in high street stores, and on limited-edition double CD from all good specialist stores, or via mail order.

Available from August 2000
DALEK EMPIRE
THE APOCALYPSE ELEMENT

A four-part story by Stephen Cole.
Starring **Colin Baker** as the Doctor
and **Maggie Stables** as Evelyn
with **Lalla Ward** as Romana.

When the planet Archetryx is threatened by a Dalek assault squad, the Doctor and Evelyn become embroiled in an ever-deepening mystery. What has become of President Romana, missing for twenty years, and what is the secret of the ancient element the Daleks are synthesising? Does Gallifrey feature in their plans?
If the Daleks cannot conquer the universe will they watch it go up in flames?

If you wish to order the CD version, please photocopy this form or provide all the details on paper. Delivery within 28 days of release.
Send to: PO Box 1127, Maidenhead, Berkshire. SL6 3LN.
Big Finish Hotline 01628 828283.

Other stories featuring the Sixth Doctor still available include:
THE MARIAN CONSPIRACY   THE SPECTRE OF LANYON MOOR

For more details visit our website at
http://www.doctorwho.co.uk

DOCTOR WHO: THE NOVEL OF THE FILM *by Gary Russell*
ISBN 0 563 38000 4
THE EIGHT DOCTORS *by Terrance Dicks* ISBN 0 563 40563 5
VAMPIRE SCIENCE *by Jonathan Blum and Kate Orman*
ISBN 0 563 40566 X
THE BODYSNATCHERS *by Mark Morris*
ISBN 0 563 40568 6
GENOCIDE *by Paul Leonard* ISBN 0 563 40572 4
WAR OF THE DALEKS *by John Peel* ISBN 0 563 40573 2
ALIEN BODIES *by Lawrence Miles* ISBN 0 563 40577 5
KURSAAL *by Peter Anghelides* ISBN 0 563 40578 3
OPTION LOCK *by Justin Richards* ISBN 0 563 40583 X
LONGEST DAY *by Michael Collier* ISBN 0 563 40581 3
LEGACY OF THE DALEKS *by John Peel* ISBN 0 563 40574 0
DREAMSTONE MOON *by Paul Leonard* ISBN 0 563 40585 6
SEEING I *by Jonathan Blum and Kate Orman*
ISBN 0 563 40586 4
PLACEBO EFFECT *by Gary Russell* ISBN 0 563 40587 2
VANDERDEKEN'S CHILDREN *by Christopher Bulis*
ISBN 0 563 40590 2
THE SCARLET EMPRESS *by Paul Magrs* ISBN 0 563 40595 3
THE JANUS CONJUNCTION *by Trevor Baxendale*
ISBN 0 563 40599 6
BELTEMPEST *by Jim Mortimore* ISBN 0 563 40593 7
THE FACE EATER *by Simon Messingham* ISBN 0 563 55569 6
THE TAINT *by Michael Collier* ISBN 0 563 55568 8
DEMONTAGE *by Justin Richards* ISBN 0 563 55572 6
REVOLUTION MAN *by Paul Leonard* ISBN 0 563 55570 X
DOMINION *by Nick Walters* ISBN 0 563 55574 2
UNNATURAL HISTORY *by Jonathan Blum and Kate Orman*
ISBN 0 563 55576 9
AUTUMN MIST *by David A. McIntee* ISBN 0 563 55583 1
INTERFERENCE: BOOK ONE *by Lawrence Miles*
ISBN 0 563 55580 7
INTERFERENCE: BOOK TWO *by Lawrence Miles*
ISBN 0 563 55582 3

THE BLUE ANGEL *by Paul Magrs and Jeremy Hoad*
ISBN 0 563 55581 5
THE TAKING OF PLANET 5 *by Simon Bucher-Jones and
Mark Clapham* ISBN 0 563 55585 8
FRONTIER WORLDS *by Peter Anghelides* ISBN 0 563 55589 0
PARALLEL 59 *by Natalie Dallaire and Stephen Cole*
ISBN 0 563 555904
THE SHADOWS OF AVALON *by Paul Cornell*
ISBN 0 563 555882
THE FALL OF YQUATINE *by Nick Walters* ISBN 0 563 55594 7
COLDHEART *by Trevor Baxendale* ISBN 0 563 55595 5
THE SPACE AGE *by Steve Lyons* ISBN 0 563 53800 7
THE BANQUO LEGACY *by Andy Lane and Justin Richards*
ISBN 0 563 53808 2
THE ANCESTOR CELL *by Peter Anghelides and Stephen Cole*
ISBN 0 563 53809 0

THE MONTHLY TELEPRESS
The official BBC Doctor Who Books e-newsletter

News – competitions – interviews – and more!

Subscribe today at
http://www.onelist.com/group/Telepress